FIRST TARGET

A LACY MERRICK THRILLER
BOOK 3

ROBIN MAHLE

HARP HOUSE PUBLISHING, LLC.

Published by HARP House Publishing
November, 2017 (1st edition)

CHAPTER
ONE

BEAMS of light shone against the contemporary limestone building, highlighting the Chinese flag as it soared in the nocturnal sky over Washington D.C. A sleek black Mercedes coupe rolled to a stop along the curb of the embassy's circular drive.

The valet approached and opened the driver's side door, where a robust man with snow-white hair stepped out. "Thank you."

"Enjoy your evening, Mr. Greiner."

Matthew Greiner placed the key in the valet's hand. "Be careful with her." He approached the entrance of the invitation-only gala, hosted by the Chinese ambassador. Security guards flanked the doors and Greiner handed over the invitation to one of the men, who appeared quite serious. "Matthew Greiner, Synergy Dynamics," he said.

"Welcome. Have a pleasant time." The guard opened the door.

Greiner arrived inside the main hall and noted the signs pointing to the ballroom. He brushed his hand atop his short, styled mane, and tugged at his fitted tuxedo jacket. He acknowledged the ushers at the ballroom's entrance with a nod and entered.

Inside the elegant room, a lone man stood in the far corner, away from the arriving guests. He lowered his head, and in a hushed tone whispered, "He's here. At the entrance."

In his earpiece, another replied, "Keep him in your sights. I want to see where he goes."

"Copy that."

In the milieu of twinkling chandeliers and soft music, the man in the corner waited and observed Greiner cavort like a statesman, but he was no political figure. Greiner was former intelligence, known to sell his services to the highest bidder. This time, it was Synergy Dynamics, a company that, before his arrival, was on the verge of collapse, but since, had dramatically rebounded. And it was no surprise Greiner was here tonight, at a gala hosted by the Chinese ambassador. After all, China had been Synergy Dynamics' savior.

"He's approaching the ambassador now," the man again whispered and looked at his colleague several feet away.

"Don't get too close." The voice in the earpiece was the agent running the operation.

"I'll get shots," the second agent replied and casually moved toward Greiner and the ambassador. Facing them briefly, he captured some images with a pinhole camera inside the button of his tuxedo shirt. He stepped aside on approach, as though he'd spotted a friend, and continued on.

Greiner offered his hand. "Mr. Ambassador, pleasure to see you. Matthew Greiner."

"Yes, Mr. Greiner. So glad you could make it. I do hope you're having a nice time."

"I am, sir. Thank you."

"Good. Good. You'll excuse me, won't you? I must be sure to greet all my guests."

"Yes, of course. Good night, Mr. Ambassador." Greiner watched him leave and began to sip on his drink, searching for anyone else who needed to take note of his attendance.

The agent in the corner whispered in the comm., "He's alone."

"Take him now."

The agents began to close in on Greiner while he ambled around the guests, nodding and smiling. Greiner caught sight of the men and slowed his steps.

One of the agents locked eyes with him. Greiner didn't appear surprised in the least and, in fact, seemed to know who these men were. The corner of his mouth upturned slightly as he halted. Drawing attention to any of this would make the situation turn ugly and no one wanted that. Not here in the Chinese Embassy. Not when tensions between the US and China were at an all-time high.

Greiner broke his smirk and bared a full, knowing smile as the agents approached within feet of him. "I can't imagine why you would be here. Let me guess." He placed his index finger on his lips and cast his eye upward. "Handley sent you?"

"Good guess. Why don't we go outside?" one of the agents replied.

"Why not?" With all the detachment of a slick operative, Greiner followed them. "Picked a hell of a time. You people got balls."

The agent pressed his hand against Greiner's shoulder. "Just keep it moving."

"Whatever you say, boss."

They emerged from the embassy and headed toward the building west of the main entrance. A few guards cast wary eyes in their direction but remained unfazed by the men.

The voice in the agents' earpieces appeared in the form of a man leaning with one foot against the wall. He pushed off and flicked away his cigarette. "Fancy meeting you here." He approached Greiner and when he was only inches from him, pulled back his right fist and unleashed a firm blow into his gut.

Greiner doubled over, coughing and wheezing, but soon stood upright. "Nice to see you too." He labored to reaffirm his resilience.

"We have enough on you to put you away for the rest of your life."

"Fabricated, I'm sure. But it does beg the question, if that is a fact, why am I not wearing handcuffs?" Greiner replied.

"Because the director wants to give you a chance to make things right."

Greiner nodded. "I see. A little *quid pro quo*?"

"Something like that. Except that if you don't comply, you will only see the sunlight one hour out of every day until you die or someone takes out your sorry ass."

"I definitely don't like the sound of that. What's he want from me?"

"Your connections."

"To who?"

The agent in charge pitched his head toward the embassy doors. "To him, first and foremost. And to his bosses. You'll meet with the director tomorrow morning and he'll fill you in on the rest. For now, go back inside. Enjoy yourself. Seems like a hell of a good time in there." He turned to his partners. "Let's go."

They began to walk away, but one of the agents stopped short and turned back to Greiner. "Oh, one more thing; it would be in your best interest to do as the director asks."

"So you said."

"Right. But don't think for one minute if you go back on the deal that I'll let you live. Not after the shit you've pulled. You're a damn disgrace."

––––––

Prison was no place for a man like former Deputy Secretary Wendell Turner. Its gray walls, concrete floors, and iron bars were contradictory to everything he knew and everything he had. But that was the man he used to be. Now he was just another inmate, waiting for trial. However, no one else in this prison was about to be tried for treason. He was special in that regard. Very special. The last person convicted of treason in the United States was in 1952. The Japanese-American was sentenced to death, but his sentence was changed to life, only then to be released by President Kennedy and deported back to Japan.

Turner's notoriety stemmed from his conspiring with the rogue Chinese agent, Lei Jian, to continue to conceal the Great Lie, as it had been dubbed by the media. The one he perpetually fed in order to keep his power, until he was exposed. But this wasn't how it was supposed to turn out. She wasn't supposed to make it to that stage long enough to tell the world what he'd done. Even if he had done it to protect the president. Or so he told himself.

The uninspired prison common room filled with metal benches and tables was nearly empty, except for the few inmates waiting to be called for visitation, including Turner. Those who remained watched the television affixed high on the wall as it broadcast the news. The anchorman, polished with coiffed hair and a jawline chiseled from stone, spoke with menacing clarity.

"*China has continued selling off its US bonds, resulting in a prolonged decline in the dollar and the yuan. According to the Treasury Secretary, their show of defiance in the face of harsh US sanc-*

tions will ultimately cost China as exports continue to rise in cost and American products continue to fly off the shelves in the US. However, he has warned that should the sell-off endure, and the dollar spiral further, the Federal Reserve Chairman will have no choice but to raise interest rates. And as unemployment continues its upward climb due to heavy job losses resulting from the sanctions, the American economy will remain in great peril."

"I warned them," Turner spoke to no one but himself. "I told the secretary what would happen if the sanctions continued. Now look at this goddam mess."

"Turner." A detention officer reached for his shoulder. "Your visitor is here. Let's go."

He adjusted his blue jumpsuit, slid back on his rubber sandals, and followed the officer. The door buzzed and clicked open. Turner was ushered into the corridor that led to the visitation rooms.

On arrival, the officer pulled open the door. "You know the rules."

Turner walked inside and spotted his wife sitting at one of the tables. He approached her and sat down. "Hi." An instant sincerity masked his face. "You look very pretty."

She smiled.

"How are the kids?" he asked.

"Missing you."

"And you?" He spotted a flash of guilt in her eyes but decided not to pull at that thread.

"Of course. We all want you to come home."

"The trial is next week. We just have to hold on a little longer." Turner had little conviction in his own words. While the prosecutors couldn't make the case against him in the deaths of Camden Meeks and his wife, they still had Kendrick's resignation letter and that turncoat staffer, Bryce Dunn, to testify against him.

A kid who he had trusted with knowledge of the letter only to have him throw it back in his face at trial. His only hope was that if convicted on this trumped-up charge of treason, the president would see his way to issuing a pardon. After all, he'd protected the president as he saw it. And he hoped his high-priced attorney would convince the jury of that too. Especially in light of the ensuing economic freefall as a result of the president taking action against China.

"We're running out of money, Wendell," she continued. "The kids' school tuition, the house—what am I supposed to do? I can't even get a job. No one in his right mind would hire me now. And what happens if you're convicted?"

"Stop." He reached for her hand, which rested on the table, before eyeing one of the guards. He pulled it away when the officer shook his head as a warning. "That's not going to happen. And I can get you money."

"How?" She regarded him with worry in her eyes. "Never mind. I don't want to know. Just make sure you do. I have to go now. I have to get back home before the kids get out of school." She started to rise.

"Will you be there? At the trial?"

"Yes."

Turner watched his wife walk toward the door. The guard opened it and she passed through without so much as a second glance at him. He closed his eyes, knowing that even if he wasn't convicted, his marriage was over. His life as a public official was certainly over. And what else did he have?

———

Trevor Axell, former CIA field operative turned inter-agency liaison, and now the head of the newly formed joint task force, stood before his team. "Where's Merrick?" No sooner had the words left his mouth did she appear in the doorway.

"Right here. Sorry I'm late. Couldn't get out of the office." Lacy Merrick's job as an FBI data analyst hadn't let up just because she was now part of the covert task force set up by the president, a direct result of her exposing to the world what the Chinese government had done—and how the US government attempted to cover it up.

"Let's get down to business." Axell sat at the head of the conference table and began, "Anyone catch the news this morning?"

"Yeah. More good news on the jobs front. The economy's still heading into the crapper. So what else is new?" Aaron Hunter wasn't usually the type to espouse doom and gloom, but they all felt it. All he'd wanted was to help Lacy, the wife of his college friend who died in the mall attack. And he had. But this was the price they would pay for their efforts.

No longer playing spy over at Langley, Hunter's full-time gig was this task force. He was an official government employee now and it wasn't his style—not by a long shot. But he was doing it for her, more than anything.

"What's new is that Wendell Turner's heading to court next week and we should all be concerned about that." FBI Counterterrorism Agent Will Caison attempted to reel in Aaron, to remind him of what was at stake, even now. He turned his sights to Axell. "From what I've heard, they don't have enough to charge him on the murder of the Meekses."

"That's the word on the vine. We know it was Shen Yang who sent his people there and Turner who told him where they could be found. The deal was that if Turner gave him the head of the man who let Martin Delgado infiltrate his inner circle, Turner would also tell Yang where we were, killing two birds."

"And that's exactly how Sajwani found us," Lacy replied. "Regrettably, any record of the phone calls between Yang and Turner has surprisingly vanished. Something we need to put at the top of our list."

"We'll just have to see how next week plays out," Axell said. "We've still got a job to do and we need to let the prosecutors do theirs."

"Speaking of jobs to do," Caison added. "As far as I know, we're no closer to finding the source behind the transfer of Dalian shares than we were when we started months ago. That's still our number one priority and I don't think we should get distracted by the trial. Turner's going to get what he gets. We can't control that. But we can and must find out how the hell Dalian and its CEO managed to avoid the sanctions and continue to have a foothold here in this country."

"Caison's right. The president put us together for a reason." Axell eyed his colleagues. "And that was to get to the bottom of the Dalian Company's finances and especially its CEO, Shen Yang. We need to figure out how that sale of shares flew under the radar of the SEC. Now, we've been busting our humps searching, but before we go too far down this road right now, I want to show you guys something." Axell stood from the table and headed toward the door. "What are you waiting for? Come on."

The team followed him into the hall, each looking curiously at the other.

"This is what we've been waiting for." Axell smiled and opened the door.

Aaron walked inside like a kid waking up to presents under the tree. "This is what I'm talking about. Finally, some decent tech."

"I thought you'd be happy with this," Axell said as he continued inside. "We have everything we could possibly want in here. And it's not just decent tech. It's state-of-the-art technology and a place to call home."

The bullpen addition had taken longer than expected, but work was now completed. And the team had a place to work. A place that meant they would no longer have to operate out of abandoned warehouses or apartment buildings. Or worry about secure connections.

"We've been given near carte blanche, people," Axell continued. "So now there are no excuses for not getting the job done. The president's come through for us."

————

With arms behind his back, Shen Yang faced the window of his office, overlooking downtown Fairfax's business district. The request had been made and his people would get the money to Turner's family through untraceable back channels. A neophyte Yang was not when it came to shifting money. To him, it was like paper cups. Try to find the one with the coin beneath it. By the time suspicions were raised, his people were already onto the next channel. Always one step ahead.

The time would come, however, when his generosity would cease and Turner would be left to fend for himself. But that decision would be made after the trial when Turner no longer posed a threat. There were still things he knew that could come back to haunt Yang. Once he was behind bars, no one would listen.

For now, Yang's chief concern was to keep the feds off his scent and the scent of the company that purchased the majority share in Dalian. The US was posturing in its attempt to make an example of the Chinese-run operation in the states. His own country was too, for that matter. Two superpowers playing chicken to the detriment of their own people. "Typical," Yang said. He turned toward his desk and pressed a button on his landline.

The voice of a young woman sounded through the intercom. "Yes, sir?"

"Arrange for one of my lawyers to be present at the trial next week. I'll need to be updated."

"Of course, sir. I'll..."

He pressed the button again, cutting off the woman's voice mid-sentence.

Dalian had suffered losses this quarter as a result of the sanctions and; more importantly, as a result of American buyers not shopping at the malls owned by Dalian. While the corporation buried itself in layers of companies and investors, some underground reports had surfaced regarding the origins of the money behind Dalian and the information had spread among conspiracy theorists online. When questioned, his media relations team denied the allegations, but if one was savvy enough, one could find the trail. And he believed that savvy person was currently working for the FBI. While she'd become a high-profile figure—a messenger of truth—she and her band of merry men were running a covert operation, but what he didn't know was who was behind it or what they wanted.

———

Snow fell lightly on the blades of grass in the front yard, clinging for just a moment before melting. Lacy closed the front room curtains as the wintery days brought early nights.

They'd survived their first Christmas without Jay. It hadn't been easy. Now that January had arrived, things were returning to normal. Well, their new normal. Therapy sessions were fewer and farther between now. Olivia was adjusting and so was Jackson.

Lacy finally felt they were safe. And the nightmare was behind them.

Although what she'd done—exposing a devastating fact to the people—had resulted in devastating consequences. She wondered how long it would be before her fellow Americans tired of the rising unemployment, civil unrest, and the battle for autonomy in the face of global economic challenges the nation had withstood thus far. Would they curse her name in the end?

It had to stop—the bluster of two world leaders proving their strengths. She understood why it had to be this way. China had to pay for what they'd done. Though they had insisted it was an act of a renegade. She knew better, and so did the president.

"Mom, it's time for you to tuck us in." Olivia approached her while still standing at the window. "Are you okay? Is someone out there?"

Lacy turned. "Oh, no, honey. I was just watching the snow. And you're right. It is time for bed." She peered into the hall. "Where's your brother?"

"I don't know."

Lacy walked toward the staircase. "Jack? It's time for bed." She listened, but there was no reply. "Jack? Where are you?" She continued down the hall in search of him and happened upon Celeste. "Have you seen Jack?"

"No, I haven't. He's around somewhere. Jack?"

The three split up in search of the young boy who turned six only weeks ago. Jack was prone to pulling these disappearing acts. It was his way of gaining attention. Lacy didn't fault him for it. Jack was still very young, and to have survived what he had damaged something in him. It damaged something in all of them. But this was his way and he always turned up in the end. She no longer feared he'd left the house or something worse. This was just part of his healing process.

"Jack? Honey, you need to come out now and get ready for bed." Lacy walked upstairs and checked the bedrooms. "Jack?" She opened the door to her own bedroom and spotted a tiny bare-foot with curled toes jutting from beneath the bed.

Lacy knelt, raising the dust cover. "Jack? It's time for bed, sweetheart." She looked into his wide eyes and broad smile.

"How'd you find me?"

"It wasn't easy. You're getting pretty good at this." She reached for his hand. "Come on. I'll help you out."

Celeste and Olivia appeared in the doorway.

"I see you found our expert hider," Celeste said. "Good. Now no more messing around. Mom says it's time for bed."

"Fine." Jackson fully emerged and slunk out of the room and to his own bed.

Lacy followed him out, regarding Celeste with a smile. "I'll go tuck them in. Thanks."

"My pleasure." Celeste made her way down the stairs.

"Okay, guys." She followed their nightly rituals until both were tucked up in bed. Lacy turned off the hall lights and walked back downstairs to the living room. All was quiet and she could try to free her mind of what lay ahead, but it would be and had always been a futile effort. She could no more forget what had happened this past year than she could reconcile with what still needed to be done. But there was still a job to do. And Lacy had made a promise to Jay. That promise had yet to be fulfilled.

CHAPTER
TWO

SWEAT DRIPPED from Will Caison's brow before rolling into his eyes. He squeezed them shut and hoisted the 200-pound barbell from his chest with a resonant grunt. Returning it to the rack, he sat up and wiped his face with a towel.

"Is that all you got?" Trevor Axell, wrapped in an overcoat, approached from behind.

Will spotted his reflection in the gym mirror and turned. "You think you can do better, old man?"

Axell had a few years on Agent Caison, fifteen to be exact, but he could hold his own. "I wouldn't want to put you to shame in front of all these ladies. Most of them look like they could take you on anyway."

"Why are you here, disturbing my workout?"

"We need to talk." Axell tossed a glance toward the door. "Outside."

Will followed him out, chugging his water bottle along the way. "What's going on?"

Axell assessed the parking lot and surrounding buildings in the strip mall where the gym was anchored. The bitter night air was noticeable on his breath as he shoved his hands in his coat pockets. "Money's been deposited into an account owned by Mrs. Turner. A large sum of money."

"When? Do we know who sent it?" Will's overheated body began to cool as the sweat turned to steam, rising from his neck and chest.

"Not yet. I'll need Hunter to look into it. My guess is it's a payoff."

"For the upcoming trial? Making sure Turner keeps his mouth shut?"

"Most likely. I can't see any benefit to Turner if he does spill the beans on Yang. Wouldn't do him any good. No way he'll get a plea deal on this. All it'll do is jeopardize his family's safety and welfare. He needs the money."

"Okay. We find out for sure it was Yang, then what?"

"Ammunition. A nail in Yang's coffin. It'll confirm to the president what we already know. That Yang was behind the conspiracy with Turner. We need that proof to bolster our case."

"Our goal is to bring down the Dalian Company, but we still don't know who the new majority shareholder is. We can get this ammo on Yang, but what will it do for us in the end?"

"It's all we've got right now. But I have an idea to get us closer to the goalpost. Which is why I'm here, freezing my nuts off." He peered over his shoulder before resuming. "I want you to do something for me."

"What's that?"

"I need a woman."

"Excuse me?" Will raised a brow.

"Someone who will get her hands dirty and is used to doing just that. I don't have anyone here that I can call on. I've known a few in my time overseas, but I just don't get involved in that arena anymore."

"And I do?"

"You work in counterterrorism. I'm sure you have resources—assets who owe you."

"Maybe. What will she need to do?"

————

A woman with blonde flowing locks and wearing a fitted black dress stood at the bar's entrance. It was an exclusive wine bar that required membership, which of course was reserved for the wealthiest of D.C., and Caison had guaranteed her access. The rest was now up to her.

"Good evening, ma'am. May I show you to a table?" The concierge approached her with hands clasped at his front. "You are a member?"

"Yes." She handed him the card.

After a momentary check of her name, he continued. "How may I assist?"

"I'm meeting someone and I think I see him over there."

"You're welcome to go over. Have a good evening."

Her stilettos clicked on the marble floor as she made her way toward the bar, putting on the necessary airs that could attract any living, breathing man on the planet. On a typical day, Madison Goodman found herself on the arm of a foreign diplomat of a Watch List country, keeping tabs and taking notes. Only tonight she was doing Agent Caison a favor. A big one. And she intended to collect when the job was done.

"Anyone sitting here?" Madison placed her evening bag on the bar top and regarded the man next to her.

"Looks like you are," he replied with a broad smile oozing with charm. It appeared he wasn't new to this game either. "What are you drinking?"

"Gin and tonic."

The man nodded to the bartender on approach. "Gin and tonic for the lady and I'll have another whiskey neat." He eyed her again, devouring every inch of her. "I'm Gary." He offered his hand.

"Madison. Pleasure to meet you. What brings you out on a cold D.C. night?"

"Just arrived in town, actually. Here on business."

"Oh yeah?"

The bartender returned with their drinks.

"Thanks. Put it on my tab, would you?" he said. "I'm a financial consultant preparing a study for a lobbying firm."

"Sounds interesting."

"Not really." He sipped on his whiskey. "And what about you?"

"I was actually supposed to meet a friend, but just as I stepped out of the cab, he texted me to say he wasn't going to make it. I decided to come in anyway since I was already here."

"His loss."

She smiled and turned away, demure, and with a youthful appearance that made it possible. On anyone else, it would have seemed insincere.

"I'm glad you decided to come in."

"Me too."

As the conversation flowed, along with the drinks, she waited for the call. At last, it came through, just when she thought she might have to take this party someplace more private.

Gary reached for his phone on the bar top and glanced at the screen. "I'm sorry, I need to take this. Would you excuse me for just a moment?"

"Of course." She watched him walk toward the exit and

turned her attention to the bartender as he moved closer. "You get a copy for me?"

"Sure did. Just sent you the photo."

"Thanks. You're a lifesaver."

"Anytime."

Within a few minutes, Gary returned. "I'm so sorry. Work. What can you do?"

"I understand completely."

"Where were we?" He pulled his stool closer.

At that moment, Madison's cell phone vibrated in her bag. "Oh no. That one's mine." She retrieved it from the small handbag. "Are you kidding me?"

"Everything all right?"

"Sorry. No, it's not. I have to go. My sitter says my kid just threw up." She stood up to leave. "Pleasure meeting you, Gary. Maybe we'll cross paths again."

"I certainly hope so." He raised his glass to her, but his expression couldn't hide his disappointment. "I hope everything turns out okay. Good night, Madison."

The bartender approached as she walked away. "That's too bad, man. She was smokin' hot."

"No shit."

———

Madison's cab rolled to a stop at the front of Will's apartment building. He stood up from the front steps and walked toward it, blowing on his hands for warmth. She rolled down the rear passenger window and he leaned in. "You get it?"

She raised a brow at his remark.

"Right. And everything went okay? He didn't suspect anything?"

"This isn't my first rodeo, Agent Caison."

"Sorry. I did it again, didn't I?"

"Don't worry about it. You'll come to understand my ways, should we need to work together again. In the meantime, give me your phone."

He handed her his iPhone.

"I just airdropped it to you. Is that all you needed?"

"Yes, ma'am. Thank you."

"You just remember this when SSA Kelly gets my bill."

Will smiled, knowing she wasn't talking about money, but favors. "Will do. Thanks again for this."

"Of course." She turned to the cab driver. "Fairfax station, please." As she rolled up her window, the cab pulled away.

Will glanced at his phone and the pictures she'd just sent. One was the credit card of the man she'd met with. The other was a picture of him on the phone as he stood outside. "She's good."

"It's cold out here tonight, Mr. Caison," the doorman said as Will approached.

"That it is." He continued through the entrance and toward the elevators.

The doors parted and he was on his way up to the sixth floor. He continued to peer at the image, as though he knew the man. But he didn't, of course. Maybe Axell did. However, he would wait until he reached his apartment and refrain from sending the pictures over the cell phone network. He'd learned enough from Hunter to know that the safest bet was to send it over a secured connection, which he'd whipped up for him within days of the establishment of their team.

Once inside, he plugged his cell phone into the USB on his computer and sent the images to a secure server at their new home base. From there, Axell could access them and take a look for himself.

With the phone to his ear, he called Axell. "It's on the server."

"No problems?"

"Not that I'm aware. She seems to be a woman of few words, though."

"That bodes well for us. Good night, Caison. And good work."

———

Inside their new cutting-edge bullpen, Lacy stared at the image on her laptop. "I know this man." She turned to Axell. "I don't know him personally, but I've seen him before. I've talked to him before."

"Where?" Axell replied.

"At Argus Solutions."

"Are you sure about that?" Will asked.

"Of course I'm sure. It's been a long time—years—but I remember him from a company party or some social event. I remember him because he hit on me." She smirked at her recollection. "Just as Jay left to get us a drink, he came up to me. He was creepy then and I'm sure he hasn't changed."

"Was his name Gary Reese?" Axell continued. "That's what shows up on this credit card, but I doubt it is his real name. That would be too easy."

Lacy turned her sights upward. "I can't remember his name. He had the same white hair though, even then. I could go back to Argus and talk to Scott Voss. He'll know him. I'm sure of it."

"I'll go with you." Aaron and Will looked at each other as they replied in unison.

Axell pursed his lips and eyed both of them. "Hunter, I need you here with me. We need to find this guy's real identity. Merrick and Caison can go to Argus and work that angle."

"Sure. Yeah. Sounds good." Hunter's disappointment was palpable.

"Good." Axell began to rise. "Then we all know what we're supposed to do. Let's meet back here this afternoon and see what we've got. Anyone have any questions?"

"Nope." Lacy stood. "You ready to go?"

"Sure am." Will pulled his coat off the back of the chair. "We'll need to check in at Headquarters afterward, before coming back here. I've got a few things on my plate."

"Same here." She turned to Axell. "That okay with you, boss?"

"Yes, and don't call me boss. You know I hate that."

Lacy smiled. "Okay, boss. See you later." She walked into the corridor.

"You're in a good mood today," Will said.

"Feeling better than I have in a while, I guess. Starting to feel, dare I say, almost normal. Not quite, but we're getting there."

"That's great to hear, Lacy. Time heals."

"That's what they say." She pushed through the exit and into the parking garage. "You want to drive, or should I?"

"Be my guest. You know where you're going." Will waited for her to unlock the door of her Lexus and slid onto the passenger seat.

"I sure do." She stepped in and pressed the ignition.

"When was the last time you were at Argus?" he asked.

"Not since I cleaned out Jay's desk. And we all know what happened after that. It'll be strange to see Scott, but I don't hold him responsible for any of this. How could I? He didn't know what Owen Ballard was doing."

"No. Of course not."

"It'll just be hard seeing everyone again, you know? I worked there too. A long time ago, but still. It's like that was a whole different life. So many things have happened since then." She gathered her thoughts and continued. "But Scott will be able to find out who he is. I'm sure of it. He was a big player a while back. Maybe still is. Who knows?"

"Why do you suppose this man has ties to Argus?"

She turned to him. "That, my friend, is a very good question."

The next several minutes passed in silence before Will began again. "How's Hunter doing with all of this? He's settled into his new place, right?"

"Yeah. I helped him unpack and did a bit of decorating for him. Tried to make it look like a full-grown man lived there and not some college kid. I mean, not that that's how he behaves; he doesn't."

"I knew what you meant."

"Aaron's a good man, though. He's helped the kids and me a lot. They've started calling him Uncle Aaron." She laughed.

"Uncle Aaron, huh? And what do they call me?"

Uh, well, I—um."

"Never mind." Will turned his attention to the passing land-scape outside his window. "Maybe I should come by more often so they can get to know me too."

"I'm sure they'd love that." Lacy turned left into the parking lot and pulled into a space near the front. "This is it."

"Did you happen to call Scott and let him know we were coming?" Will opened the passenger door.

"I did not. But he'll be here. It's not a Friday afternoon. Then we'd stand no chance. He enjoys a game of golf on Fridays and usually takes the sales staff with him."

"Sounds like a good guy."

"He is." Lacy stepped out of the car and pulled on her coat.

They entered through the glass doors and approached the front desk.

"Lacy Merrick? What on earth are you doing here?" said the woman who sat behind the reception desk.

"I'm here to see Scott Voss. Do you know if he's in?"

"I believe he is, but I'll call up to him. Wow, it's really good to see you. I hope you're doing well—after everything."

"Thanks, Nora. I am. And it's good to see you too."

"Hi, Lacy Merrick is here to see you, if you have a minute." Nora paused. "I'll send her right up." She replaced the receiver and smiled at Lacy. "Go ahead on up. You remember where his office is at?"

"I sure do. Thank you." She nodded for Will to follow.

"She seems very fond of you," Will said.

Lacy pressed the elevator button. "She's a good kid. Bright. Much too bright to still be answering the phones. I'll have to mention that to Scott."

Scott Voss was already on his feet with open arms on their arrival. "Lacy. It is so good to see you. How are you?"

"Doing well, Scott. Thank you." She pulled from the embrace. "This is Special Agent Will Caison."

"Oh. This is an official visit, then?" He returned to his desk. "Please, why don't you both have a seat."

"Thanks." Lacy began, "Sorry to arrive unannounced, but I was hoping you could help me with something."

"Of course. Anything. You know that."

Lacy pulled out a file folder from her carrier bag and retrieved the photos. "Do you know who this man is?" She placed the images on his desk and pushed them forward.

Scott held one of them in his hands and examined it. With a furrowed brow, he shook his head. "I don't think so. Should I?"

"2015-ish. Company Christmas party, I think. We were here at the office and you invited some of the bigger clients."

He studied the picture again, seeming to concentrate a little harder.

"I don't know who he worked for at the time," Lacy continued, "but I remember him there. I just need your help placing him. The company. His name."

"2015 Christmas party," Scott said under his breath. "One of our clients." He continued listing parameters in an attempt to recall the man's name. "Hang on a second. He was Bruce's client. That's right. But Bruce isn't here anymore." Scott looked at Lacy. "We lost quite a bit of business after that whole Nova thing."

"I'm sure," Lacy replied.

"So, who is this guy to you?"

"Just something we're working on. Any other thoughts?" This time, Will chimed in.

"Yeah." Scott nodded. "That's right. I remember him now." He turned toward his computer and began typing. "He was with a company called.... Damn, I can't recall off the top of my head... Wait, here it is. "Synergy Dynamics." He faced them again. "His name is Matthew Greiner. And he was Bruce's client."

"What did he do for them, this Synergy Dynamics?" Lacy asked.

"Couldn't tell you. I do know that they were contracted to do work for the government and I only recall that because of the amount of paperwork we had to file in order to become an approved subcontractor."

Anything else you can tell us?" Will added.

"Not really. I didn't have much to do with him. Although I do remember him being at that Christmas party now. In fact, if I recall correctly, he'd hit on a few of the staff and I got an earful about it."

Lacy smiled. "Yeah. That's pretty much what I remember

about him." She began to rise. "Thank you so much, Scott. I can't tell you what a help this is."

"Listen, can I take you two out to lunch or something? I'd love to catch up."

"We appreciate the offer," Lacy began, "but we have a packed schedule today. I'll tell you what, though. I'll shoot you an email with some dates and we'll get something on the calendar."

"I'd like that, Lacy. I really would."

"Me too. Thanks again, Scott."

"Anytime."

CHAPTER
THREE

ON THE BALCONY of his high-rise apartment, CIA Agent Caleb Shaw peered out over the bustling streets of Beijing. He pressed his cigarette into the ashtray that rested on a table and walked back inside. "Air's getting pretty thick out there. Might have to break out the masks before too long." He walked toward the kitchen. "Want a beer?"

"Thanks," CIA Agent Brent Maddox replied.

Shaw returned and offered the beer. "What happened over there?"

"Something's going on." Maddox tossed back a swig. "I don't like it. Whatever it is. This shit assignment is throwing me off my game. You know I don't like playing with this kind of fire."

"Yeah. I know, man. Your job is to grow the network here. Keep your eyes on the up-and-coming hackers and work them. But we got lucky. You found her."

"Luck doesn't play into it. In fact, I'm pretty sure I drew the short stick on this deal."

Shaw laughed. "You might be right. But what could you do? She knew your boy and your boy said you should know her."

"I know. I was there. Anyway, she says he's been coming to visit. Which wouldn't be hard to confirm."

"Just need to check his passport."

"Right. But he's been meeting with others from the village. And some heavy-hitters here in Beijing."

"Why?"

"You want the truth?" He eyed Shaw. "He's planning something. And I think he's about to test the waters."

"What's going down?"

"So far as she knows, word got back to her that he was going to start small. A car bomb, like the one a few years ago."

"Here?"

"Yeah. Don't know where yet. But it's going to be soon."

"We stand a chance at stopping it?"

"She didn't get enough intel to know dates. But why would we, huh? After what those assholes did to ours?"

Shaw cast his gaze downward. "Hard to argue that point. But he's the CEO of Dalian. Man, we can't ignore that. Because if he's testing the waters here, what do you think could happen back home?"

Shaw's cell phone buzzed in his pocket. He glanced at the caller ID. "I have to take this. Hang on." He turned away. "Shaw here."

Maddox looked through the sliding glass door and onto the city, finishing his beer while Shaw continued with his conversation.

"No. When did this happen?" He promptly turned back to his colleague with wide eyes. "Our guys okay?"

Maddox stood at attention and held Shaw's gaze.

"Son of a bitch. On our way." He ended the call and reached for his keys.

"What happened?"

"Guess we don't have to wonder anymore."

"What the hell are you talking about?"

"A bomb went off in the Tiananmen West Station. Chief wants us now."

———

The FBI investigation into the entire State Department came on the heels of the president's speech some eight weeks ago. The one he was forced to deliver in light of events brought forth by Lacy Merrick.

Transparency was key to ensuring the public was satisfied with the president's remarks, and while the investigation itself had been deemed classified in the interest of national security, the president often remarked upon their progress, suggesting, "The truth will prevail" in his words.

This offered little comfort for Lacy as nothing had yet been disclosed. However, she still held the president in high esteem and expected he would continue to get to the bottom of the complete breakdown of his State Department, and discover if the lie had truly ended with Wendell Turner.

Lacy turned off the radio as she and Will made their way back to base. "You think anything will come of this?"

"The investigation?" Will glanced at her. "I don't know. Director Mobley might shed some light on it for us."

"It's classified, remember?"

"Axell's got the clearance. But we can't worry about that right now. Our job is to find out if Yang is sending money to Turner and what this Matthew Greiner has to do with any of it."

"Maybe Aaron was able to get somewhere." Lacy killed the engine and stepped out of the car. Noting precise details of her surroundings, something she did now out of habit, the two made their way into their new headquarters.

"You're back." Trevor Axell raised to full height as the two caught his attention. "Hunter's been working on the money transfer."

"And?" Will asked.

Aaron spun his chair away from his monitor. "It's looking like it was dark banking." He noticed mild confusion mask their faces. "When individuals make money transfers between branches. It's just another way to shield transactions. Anyway, I'm still working on it. How'd you guys do?"

"We got a name." Lacy approached the two inside the bullpen. "Matthew Greiner. He worked for a company called Synergy Dynamics."

"Government contractor," Will added.

"Really?" Trevor rubbed his chin stubble. "That's interesting."

"That was back in 2015, though. The salesman who handled that contract has since left Argus and his clients along with him," Lacy replied. "Nevertheless, you should be able to find something now that you have a name, a face, and a credit card."

"It was a secured card under a false name. Hunter pulled the information on the name and got a big fat zero. But now we have this. It might still open some doors for us," Axell replied.

"I assume you think he's got ties to Yang. What intel do you have?" Will began. "You asked me to get you someone who could give us pictures and I did. But that means you had to have found something suggesting a connection to Yang."

"I did. And I should've shared that with you." Trevor returned his attention to Aaron. "Can you pull up the satellite images from Dalian from Monday afternoon?"

"We have satellite imagery?" Lacy asked. "I didn't realize we had that sort of clout around here."

"I take Director Mobley at his word when he says the president's determined to let us do what needs to be done about Shen Yang and Dalian. Lacy, we've been given unprecedented resources usually reserved for foreign surveillance."

"Not domestic," she added.

"I got it." Aaron displayed the images on the large screens mounted on the wall. "These are from last Monday around 1 pm."

"Perfect." Axell approached the monitors and pointed with his index finger. "This is our guy right here. He's been showing up at the Dalian offices more frequently and I wanted to know why. Then, when I got word Turner's been getting money, I thought why not start with this guy? So I started following him. Where Caison's asset met him was one of a handful of hangouts I followed him to. I'd hoped he would be there the other night because he was there that same time the previous week. My hunch was right. He's not our only lead, just our best one."

"Has he shown up at the prison too?" Will asked.

"No such luck. But now we have a name, a real name, thanks to you two."

"The problem is, as I see it," Lacy began, "is that he's tied to Argus—or was."

"Meaning he could've been in the picture from the very beginning," Trevor began. "But since we weren't looking at him, he slipped under our radar. Now that he's popping up, it's time we learn a little more about him."

———

Matthew Greiner finished his whiskey neat as the announcement stated the plane would begin its descent into Beijing. He returned his first-class seat to its upright position, folding the legrest down and turning off the television monitor.

"May I take that glass for you, sir?" A pleasant-looking flight attendant flashed her smile and held out her hand.

"Of course. Thank you."

"Thank you, sir."

He watched her continue collecting miscellaneous items from the others in first class, noting the sway of her hips. "Maybe next time," he whispered under his breath.

Within minutes, he was ready to deplane and reached for the carrier bag stowed in the overhead bin. Inside the terminal, he started toward baggage claim. He pushed his hand through his white hair to straighten it after the long flight. Having turned gray at the age of thirty-five, now in his early fifties, his hair was completely white. It was his belief that it made him appear distinguished and Greiner thought highly of himself when it came to most things. Sexual conquests, business dealings, political friendships; he believed himself better than most. The hard work of making backroom deals, shaking the hands of dictators, royalty, and the political elite in Washington lent him exceptional confidence that could easily be mistaken for arrogance.

But his job now was something of an anomaly. A request, or rather, a demand made by a powerful man who'd engaged him to lay the groundwork some months ago. And there was still much to be done.

His leather-bound case rolled down the belt and onto the carousel. Greiner stepped closer and reached for the bag, but not before someone else reached for it. "Excuse me. I believe this is my bag, sir."

This person didn't appear to be some distracted tourist or foreign businessman. Greiner eyed him and didn't like what he was seeing.

"My sincerest apologies, sir." The man bowed only slightly, his eyes never leaving Greiner's. "My mistake." He released the bag and turned on his heel.

Greiner wasn't under the impression that what just happened was anything but intentional. A warning from someone who knew he had arrived, but was possibly unaware of his purpose. He was in foreign territory. A country that was on the receiving end of severe sanctions and it was only a matter of time before US citizens would no longer be allowed to travel here.

———

The lobby of the five-star hotel in the center of Beijing boasted a stunning bar area, complete with a karaoke stage tucked in the corner. A young Chinese man in a white oxford and loosened tie belted out a peculiar rendition of a recent Madonna song. The form of entertainment that had been so popular in Japan had grown even more popular in China.

Greiner sat at a bar top table for two as he looked with curiosity at the singer, waiting for his drink. His phone buzzed with an incoming message. "I'm here." The text came through on the country's popular texting app, one he had downloaded some time ago when he began this mission.

He turned toward the entrance and raised a hand to signal his location to the one who had texted him.

"How was your flight?" A man in a black suit and grey tie took a seat across from him.

"Decent."

"You must be exhausted."

"I'm all right." He raised a hand to garner the attention of the cocktail waitress. "What are you drinking?"

The man turned to the waitress on her arrival. "Kweichow Moutai."

"What he said. *Xièxiè*. (thank you.)" Greiner was familiar with the popular drink that had become the calling card of the politically connected and well-to-do in China. However, the vodka-like liquor wasn't his cup of tea and he preferred his scotch whiskey like every other red-blooded American man. Which, frankly, wasn't that easy to find here.

After the waitress left, he continued. "You called this face-to-face. What is it that I can do for you, Minister?"

"As you know, it seems we've gone from bad to worse with US relations."

"That's an understatement."

"Indeed, it is. However, it must be this way until we can come to a mutual understanding with the current administration."

"They won't call off the investigation if that's what you're asking. Not a chance that will fly with the American people."

"No. I don't suppose it would. That is not what I am alluding to, however. As I see it, my government intends to continue to dispose of US bonds, which, as you know, will continue the decline of our currency."

"Which of course, you can manipulate, should you choose to do so."

"It's not that easy and certainly not under this political climate or economic one."

"China keeps dumping stock, then what?" Greiner pressed on.

"Let me backtrack for just a moment and get to the point of why I called you here."

The woman brought their drinks, placing them on the table. "Enjoy." She turned on her heel and walked away.

"It's about Yang. There was—an incident. And we've begun to feel as though he might not be looking out for the Party's best interest."

"I am aware of what happened." Greiner had already been

briefed about the bombing. "Do you know for sure Yang was involved?"

"We do not. However, with the sale of Dalian majority stock, we believe this has emboldened him to move in a direction that is making the Ministry quite uncomfortable."

"If anything, he's become your lap dog. Apologies if I offend, but he cannot move right now. Not with the scrutiny Dalian is currently under. Yang's hands are bound, I assure you."

"While I agree with you on that front, I'm speaking more about his association with certain individuals who, how should I say it? Have a difference of opinion from those of the Party."

Greiner began to understand the minister's meaning. "I'm not seeing that on my end and I have spent a fair amount of time with Yang in recent months. Even after the sanctions, I still believe him to be loyal to the premier and the president."

"I'm sure you're probably right. But..." He cast his gaze for eavesdroppers. "Perhaps it's best if we meet in my office tomorrow. Would that be acceptable to you?"

"Of course."

"I have something that I'd like to show you. Then you can decide if we are on the same page, as you say."

"Absolutely. How about another round? It's on me. Well, Yang, actually." He nodded to the waitress once again.

"I'd like that, thank you."

————

A woman lay next to Greiner in the early hours of the morning, her bare skin exposed. Her long black hair scattered across her pale back. And while she slept soundly, he sat up in bed, staring at her perfectly petite figure. Still jet-lagged, he regretted the late night, too much alcohol, and the energy spent on her. He was no longer a young man who could easily recover from such excesses, though he often pretended to be.

She began to rouse as he stood from the bed.

"I have to leave soon. Please show yourself out," he said before continuing into the bathroom. Not long after he turned on the shower did he hear the door close. Greiner was an unsentimental man who had never been married nor did he have any children, that he was aware of.

He straightened his tie and glanced at himself in the mirror a final time before leaving his hotel room. Bags in hand, he would head straight back to the airport after the meeting. The quick turn-around was necessary to avoid any concerns on Yang's part that he'd been gone for too long. Yang had no idea of his whereabouts and it was best kept that way.

He pushed through the lobby doors and made his way to the waiting black BMW ready to whisk him to the offices of the MSS. China's Ministry of State Security operates out of two locations. The first and public location was near Tiananmen Square. However, Greiner was not headed to that location. Instead, he would be taken to the clandestine compound located in Xiyuan, on the outskirts of Beijing. The MSS employed some 100,000 offi-cers, roughly half of whom operated in-country. The rest were dispersed throughout other parts of the world. Many of its opera-tions ran from this secret location, such as Bureau 17, the Enter-prises Division. This was where the minister requested to meet. And Greiner had just arrived.

He stepped out of the car where two MSS guards awaited him. "I'm here to see Minister Cheng."

Greiner produced the required identification, most of which he'd been given, not by his current employer, but by the highest ranking foreign intelligence officer in the US. Within moments, he was escorted to the appropriate area. The high-security measures were far greater than what he'd seen in any intelligence facility in the United States. And he knew that one false step here would mean certain death. Sometimes the thought crossed his mind that he'd played with fire for too long and it would catch up with him. But with any luck, it wouldn't be today.

In his native tongue, and with stiff arms, the guard slapped the sides of his thighs and bowed. "Sir, Mr. Greiner is here to see you."

"Thank you, you may leave now." The minister emerged from behind his desk and offered his hand. In English, he continued, "Thank you for coming."

"Of course. It must be important, or else why would I be here?"

"Let me show you something." Cheng approached an adjacent door and opened it. Inside was what appeared to be a surveillance post, manned by four men, none of whom donned the MSS guard uniform. These were likely key operatives monitoring satellite feeds from across the globe or wherever the minister deemed was the biggest threat. And in this case, Greiner noted one such location was the Dalian Company headquartered in Fairfax.

He turned to the minister. "CIA hasn't caught on to the fact that you hacked into one of their satellites?"

The minister smiled. "We aren't inside long enough for them to notice. And you can't pretend they don't do the same thing."

"Good point." Greiner knew well the tactics employed by the Central Intelligence Agency. He should, considering he was one of their operatives many years ago before realizing the money was in selling secrets to foreign entities. It was as simple as that.

"What am I looking for here? What did you want to show me?"

"Since the sanctions were put in place, we had no choice but to establish an organization through which we could fund the purchase of Dalian stock through our American partner and we wanted to ensure our investment was secure."

"Of course. And as far as I'm aware, that hasn't changed."

"Our sources inside have ensured the proper SEC filings and funneled the purchase through several shell corporations in order to avoid exposure. However, and this is the reason you're here today, we've seen some activity at Dalian and Yang's personal residence that forces me to take pause and question his loyalty to us, as we briefly discussed last night."

"You're monitoring his residence too?"

The minister only eyed him. "And at those locations, we've noticed a man who has held numerous meetings with Yang over the past several weeks."

"Since the sanctions."

"Yes."

"And who is this man?"

"That's what I need you to find out. Since you're operating the bogus fronts, you have Yang's ear. Right now, we suspect this man could have ties with the Uyghurs and is one of their American operatives."

"You believe Yang is tied to the terrorist group?"

"That will be your job to figure out. As you know, since the Xinjiang Communist Party chief was appointed to the Uyghur region last year, and is the primary location of dissension, they've banned fasting during Ramadan. Changed the prayer callings to playing the party national anthem and doing everything in their power to assimilate their minority Muslim population."

"Which, let's be honest here, isn't such a minority in that region," Greiner added.

The minister glowered at him. "You need to find out who this man is and whether he has ties to the group. And—if Yang is working with them, he will need to be replaced at Dalian."

"Of course. But you understand, if that is the case, the US government will grow increasingly concerned and perhaps begin to look closer at the shell companies—and me."

"Let me deal with that. You handle Yang."

CHAPTER
FOUR

UNDER COVER of Lacy's front porch, Will stood wrapped in a black overcoat that fused into the night sky. He was about to knock, but with his knuckles at the ready, she opened the door.

"I saw you pull up. Come in before you freeze out there."

"Thanks." Will rubbed his hands together before pulling off his coat. "Sorry I'm late."

"Don't worry about it. Lasagna keeps. Here, let me hang that up for you." She approached the coat hanger to the left of the door and draped his coat over the top hook. "Can I get you a beer, wine?"

"I'll take a wine actually. It'll warm me up." He followed her into the kitchen. "Smells good."

"I went ahead and had the kids eat with Celeste. She's upstairs getting them ready for bed now."

"Aw, man. I was looking forward to having dinner with them. Oh well, it's not like I'm Uncle Aaron or anything."

Lacy peered over her shoulder on the way to the kitchen. "What's that?"

"Nothing. How about I pour the wine and you can dish out the plates?"

"Sure." Lacy returned to the oven and retrieved the leftover lasagna. As she set the portions on the plates, she began, "Listen, I appreciate you coming over. You didn't need to, though. I'm fine, really."

"After what happened? I didn't want you to be alone."

"It wasn't the first time and I'm sure it won't be the last." She sat down, placing her napkin on her lap. "People are upset. I can understand that."

"I get they're upset, but this isn't your fault."

"Isn't it? I was the one who came out in front of the world and told the truth. Now look at what's been happening. People have lost their jobs. Riots have cropped up everywhere."

"That's no excuse for some damn reporter to shove a live mic and camera in your face as you're leaving HQ and ask if you regretted coming forward. He harassed you. He followed you to your car."

"What did you think would happen, Will? I wish I would've had the courage to respond to him. Instead, I crawled into my car and drove away."

"This country owes you, Lacy."

"Not everyone sees it that way. They want things the way they were. It made them feel safe."

"It was a false sense of security. No one's safe. Not anymore."

"Exactly." She sipped on her wine. "I didn't tell Trevor. Aaron knows, but I figured Trevor had enough to deal with right now. But I do appreciate you checking up on me. I do feel safe here, though. The association put in a guard shack. And the guard's a good guy. He already said he wouldn't let, oh, how did he put it? He wouldn't let those leeches in unless I said it was okay." She took a bite of her food and the two were silent for a moment before she continued.

"Look, this whole joint task force thing? It is kind of crazy. I mean, you and I work at Headquarters, do our jobs, and then have to make time to go to our new digs and do a whole other job. I'm glad to be a part of it, don't get me wrong. But I feel as though we're living double lives. We can't talk about the task force—to anyone. My staff is starting to think I'm trying to skate my way through the job because I'm hardly ever there. I feel as though it could come to a head. That we could be exposed. And frankly, I don't know what that might do. I suspect Trevor's feeling some of those same pressures. Like we're all double agents."

"You're right about one thing," Will began. "It does feel like I'm leading a double life. I can't tell SSA Kelly what's going on, or anyone on my own team. Makes it hard to work on the kind of stuff that drew me to the CTD in the first place."

"Fighting terrorism."

"Yeah."

"You're still doing that, but on a different front."

Will swallowed down the rest of his wine and began to cut away a piece of lasagna. "Lasagna's great, by the way. Family recipe?"

"Yes and no. It's Celeste's recipe. Can't take the credit for the food, unfortunately."

Celeste soon approached. "Sorry to interrupt, but the kids are asking for you to tuck them in."

Lacy wiped the corners of her mouth and stood from the table. "Excuse for a minute, would you?"

"Of course," Will replied.

She walked upstairs and into Olivia's room first. "Hey, sweetheart. All ready for bed?"

"Yeah." Her favorite stuffed animal was by her side and the covers were pulled to her waist.

Lacy sat down on the edge of the bed and pulled them up to her chin. "Goodnight, baby. Sleep tight and I'll see you in the morning." She leaned over to kiss her cheek.

"Don't forget Bunny."

"How could I forget Bunny?" Lacy held the pink rabbit and kissed it on its nose. "Goodnight, Bunny. Sleep tight."

Olivia had come a long way to forgiving Lacy for putting her in danger. She didn't really understand the kind of danger they had been in, but that it took her away from her mother shortly after her father died. That was all she cared about.

"Goodnight, Mom."

Lacy walked to the door and switched off the light. Jackson's room was just around the corner and she continued inside. "Hey, buddy. You ready for bed?" She noticed he was already asleep. A smile spread across her face and she pulled the covers up over his chest and kissed his forehead.

It was times like these that made her miss Jay all the more. The children had already grown taller, their faces looking more and more like young kids instead of toddlers. And of course, all they'd been through. That aged them perhaps more than anything. As it had her.

On her return to the kitchen, she spotted Will at the sink washing the dishes. "You don't have to do that."

He turned, wiping his hands on the towel that was draped over his right shoulder. "I know. But I have to repay you somehow for the meal. If I was at my place, I'd be eating ramen noodles and drinking a Bud Light."

She grabbed the towel from him. "Fine. You wash and I'll dry."

———

With his feet resting on the coffee table and his arm hanging over the top of the sofa, Trevor raised the shot of bourbon to his lips and tossed it back. He pressed a few more keys on his laptop and continued to search for the man he'd seen more times than could be considered a mere coincidence at the Dalian Company offices.

And there were still so many unanswered questions as Wendell Turner faced his upcoming trial. The defense still hadn't had the two witnesses to attest to the act of treason, a requirement in order to be convicted of the crime. Bryce Dunn was the only one. Everyone else was dead. Strange how it was harder to be convicted of treason than it was to be convicted of murder, which in most states required substantial proof, DNA, prints, motive, etc. But for treason, the act itself was defined as charging war against the United States or giving aid and comfort to its enemies. A crime punishable by death, but mostly, and most recently, punishable by time in prison and a fine. Hardly seemed equal to the crime, in his opinion. Wendell Turner was complicit in the cover-up in order to save his own ass, but to prove treason was a different ball game. And of course, there was still the question of the murder of Camden Meeks and his wife. That was what Trevor had wanted to prove more than anything, but his efforts had thus far amounted to zilch. Nothing he could find in phone records, emails, or anything that tied him to that. He suspected it had gone through Lei Jian and if that was the case, then there was no case. Jian was dead and his secrets along with him.

But Trevor had to remain focused on the task at hand. He was responsible for uncovering any wrongdoing on Dalian's part in the wake of the economic sanctions placed against China. What he hoped to accomplish was discovering that wrong-doing and tying it together with Wendell Turner, but he was running out of time.

Turner's trial had been expedited and a case of this magnitude should have taken a year or more to come to trial, but it was in the president's best interest to bring this to closure. The public demanded it. So they found loopholes and Turner's lawyer had exhausted his resources.

Trevor zoomed in on an image on his screen. He studied the man in the photo. White hair, stout, above average height. This was the man they knew to be Matthew Greiner. But Trevor knew him as someone else. And began to recall their last meeting.

Egypt, 2001, a few months before the attack on the towers, before the world flipped on its end. Trevor was an intelligence officer at the Cairo station. He remembered well the day he met Casper Janz, now known as Matthew Greiner. The man had arrived at the station and met with the Station Chief. In an infamous program begun by former President Bill Clinton and significantly ramped up after 9/11 by then-President George W. Bush, the program was called the Extraordinary Rendition and Detention Program. CIA operatives from around the globe in conjunction with several other participating nations hunted down suspected terrorists, flew them to other parts of the world, and detained them for months.

While Trevor hadn't been one of the operatives involved, he certainly was well aware of the program. And the day Janz arrived with one such suspected terrorist, who might or might not have been involved in the bombing of the USS *Cole* in October of 2000, was a day Trevor would never forget.

He'd been witness to the "enhanced interrogation techniques" employed by the CIA and other intelligence agencies. His job in Cairo was to recruit assets and nothing more. But he witnessed this man, this man who now stared back at him in the photo some sixteen years later, interrogate his prisoner. Ultimately, the man was following orders so Trevor didn't question it further. It wasn't until after 9/11 that the program had grown nearly out of control and he watched as several of his colleagues participated. At the time, of course, he agreed that this was what the terrorists deserved. And perhaps that was still how he felt, especially in light of his current task. But Janz took a little too much pleasure in the torturing of others. And that was what frightened him now. He was older, grayer, but those kinds of people didn't change. The lengths he would go to ensure he remained Matthew Greiner were lengths Trevor didn't want to test. So far, he'd kept his knowledge of Greiner's true identity a secret from his team. Something he hated doing. But until he knew what Greiner, aka Janz, was up to, he felt it was better to keep them in the dark. Especially if it involved Argus Solutions. Lacy didn't need to be made aware of anything potentially damaging on that front. It was a decision he might regret.

Trevor checked the time and retrieved his cell phone. "Hey, it's Axell. Listen, I need a favor."

———

The J. Edgar Hoover building loomed in the distance as Lacy approached the parking garage. On her arrival, she stopped at Michelle Vogel's office. Her supervisor and friend had helped Lacy through much of what she'd faced this past year. And now, she wished she could tell her about the task force, but it was something that couldn't be shared—with anyone. "Morning."

"Lacy, how are you?" Michelle removed her reading glasses. "Come on in. I feel like we haven't talked in a while."

"I know. Things have been pretty busy around here."

"Uh-huh."

As Lacy took her seat, she realized Michelle must've had an inkling as to what was happening. After all, she was an intelligent woman. How could she not?

"Listen, I'm sure you'll hear it soon enough, but I wanted to tell you that Eckhart is putting in for a transfer."

"Really?" She recalled how Eckhart had been after the promotion she'd received, but didn't think he was so upset as to leave because of it.

"Actually, he's been recruited. He'll be heading to Quantico and then, well, who knows?"

"That's great. I didn't realize it was something he was interested in doing."

"I think after all that happened with the mall attack. I think it changed some people. Brian included. Made him want to take a greater role in stopping things like that from happening again."

"I'm sure. Well, good for him. I'll stop by and talk to him in a minute."

"Good. Everything else okay?"

"Sure."

"You know, it's not too late for you. If it's something you wanted to pursue."

"What? The Academy? No. That's not for me. I thought about it—once. But I like this side of things. And, after the attack, we've really come together. The law side and us civilians. Things have gotten a lot better."

"They have. Just thought I'd throw that out there."

"I appreciate the sentiment. But I'm not going anywhere."

"Glad to hear it. I'm sure you've got another busy day ahead of you, so I'll let you get to it."

"Right." Lacy stood. "I'll talk to you later." She watched as Michelle returned the glasses to her face and didn't reply.

As she arrived at her desk, Lacy wondered how long this would last. If they were successful in pinning something on the Dalian Company, would her position inside the task force be permanent? Right now, there was no telling if other corporations, foreign or domestic, had any such dealings as Dalian. That was the job of the task force, after all. But keeping up with her duties at Headquarters required dedication. The idea she might let something slip through the cracks and miss a sign of another imminent attack sickened her. And how long might it take to get Yang without their full efforts? The part-time job seemed absurd. But that was what it was.

Nonetheless, she would do as Trevor asked and continue to play the part. Perhaps he, or the president, had reason to set it up this way, keeping the task force well under the radar.

An email appeared in her inbox that drew her away from her current thoughts. It was the weekly report from her staff, the one they were due to discuss later today. Her advanced copy was to be approved by Michelle and her prior to the meeting.

As she began to read the report, she found that a disturbing trend had emerged. Traffic on certain websites contained within the dark web had exploded. The source of her concern was that these sites originated in the US and appeared to be channeling hate to a certain ethnic group. They were showing up on their data due to the nature of the language used. Meaning terms that were also flagged on the internet. Hate, violence, threats. She printed the report and headed back into Michelle's office. "Hey, have you seen the report this week?"

"I was just reviewing it now, actually. I assume you, too, picked up on the trend?"

"Yes. This is a problem."

"We need to make the head of Cyber aware of what's happening on our end. Understand if they are seeing it on their side of things too. They'll have better insight as they're monitoring the chatter as well."

"I guess it was only a matter of time before this happened."

"Same thing happened after 9/11. People were angry and afraid. Only now that fear is directed at another group."

CHAPTER
FIVE

SYNERGY DYNAMICS, the enigmatic corporation that employed Matthew Greiner, seemed to have materialized from thin air. Records were scarce. Corporate filings, tax returns, all seemed to be protected under the guise of national security.

Lacy leaned over Aaron's shoulder as he sat at one of the workstations. "It's beginning to look as though it was the government contract that brought this company back from the verge of bankruptcy."

"Which also happened to be around the time Greiner came on board, from what I can find," Aaron replied.

"Tell me that's not a coincidence. There seems to be a lot we don't know about Matthew Greiner, except that where he goes, money seems to follow. Synergy Dynamics, now possibly a Dalian connection." Lacy considered the situation. "Scott mentioned having to jump through hoops to become an approved vendor because it was a government contractor. What government work was this company performing? That's what we need to know."

"I don't know what to tell you, Lace, but from where I sit, it's like damn musical chairs. Companies, banks, money. All vying for a seat before the music stops."

"I need to track down Bruce, then."

"You know where he works?"

"Nope. But I'm sure you can find out for me." She patted him on the shoulder.

Aaron shrugged. "Please. It's a cakewalk. It'll take me like two minutes. Just give me a last name."

"Quintero. Bruce Quintero."

Within minutes, he rolled back from his desk and presented his accomplishment. "*Voila*. Bruce Quintero, thirty-two, lives in Fairfax. Currently unemployed."

"Unemployed?"

"Well, he's not paying payroll taxes. I suppose he could be working for someone and getting paid under the table. But it doesn't appear as though he's working for any legitimate company."

"You have his address? I'll have to make a trip to see him."

"I do. But I'm coming with you."

———

Lacy pulled alongside the front of the townhouse and cut the engine. "This is the place. I hope he's home."

"And if not?" Aaron said as he stepped out of her car.

"I guess we'll have to wait for him." She joined him on the sidewalk. "By the look of this house, I'd say he's working for someone."

"Yeah. Doesn't look like he's unemployed to me. Maybe he won the lottery."

They continued their approach along the driveway of the

upscale townhome in Merrifield, not far from Lacy's home in Annandale.

"I had no idea he lives so close to me." She was the first to approach the steps and climbed up to the front door with a quick glance at Aaron before she knocked.

The two stood silent for a moment when the sound of a dead-bolt disengaging caught their attention. Lacy smiled and nodded to Aaron.

The door opened only slightly.

"Hi. Bruce Quintero?"

The man creased his brow, and with a spark of recognition, he pulled open the door. "Lacy Merrick? Is that you? What on earth are you doing here?"

"It is me. Hello, Bruce. How are you? It's been a long time."

"I'd say so. What, a couple years at least?"

"Something like that. Listen, I wanted to talk to you about Argus Solutions. Do you have a minute?"

He eyed Aaron before returning his attention to Lacy. "What about them?"

"This is a friend of mine, and Jay's, actually. Aaron Hunter. Do you think we could come in? We just have a couple of quick questions."

"Um, yeah, sure. You still with the FBI?" He stepped aside while they entered.

"I am, yes. Just a civilian, though. And this isn't an official visit. I just wanted to talk."

"I'm so sorry about what happened to Jay. Still can't believe any of it happened, really. And then all that stuff with what you did. I mean, that took guts—what you did." He closed the door.

"Thank you. About Jay, I mean. As far as what I did. Well, I think anyone in my position would've done the same."

"I don't know about that." He offered his hand to Aaron. "Bruce. Any friend of Jay's is a friend of mine."

"Appreciate that. He was a good man and we all miss him."

"Why don't you two have a seat? Can I get you a glass of water, coffee? Something stronger, maybe?" He was quick to check the time. "It's after five, right?"

The fleeting moment of laughter among them helped to break the ice and open the door for Lacy to ask what she came here to ask. "Thanks, I'm okay."

"Suit yourself." Bruce followed them into the living room and sat down on the side chair. "What do you need to know? You said it was about Argus?"

"I did, yeah." Lacy took in a breath and tried to find a good place to start. Much of what she was doing was classified and so she had to tread lightly around the issue. "Do you remember a company called Synergy Dynamics?"

"Yeah, of course. They were one of my clients."

Lacy noticed him clasp his hands and begin rubbing his thumb inside the palm of the other. "I understand they were a government contractor and in order for Argus to be a sub, they had to fill out quite a bit of paperwork and go through some other checks just to get approved."

"I remember all that. But, to be honest, I just forwarded the forms to accounting and let them handle it."

"What were you contracted to do for them?"

"The usual. Cyber security. Program monitoring. Nothing out of the ordinary. Why are you asking about them?"

Lacy eyed Aaron and continued. "I guess you could say I'm really here more as a friend. There are still some unanswered questions surrounding Jay and Argus."

"Oh, right, of course. I can tell you with confidence that Jay had nothing to do with Synergy Dynamics. Those guys were mine and I don't recall ever mentioning them to him, except maybe in a sales meeting."

She was beginning to lose her footing. This was not her area of expertise, but she would have to think on the fly or risk raising Bruce's suspicions. "Okay, you got me." She raised her hands in surrender. "I'll be straight with you." She noticed Aaron's eyes widen a little. "I am still looking into a few things regarding Jay and his dealings with companies during his time at Argus. Now, I can tell you that this doesn't really have anything to do with you. More to do with the type of companies Argus was contracted with."

"Oh, okay. Lacy, I was sorry as hell to hear about Jay. But I just don't have much that I think could help you out. SynDyn, which is what we called them, was just another client. I got them to sign the deal and that was just about the extent of it."

"Sure." She nodded. "Can I ask you one other thing, then?"

"Shoot."

"I've asked Scott for their file, but you know, I don't have a warrant or anything. Like I said, this is more for me and I'm not a Fed. But just so I know and can rule out any involvement Jay might have had with this company, do you happen to have any of the paperwork on them?"

Bruce rubbed his thumb harder. His palm turned red from the pressure. "I don't have anything, except my contact. I can give you a name, phone number, and email. But I'm sorry, Lacy. That's all I've got."

"Is your contact Matthew Greiner?"

"I-um, yeah. I believe that was his name. Like I said, it's been a while. You know I'm out of that line of work now."

"Oh? What do you do now?"

"My own thing. You know, consulting and stuff."

"Sure. Anyway, I'd be grateful for your contact. If nothing else, maybe I can set up an appointment to go to their offices or something."

"I'm sure they'd be happy to answer your questions."

————

Lacy pulled her coat around her waist as the door closed behind them and she started back down the steps.

"That was kind of a bust," Aaron said.

"Not necessarily." She pressed the remote to unlock her car and stepped into the driver's seat. When Aaron joined her, she continued. "Did you notice his body language as soon as I mentioned SynDyn?"

"I guess so. I suppose he seemed caught off guard. I don't think I'd classify it as nervousness or something like that."

"I would. And I can tell you for a fact that he would still have their contract, at the very least, in his possession."

"Why is that? He doesn't work at Argus anymore."

"Because of the way Argus pays their salespeople and to keep management honest." She started the engine and pulled away from the curb. "I can't tell you how many times Jay had to produce copies of executed contracts because accounting lost theirs or there was a dispute as to who was paid commission. Sometimes there were commission splits. I have friends at Argus and they were very good to Jay, but make no mistake, they are a company like any other. And if they think they can get away with screwing someone out of commission, they will. So Jay and I know others kept their contracts—just in case."

"Geez. I had no idea. Do you think Scott might be able to produce a copy of SynDyn's contract?"

"I don't know. I didn't want to get him involved. And he might not be so willing to hand over confidential client information without a warrant. They're a cyber security firm—noted for taking extra precautions. If a contract got out to a competitor, it wouldn't make Scott look very good."

"What do you want to do?"

"It was clear to me that Bruce was hiding something, or feared some sort of backlash should he reveal what he knew of SynDyn."

"Do you think he's being watched?"

"Hard to say. But I wouldn't mind keeping tabs on him for a while. He's a consultant, right? Where does he go every day? Who's he talking to?"

"You really think he's that important?"

"I think SynDyn and Matthew Greiner are important. To me, that makes Bruce important."

———

The "shop," as the team had dubbed it, was a nondescript building that lay near Langley in a warehouse district that at first glance would easily be discounted as just that. However, Lacy was skeptical that theirs was the only covert operation in the area. The buildings were set far back from the street, shrouded in lush landscaping, but maintained the warehouse appearance with tractor trailers parked against large rolling doors at the rear.

In the dusky light, it was difficult to see the front entrance, but Lacy pulled around to the back of the building. "Looks like Will and Trevor are still here." She walked through a rear entrance with Aaron trailing. Emerging from the corridor, Lacy heard Will's voice.

"You're back. How'd it go with Bruce Quintero?"

"How did you know where we were?" Lacy replied.

"Had a hunch." Will looked at Axell. "And he might've mentioned something."

Lacy was about to ask how he knew but thought better of it. "I see. We didn't get the information I'd hoped for. I think Argus' former employee could be nervous about speaking to us, at least, regarding the topic of SynDyn. That's what he called them. He said he'd email me his contact, which I don't really need, to be honest. We know Greiner worked there. What I need is to keep tabs on him and see who he's talking to. Might get us somewhere."

"I'm not sure that'll be necessary," Axell replied. "We need to keep our focus on Greiner."

"That's what I'm trying to do. He was a part of SynDyn when Bruce signed them. I think there's something there. Don't you think it's best to find out before dismissing it?"

"Maybe, but not enough to pull your resources. I'd prefer if we kept our eyes peeled for Greiner and what he's up to. Whatever his role with SynDyn was or is doesn't seem to be important any longer. He's been seen with Yang. He's who we need to keep tabs on."

"So I just wasted our time?"

"Not necessarily. You found a connection between Greiner and Argus. Whatever that is, it's not a coincidence and maybe when the time is right, we can pursue that lead."

Resigned, Lacy continued, "Okay. Then how should we get a handle on Greiner?"

"I'm glad you asked." Axell stepped closer to his workstation. "While you two were out, Caison and I got a hit on Greiner's passport. He just traveled to Beijing, having returned yesterday evening."

"Any idea who he met with?"

"No. That's what I'll be working on. I'll get more intel on that. In the meantime, I'd still like Hunter to continue his probe into Greiner's finances."

"And what about Yang himself?" Lacy began. "What direction

are we taking that?" She was growing concerned that Axell's priorities were shifting toward Greiner and not taking into consideration they still had Yang to contend with.

"Our goal is to find out who the buyer was of the fifty-one percent of Dalian Company stock. Because whoever that person or company is will, I believe, lead us back to Beijing. First and foremost, if Dalian is circumventing the sanctions and we can prove Beijing is behind it, Dalian goes—and so does Yang. It's the easiest solution to this problem. Remember what our jobs are here."

"I do remember. Prevent another attack. Prevent the government from covering it up again. And make sure those involved pay the price," Lacy replied.

Will stepped in between them. "I think our goal is to do all of that. Including Axell's point of finding out who the money man is behind Dalian right now. Maybe that's Greiner, maybe not, but remember, we all want to get Yang for reasons well beyond the president's mandate. All of us in this room know he helped Turner kill the Meekses. Now the courts will have to decide what happens to Turner. There's nothing more we can do on that end. But we still have Yang."

"Lacy, I promise you, Yang will pay for the Meekses deaths and Keith's. I haven't forgotten about him either. I'm just trying to handle this as it comes. Right now, we have a lead on Greiner. He went to Beijing. Let's find out why. If what I'm thinking rings true, it will lead us to Yang's front door."

"Okay. I trust you," Lacy said. "We'll take it one step at a time."

———

As she was dressed in her nightshirt, with the kids tucked up in bed, a knock sounded on Lacy's front door. She squinted through the peephole lens and stepped back to open it. "Hi."

"Is this a bad time?"

"No. Not at all. Why am I not surprised you're here?"

"It's okay, isn't it?" Trevor walked inside and shed his coat, hanging it on the rack.

"Of course it is. Come in, take a load off." She secured the door. "You want a beer or something?"

"Sure. Why not." Trevor walked into the living room and sat down.

Lacy returned and handed him the bottle. "Here you go." She continued toward the sofa and took a seat.

"I just wanted to clear the air. Make sure there are no hard feelings. I don't like the thought of you being mad at me."

"I'm not mad. Is that what you think? Look, I get where you're coming from with regard to Greiner. I really do. I was just hoping I could work what I believe could be a lead. But I understand."

"I know it's tough. Especially since we've been after Yang and Dalian for so long. But you have to trust me, Lacy. Everything I'm doing—we're doing—serves a purpose."

"I trust you with my life, Trevor." For a moment, she noticed his cheeks flush a pale shade of pink. She adored him so much. While he wasn't old enough to be her father, he was, at the very least, like an older brother to her. Always watching out for her and keeping an eye out for her best interest. She'd grown to love these men very much and was still heartbroken to have lost Keith. "We're not going to find anything on Turner before the trial, are we?"

"I haven't given up on that. We'll just have to hope justice prevails. He won't be tried for murder right now, but he sure as hell can be at any time down the road. That's what keeps me going. That, and knowing that you three have my back. Just like

Keith did." He finished his beer. "I'll get out of your hair. Looks like you're ready for bed." He checked the time. "I guess it is getting late. Sometimes I forget, you know? I don't have kids or a wife to remind me to come home." He stood to leave.

"I'll walk you out." Lacy led the way to the door and pulled it open. The icy air pierced her skin. "I hear it might snow tonight."

"That's what they say." Trevor pulled on his coat. "Listen, there's one other thing I wanted to mention away from the boys."

"What's that?"

"It's pretty clear, to me anyway, that there are a lot of emotions floating around our little group."

This time, Lacy turned flush.

"I may be in my fifties, but I'm not dead. I can see when a man has feelings for a woman. But the problem is, I think you may have one suitor too many, you catch my drift?"

"I can't think about that right now, Trevor."

He held up his hands. "I'm not saying you want any part of whatever they got going on. I just want you to be aware that it could and probably already has affected certain decisions those boys have made. Now, they are grown men and I don't think for one minute that they'd crumble under the weight of any sort of rejection coming from you. I just don't want there to be any problems between any of us. We need to maintain focus on our objective. We need to be able to depend on one another."

"I know. If I need to set someone straight, then I can do that."

"Okay." Trevor kissed her cheek. "Now close this door before you catch your death." He stepped outside. "I'll see you tomorrow."

"Tomorrow's Saturday."

"Is it? Well, shit. Guess I'll see you Monday at the trial."

CHAPTER
SIX

THE THRONGS of media outlets with their cameras and microphone-wielding reporters descended upon the courthouse steps like killer bees on the attack.

Several police and Secret Service escorted disgraced former Deputy Secretary Wendell Turner toward the building.

Lacy was several feet away and turned to Will. "Glad to see the press is finally showing an interest." Behind her shaded lenses and beneath a wool hat and coat, she observed the spectacle.

"Just so long as they don't spot you. That's the last thing we need."

"They won't. They're not looking for me. Not anymore."

"I wouldn't be so sure of that. You did just have a run-in with a reporter the other day. Still, it does feel surreal watching this unfold. That should've been Drew Kendrick. The rest of it might never have happened."

"Yes. It should have. It didn't have to end the way it did. And Keith might still be here. But things didn't work out the way we planned. And now look at us. Standing here, hoping we aren't spotted, and watching this charade unfold. He should be going down for murder."

"He should, but like you said. Best laid plans."

"Right." She watched as the mass inched their way toward the stone steps. "Doesn't look like they've got him handcuffed."

"Maybe they're trying to let him keep some dignity. Not that he deserves it." Will surveyed the growing crowd. "I thought Axell was coming? Do you see him anywhere? He said he didn't want to miss one second of, how'd he put it? 'That traitor getting what he deserves.'"

Lacy checked her cell phone. "I don't have any missed calls or texts from him. But yeah, that's what he said. Should we call him?"

"No. It's not like he doesn't know what's happening. Something might've come up. You never know with Axell."

"I suppose. He could be with Aaron. I haven't heard from him yet this morning either."

"Good point." Will adjusted his sunglasses and folded his arms. "They're bringing him to the front now."

The reporters began to shout questions, or rather, demands for answers. One asked if Turner thought he was a traitor to his country. Another asked if he had anything to do with the death of Drew Kendrick.

Lacy appeared repulsed. "It's a little late for those questions now." At that moment, she locked eyes with Turner. He appeared to recoil and continue on the never-ending walk to the courthouse doors, but then he glanced over his shoulder, and this time, his face was masked in regret.

But what she didn't know was regret for what? His lies to the American people or regret for ordering the deaths of Mr. and Mrs. Meeks and quite possibly the death of Keith Colburn? Or maybe he only regretted getting caught.

"Keep moving." One of the men flanking Turner on the right

grabbed his arm and ushered him while his counterpart pushed aside the onlookers and others in their path.

Turner lost his footing for a moment until he was yanked up again by the men. "For God's sake, can you just get me inside, please?"

"That's what we're trying to do, sir. Just do as we ask and this will all be over soon."

As they reached the top step, a final question was shouted from someone in the crowd. Turner peered into the mass to find the one who asked the question.

There it was again. "Were you responsible for the death of Agent Keith Colburn?"

"Let's go." The agent pulled him again. "You need to go inside —now."

"I did what I did to protect the president and the country." Turner's body instantly pitched forward as if he'd been sucker punched in the gut. Except that when he peered at his chest, blood spilled from a hole. His eyes widened and he began wobbling on unsteady legs.

"Get down! Get down!" The guard pulled him down.

People screamed and scattered like cockroaches. Some fled, some hunkered down behind cars parked alongside the road.

"Jesus!" Will said.

He grabbed Lacy and before she knew what was happening, she was on the ground.

"Stay down!" He shielded her and quickly drew his weapon.

Lacy instinctively threw her hands over her head when another shot sounded. "Who's shooting? Where's it coming from?" She had to raise her voice to be heard over the shrieking crowd.

"Follow me and stay low!" Hunched down, he pulled her to a safer location, hidden behind a media van. "Stay here. I'll be right back."

"Wait. Will!" She watched him tear through the area in search of the shooter and all she could do was sit there. Lacy didn't carry a weapon. She wasn't a field agent. But too many times, she'd been in this very same spot and no longer wished to rely on her cohorts to protect her.

"Damn it." She peered around the van but could no longer see him. Her eyes were drawn to the innocent people cowering where they stood. Frozen in fear and easy to pick off, if that was what the shooter was going for. But as the seconds passed, it became apparent this was not random, nor was it intended for maximum carnage. There was only one target and that target was Wendell Turner. And from Lacy's vantage point, whoever it was had accomplished the goal. Turner was still on the ground. Officers, courthouse guards, and Secret Service formed a circle around him, weapons drawn. Other law enforcement had begun to corral the crowd to safer locations in and around barriers and vehicles and anything they could find to protect the people.

There were no more shots being fired. The screams began to quiet, only to be replaced by sobs from frightened reporters. Lacy emerged from behind the van, still low and still eyeing everything and everyone around her. But she could not find Will. "Where the hell did you go?" She reached for her phone and began to dial, but there was no signal. "What the...?" On surveying the crowd again, there were too few people to have caused the signal loss. And it dawned on her that the cell towers could have been jammed. No calls in or out. And that maybe this wasn't a one-man operation.

———

Turner clutched his chest as his breathing became shallow.

"Keep pressure on the wound!" The Secret Service agent, weapon still at the ready, shouted the order at his counterpart.

"Jesus. Where the hell is the ambulance? We need to get him inside."

"We can't move him!"

"We have to. He's too exposed out here. We all are." The man cast his eye in every direction. Toward the adjacent buildings, toward the street, into the crowd that had splintered into several smaller groups protected by police officers. "Let's go. Now."

One of the guards stood at Turner's head and reached under his shoulders. "Just hold on, sir. We're taking you inside."

Turner moaned as the man clutched under his arms.

The other reached for his legs and another stood in the middle, one hand on Turner's chest and another against his back.

"On the count of three," the officer at the front began. "One, two, three."

Turner howled in pain while they began to step toward the courthouse entrance. The agent still held his gun, ready to fire on anyone who posed a threat.

"Open the door!" one of the men called out.

Others pulled open the heavy wooden doors of the courthouse while Turner was carried inside.

The guard at Turner's head spotted the bench and began walking toward it. "Set him down over there."

Once they were inside, the door was secured, and the agent who'd held his weapon finally holstered it, but not before barking another order. "Secure all the entrances. And get that damn ambulance here now!"

Trevor Axell jogged to catch up with the agents who'd just brought in Turner and held out his ID. "What the hell happened out there?"

"Someone took a potshot at Turner. Son of a bitch got one off and hit him in the chest," the officer replied. "Goddam ambo hasn't arrived yet and he needs to get to the hospital."

"For God's sake." Axell rushed to Turner, who was still on the bench. "They'll get you out of here ASAP."

Turner eyed Axell. "We both know it was Yang."

"Just relax. Save your energy."

"I didn't kill Camden Meeks or your friend. You have to believe me."

Axell ignored Turner's plea. "Just hang tight. Help is coming." He walked back toward the officer. "Secret service?"

"Yeah. CIA?"

"Yeah. What's it looking like out there? Is the scene secured?"

The agent retrieved his radio. "All clear?"

"Affirmative. Bystanders are safe. Officers still searching the area."

"There's your answer," he said to Axell. "I told them not to bring him through the front. I fucking told them. And now look at this shit! Did they really think there wouldn't be some crackpot out there just waiting for him? Som' bitch was asking to be taken out. You know that as well as I do."

"Yeah. I have to find my people and make sure they're safe."

"You got people here? Outside?"

"I do."

"Good luck." The officer's head turned at the sound of the door opening. "Bout fucking time you got here!" He rushed toward the EMTs, leaving Axell on his own.

Axell grabbed his phone. "Caison? Where are you? Where's Merrick?"

"I'm with the Secret Service. WFO agents are on the way. We're clearing the buildings. I told Lacy to get back to head-quarters."

"Ours?"

"She's heading back to the shop now. Told her I'd be there as soon as possible and to get in contact with Hunter. Unless you've seen him?"

"No. I'll stick around here and see what I can do. I'd be surprised if Turner makes it through this."

"Jesus. Who did this, Axell?"

"I have my suspicions."

―――――

The glow from the wall monitors reflected off Lacy's face as she stood before them, captivated. Each one with a different news station that broadcasts the breaking story. Several cameras had been rolling at the time of the shooting and she tried to spot what they all seemed to have missed up to that point. Who took the shot and from where?

"We need to get our hands on all the CCTV in the area."

She whipped around at the sound of the voice she recognized. "Where the hell have you been? I've been trying to reach you since this morning."

"I'm sorry. I was working on some stuff at the house Axell needed right away." Aaron approached and stood next to her. "Any news on Turner's condition?"

"No. Not since he got out of surgery. He's still in critical condition last I heard."

"Son of a bitch deserves to die."

"Of course he does, but it wasn't supposed to go down like this. He was supposed to stand trial. Show everyone how guilty he was. That would've been justice. This?" She shook her head. "Now no one will know what really happened. They won't know what he did."

"Only if he dies."

"If that bullet doesn't kill him, they'll find another way. I just wish I knew who 'they' were."

"You hear anything from the guys yet?" Aaron continued.

"Will was helping the FBI field office. His team was called out too."

"They're calling it a terrorist attack?"

"They'll have to rule it out, as usual."

"And Axell?"

"Haven't heard from him yet. Will has, but only relayed to me that he'd be here later. That we were all to meet here later today."

"Shit, it's almost four."

"I know. We'll just have to stay put until further notice." She turned to him. "I thought you and Trevor were meeting us at the courthouse this morning. What happened? What was so urgent you needed to work from home?"

"Axell asked me to find account info on Greiner."

"Yeah. I know about that. That was days ago. You finally get a hit on something?"

"I did. Late last night, I was up. Couldn't sleep. Guess I was a little wound up about the trial starting today. But anyway, I started tinkering around and found something that caught my eye."

"What was that?"

"Seems our Mr. Greiner has a bit of a checkered past."

"What else is new?"

"Right. But this—this was something else. Greiner appears to be an alias. I couldn't figure out why there were no tax returns or any other financial records prior to 2010. He was basically a ghost."

"An alias?"

"Seems so. Although I'm still trying to find more. Except that something changed in 2010 for this guy. That's what I was working on all night and into this morning. That's why I wasn't at the courthouse. I wanted to get a name."

"But you didn't?"

"No."

"Well, it's a decent lead. At least we know we're dealing with an expert."

"No question. An expert who has help covering up whatever he was into back in the day."

"Did you mention this to Trevor?"

"Not yet. I will when he gets here."

"Mention what?" Axell walked into the bullpen.

"There you are." Lacy approached. "Any word on Turner? Any word on who they think took the shot?"

He raised his hands. "I know about as much as you do right now. That's why I came here. Nothing more I can do for those guys and I needed to know where everyone was at." He looked around. "Where's Caison? I thought he'd be here by now."

"Last I heard, he was still helping WFO on the search."

"Figures."

"Who do you think did this, Trevor?" Lacy continued.

"I wish I knew. We can speculate, but there's not much point in that."

"I'd like to request CCTV footage from the area," Aaron said.

"You and everyone else. FBI's got priority on this one. Caison can probably get us copies of whatever they get. But our request will fall on deaf ears. CIA doesn't get involved in domestic shootings. And neither does this task force."

"Unless the shooter is an international terrorist," Aaron added.

"We just don't have any idea yet."

"You sure about that?" Lacy moved in toward the screens as they continued to show on a loop the events of the morning. "You can't tell me you don't think this has everything to do with Yang and Dalian Company."

"It's a possibility. A likely possibility," Axell replied. "And there are things we can and will do to find out what happened. We'll just be doing it on our own."

"So nothing new there," Aaron replied.

"Nope."

Lacy spotted a Breaking News banner flash on the screen. "Hang on." She reached for the volume control and turned up the sound.

"We've just been informed that the former Deputy Secretary of State, Wendell Turner, has died as a result of the gunshot wound he sustained this morning while arriving at the courthouse for his trial. Mr. Turner, if you'll recall, was to be tried for Treason against the United States. A laborious and often difficult-to-prove charge that could have seen Turner suffer the death penalty, but likely would have resulted in life imprisonment. Wendell Turner was 53 years old and is survived by his wife and two children."

"Damn it," Lacy began. "I'm not the only one who thinks it was Yang, am I? He made sure Turner kept his mouth shut. What are we going to do about this?"

"What do you think we should do?" Axell asked.

She looked at Aaron. "You found out that Greiner was a ghost prior to 2010. We know he worked for SynDyn at least in 2015. And now he's what, a consultant for Dalian?" She returned her sights to Axell. "You said he's been seen with Yang on too many occasions. It could've been him. This guy arrives pretty much out of nowhere and now Turner's dead? Trevor, we have to find out who he is now. If Yang's willing to go to the trouble of killing a former government official in front of the country, what else do you think he's capable of? You know, all this time, I thought it was Jian we needed to worry about. But for all we know, Jian was one of Yang's pawns too. And if that's the case and Yang's running this show, then we need to go after him hard."

Axell's cell phone buzzed in his pocket. "Axell here. Yeah. We're all here. What's going on?"

Lacy and Aaron watched as Axell listened and nodded.

"They did? Where?"

Lacy drew near and whispered to Axell, "What's going on?"

He raised his index finger and continued the conversation. "Get here when you can. We've got plenty to keep us busy right now. Hunter got some new intel on our friend Greiner. We'll dig into that until you get back. Keep me informed of any new developments." He ended the call.

"Well?" Lacy asked.

"Caison said they found where the shot came from. It was a building across the street. It wasn't a sniper-quality shot, but it was someone with at least medium-range skill."

"No weapon found?"

"No. It was a professional hit, as we probably already figured. Except for one thing." He looked at Aaron and Lacy. "Caison said they think they caught him on surveillance footage."

"Who was it?"

"No positive ID yet. They're running it through the system now. The guy was wearing a ball cap, overcoat, but that's all they've got right now until they can get computer forensics on it."

"That's something positive out of this shit day," Aaron replied.

"It is. But until they know more, we'll keep moving forward on our end. Hunter, let's keep looking for signs of Greiner before 2010."

CHAPTER
SEVEN

THE MOUNTAINOUS DESERT region of the Xinjiang province is located in the far northwest of China. With borders alongside Russia, Pakistan, India, and others, it had more in common with its Middle Eastern neighbors than its own country. And had for centuries, remained largely autonomous, until recently.

As Shen Yang walked along the streets of the impoverished area which had been the source of unrest in recent years, he began to miss his home. Having moved to Beijing in 2005, still a young man with notions of wealth and greatness, Yang soon became entrenched in the society of the Han Chinese and left behind his roots based in the Muslim faith as a Uyghur. He changed his name and assimilated, becoming what he had desired—a wealthy businessman with ties to the government that had allowed him to become what he was today. But as he observed what he considered the "ethnic cleansing" of his people, Yang grew resentful and sought out those who he knew well in his youth; those who had also grown tired of the persecution they'd faced day after day.

The Communist Party of China was atheist and ruled in such

a manner. However, with ten million plus Muslims in the Xinjiang region alone, things had begun to change after the terror attacks in America. The Chinese government used those attacks as justification to crack down on what they saw as a growing extremist problem in the area.

And today as Yang again traveled through Kashgar, a part of the famed and ancient Silk Road, he noticed the dramatic changes the Party had already implemented and it sickened him. Mosques had been barred from broadcasting the call to prayer. Now they broadcasted the Party's national anthem. And as he walked the streets, he noticed the banners hailing the Party. The Uyghurs were being wiped out, little by little, day by day. Though he'd been in America for the past five years, running the Dalian Company and minding the call of the Party, it now served a higher purpose. The reason Yang was so fortunate and had the ear of the Ministry and powerful businessmen around the world was to bring his people the religious freedom they once had and continue the separatist movement that had already started. Yang, along with others in the Movement, wanted an independent Xinjiang. The Beijing attacks just prior to the Olympics were organized by the Movement and was the first time he'd seen their capabilities. Several recent attacks on the police and others were also a result of the Movement. Yang believed such attacks were necessary to revolt against this ethnic cleansing the Party had invoked, deeming it as containing the spread of extremism.

Religious restraints were being defended by the government, but in doing so, they were creating an even greater extremist movement. And Yang was now entrenched in it.

He knocked on the door of a modest home inside a community that had seen recent economic investment. And as Yang saw it, the Chinese government's handouts and subsidies were yet another way it had exerted control over the people. Lift them from poverty and they would become loyal.

"My friend." A man of similar age smiled and greeted Yang with open arms and continued to speak in their native Turkic language. "Please come inside where it is warm."

Yang followed the man inside and guilt swept through him, for his life was so much better. His home was filled with grandeur. This was the home of a poor man who clung to his faith in any way he could, regardless of those who would attempt to steal it from him.

"I'm sorry it's taken so long for me to return, Mehmut. Especially after the success of our last efforts at the train station."

"You are very busy in the US, no doubt." He patted Yang on the shoulder. "You are here now and that is what matters. And you do look well, my friend."

Yang bowed his head. "As do you. So tell me, when will the others arrive? I am anxious to get started. I can't stay long."

———

Aaron stared at the screen. "Hey, Lace? Come take a look at this." He turned to her while she stepped closer.

"What is it?" She placed her hands on the back of his chair and leaned over his shoulder.

"SynDyn. I was able to retrieve government records listing its subcontractors. Most of that's public info anyway, but these guys had clearance. TS clearance."

"What were they doing that gave them Top Secret clearance?"

"IT work for the Pentagon. Or at least, a division of the Pentagon."

"Okay. What does this mean for us?"

"Well, take a look here. I've pulled the contract. Whose signature does that look like to you?"

She leaned closer and noted the pen scrawl across the bottom. "Is that...? Does that say, Matthew Greiner?"

"Looks like it to me."

"This was what, 2014?" She leaned back and studied the image. "So he'd been going by the name Greiner at this point. Meaning he already had all the background info he needed."

"Right. Social, prints, previous employment," Aaron added. "All the things required to get clearance. Including a personal history."

"Only back until 2010, by our account. Makes me wonder how he got the clearance if his history only went back that far."

"That's what I'm thinking. He either had it..."

"...Or it was erased. Can we get our hands on any of what you just found?" Axell walked into their conversation. "Didn't mean to eavesdrop. Heard you talking."

"That would depend on what strings you could pull for us, I imagine," Aaron replied. "It's not something I think I could dig up. Not through approved channels, anyway."

"Since when are you worried about approved channels?" he asked.

"Since I nearly got thrown in jail a few months ago."

Axell smiled. "Right. I think I can get us more on him. Good work, Hunter. You two should go home. It's getting late. We'll reconvene tomorrow."

"I've got a meeting in the morning. It'll have to be after that."

"Whatever you have to do, Merrick. Just get here when you can." Axell returned to his office and closed the door.

She eyed Aaron. "Something's off with him. It isn't just me, is it?"

"No. Something's off. And I think it has to do with this guy." He pointed to the monitor.

"Should we be concerned?"

"Probably."

She lowered her voice to just above a whisper. "Does it bother you that we don't know where Trevor was this morning when the shooting happened?"

Aaron whipped his head back. "What?"

"Shhh. I'm just saying, he's been quiet about his whereabouts. You don't think..."

"No. I don't. And neither should you. Look, I know how much he hated Turner. We all hated him, but Trevor's not a murderer. Even after losing Colburn and his old boss. I just don't think it's something he's capable of doing. He knows what's right and wrong."

"We all know. But how many times in the past year have both of us—all of us—teetered on the edge of that line? You do remember Sajwani? How much can one person take before dipping a toe in those waters?"

———

Lacy made her way to the car and was ready to head home for the night. But as she started up the engine, Will pulled alongside her. She rolled down her window as he stepped out. "Hey. Didn't think I'd see you today. How'd it go?"

"You heard Turner died, right?" He leaned over her door.

"Got what he deserved in the end."

"He did. Still. It shouldn't have gone down like that. He should've faced trial."

"They weren't going to get him on the murders. And as far as I'm concerned, that's what he should've been charged with. And getting a conviction on the treason charge? You and I both know that was going to be a tough sell. Especially in light of what happened to Drew Kendrick. He would've just copped some plea that he feared for his life or some bullshit like that."

"You're probably right, but now we'll never know. Sorry, I don't want to keep you. We can catch up tomorrow. I need to talk to Axell anyway."

"You told Trevor they found surveillance footage. Any idea who the shooter was or if he acted alone? I lost my cell signal right after the shooting. I think it was intentional."

"I don't know if they'll get a positive ID. And, the signal, well, that could've been a flood of emergency calls. But whoever it was knew there were cameras and kept himself well hidden."

"Sounds about right. No one's going to make it easy on us."

He regarded her with concern. "What happened today..."

"I'm fine if that's what you're worried about. It seems like this has become our new normal."

"No. It's not that. I know you can handle yourself—and you did. Which was why I didn't hesitate to take care of business on my own. I knew you would be fine."

"Then what?"

"Look, I would never even suggest this if it hadn't been odd that Axell wasn't with us this morning like he said he was going to be."

Lacy's expression fell.

"It's just. Well, looking at that surveillance. I mean, shit, I have no idea who it was, but the height, the build. He was wearing an overcoat, but still. And the demeanor."

"You think it was Trevor?"

Will shook his head. "I hate to even think it, to be honest, but Colburn's death, Camden Meeks' death. We know who was really responsible."

"Before you go any further, have you mentioned this to anyone else? Anyone at WFO or Headquarters?"

"No. Absolutely not. But I thought it was important that I talk to you about it. I could be hitting out in left field here, but it's just something."

"Something that keeps popping up in your head. No matter how hard you try to dismiss it."

"Exactly."

She was reluctant to continue, but this was Will. And he could be trusted with anything, even this. "The idea had occurred to me. And I did mention it to Aaron."

"What did he say?"

"No way in hell, basically."

"Which is probably what I would've said, were it not so damn coincidental."

"What do we do about this, Will? Do we confront him? Ask him straight out?"

"That's probably what we should do. He's our boss. He answers to Mobley and Director Handley."

"Who happen to also answer to the president."

"And there's that." He paused. "If he did, it changes things, Lacy."

"I know it does. But, maybe we should talk to him. He's first and foremost our friend. We owe him that much. And if we're wrong, then we'll apologize."

"And if we're right?"

"With everything we've been through together, would you turn your back on him for doing something we all would have done if given the chance? Will, let's keep this between ourselves for a while. Keep our focus on Greiner. Let it die down a little and then we can mention it to him—maybe. Turner's gone and there's nothing we can do about that now. I don't want to condemn

Trevor. I'm sure there was a very good reason why he wasn't there this morning. And I'd like to keep thinking that for just a while longer."

"Yeah. Okay."

"There is one thing I'd like to do, though," Lacy continued.

"What's that?"

"Aaron uncovered more about SynDyn and Greiner earlier this evening. He found a government subcontract agreement signed by Greiner back in 2014."

"Meaning he's been using this cover for a while."

"Seems like it. The contract was for some IT work at the Pentagon. Which stands to reason, given that's what they did. I guess what I'm saying is that do you think Fraser could do us another favor?"

"I'm sure he would." He appeared to realize what she was about to ask. "You want me to ask how Greiner got the clearance?"

"I think we need to know who granted it. Who they interviewed. And see if any of these people—friends, family, whoever—actually exist."

"I'll talk to him. I think he can get that information. I can't say for sure, but he's already pulled rabbits out of hats for us. He'll do it again with good reason."

"We need more history on Greiner, or whatever his name is. When he got involved with Dalian, who made the introductions. Whatever we can get so we can figure out who we're actually dealing with here."

Will nodded. "Sounds good. I'd better go in." He tapped on the ledge of the door. "Drive safe."

CHAPTER
EIGHT

IN A FLURRY OF SNOW, Matthew Greiner walked alone through the parking lot of the Dalian offices. Light from a lamp post captured tiny flakes whirling and landing on his Mercedes, dusting it like confectioner's sugar. And in this beam of light, another item sparked his attention. A note tucked beneath his windshield wiper. He pulled it out from beneath the blade and double-checked the lot. He was alone with only a few other cars dotting the area.

Greiner slipped into the driver's seat of his car and keyed the ignition. A blast of cold air gushed through the vents until the engine warmed. On the note were the cryptic words "Cairo. 2001. Meet at The Office tonight." The handwriting didn't trigger a clue, but this was someone who knew him well enough to know the places he frequented. And who knew about Cairo, a time and place he'd tried to put in his rear view?

In the late hour, he questioned whether this individual would still be waiting. But the more he considered the idea, the more he realized it was likely this person knew the moment he stepped out of the building. The note wasn't wet, as though it had only just been placed. He was being watched, and while this was to be expected, per the agreement he made months ago, this watcher was someone new in the equation.

Within minutes, he'd arrived and parked across the street from the bar, ironically named The Office. He eyed the few passersby wandering the streets as it came upon midnight. Greiner placed his gun in the waistband of his pants and stepped out, pulling his coat around him. And with his head down, rubbing his hands together, he made his way over. The dive bar was located in a sketchy part of town, and he preferred the people there as opposed to those in the downtown D.C. bars. He came here when he wasn't looking to get laid, which was rare in any event. But the people here were real and they didn't give two shits about him. He liked that. No one cared. No one asked questions.

The bar was nearly empty as he opened the door and hesitated a moment before committing to enter. In his line of work, it was that hesitation that could get you killed. But here in D.C., even in a place like this, he figured the one who left the note was intelligence and wasn't likely to whip out a gun and start blowing holes in him. That was his expectation anyway.

"What can I get you?"

Greiner pulled up a stool. "Blue Moon, thanks."

The bartender placed the bottle in front of him. "Six fifty."

"I got this one." Axell placed a twenty on the bar top. "And I'll have a whiskey neat."

This was the guy. He even knew what he liked to drink. Still, Greiner couldn't place him, though his wheels spun with his best efforts. "Thanks."

"No problem. Appreciate you meeting me."

"Sorry, but do we know each other?"

Axell turned until he was squarely facing him. "The note

didn't ring any bells? I figured Cairo would've been a dead giveaway."

Greiner knitted his brow. "Sorry, man. I—hang on."

Axell sipped on the whiskey shot that had just arrived. "Last I saw you, you'd brought in some poor Hadji you thought needed some extra special attention."

With a flicker of recollection, Greiner began, "Axell. Trevor Axell. What the fuck are you doing here? And how did you find me?"

"Wasn't easy, Janz. Casper, right?"

"Yeah. That's right." He tipped the bottle of beer to his lips and licked the froth away. "So, who sent you? Who've they got looking out for me? Don't tell me you were feeling nostalgic and just wanted to play catch up."

"And if I was?"

Greiner laughed. "If memory serves, I seem to recall a fairly uptight, by-the-book punk kid fresh out of Langley who looked down his nose at me any chance he got."

"Oh, I wasn't fresh out of Langley. I'd been around the block a few times when we crossed paths in Cairo."

"Sure. Right. Sitting behind a desk, safely away from all the bullshit we were dealing with."

"Recall it however it suits you, Janz, but I remember you. Oh yeah. I remember you." He tossed back the rest of his drink.

"You haven't answered my questions. What do you want? Why the hell am I here?"

"You must be slipping in your old age. Honestly, I didn't think you'd show at all. Feeling guilty about what you did back in the day? Or were you worried I might have something on you? Something that might put a wrinkle in your current gig? I hear you're making bank now."

"Fuck this shit." He stood up to leave.

Axell grabbed his forearm. "Sit down. We need to talk."

"Then let's dispense with the speculation, shall we?" Greiner yanked his arm away. "You want to talk? Talk."

"What are you doing for Shen Yang and the Dalian Company?"

"What the hell are you talking about?"

Axell eyed him. "Don't insult me. What are you doing for Yang? You know his people took out a few of our own. And you're working for the son of a bitch. Maybe you just don't give a shit about your brothers, or those who used to be your brothers before you sold out."

"Man, fuck you."

"You're going to tell me what I need to know because you don't want me up your ass on this, you catch my drift?" Axell scanned the bar. "Yang has powerful friends if you don't already know that."

"Yeah, well, so do I. Friends who want to keep Yang on a short leash."

Axell creased his brow for only a moment. "Our side? Because of the sanctions?"

"You have no idea what you're stepping into, Agent Axell. You should go back to the comfort of your little office at Langley and pretend to be useful. I can only assume that's where they've put you. You're getting up there too, you know." He tossed back another swig of his beer.

"You recently traveled to Beijing. Why? Are they concerned about Yang?"

This time, Greiner only eyed him.

———

Yang waited in the customs and immigration line at Dulles Airport on his return from the Xinjiang region.

"Step up, please," the immigration officer said.

Yang handed him his Chinese passport and inside was his Visa and work permit.

The officer examined Yang and again peered at the photo. A contemptuous air about the man permeated his every gesture and Yang grew concerned of trouble ahead.

"Surprised you're still allowed here after what your people did." He stamped the passport.

And there it was. The growing hatred for him and his "people." Tensions had mounted since the truth behind the attack was revealed and it was making Yang's job that much more difficult. "I'm sorry if I've offended you, sir. I'm just here to do my job." He avoided direct eye contact, eager to douse the fire of resentment and be granted entry. The alternative would mean spending hours in holding while they searched his bags, only to come up empty-handed. But the desired effect would have been achieved.

"Have a good day—sir." The man returned Yang's passport. His disdain was not lost in translation.

Yang walked past the checkpoint and made his way outside the terminal. Greiner stood in front of the car. "Welcome back. I trust you had a pleasant flight?" He opened the passenger door for Yang.

"It was fine. We have much to discuss, Mr. Greiner. I hope you have cleared your schedule." He slipped into the passenger seat.

Greiner closed the door and returned to the driver's side. "Of course. Where would you like to go?"

"Home, please."

The sky was overshadowed by the dusky haze of nightfall as they drove to Yang's palatial estate. Greiner pulled the car around the circular drive to the front of the home. They both emerged as Yang led the way inside where they were greeted by Yang's wife.

"Hello, sweetheart." Her plump red lips pressed against his. And when she pulled away, her eyes landed on Greiner. "Mr. Greiner. Pleasure to see you again." She tipped her head slightly and her thick black hair fell against her cheeks.

"Ma'am," he replied.

"We'll be upstairs in my office for a few moments. Then you'll have me all to yourself." Yang looked to Greiner. "Let's go."

"Should I bring you drinks?" she asked.

"Thank you, no. Mr. Greiner won't be here long enough, I'm afraid."

He trailed Yang up the marble curved staircase and into the office that featured hard lines, sharp corners, and stark-white walls.

"So, I've yet to hear about your trip to Beijing, Matthew." Yang began to pour himself a drink without offering one to his guest.

"They would like me to keep a closer eye on you. More closely observe those in your circle. Visitors. Things of that nature."

"I see. And why do you suppose they're concerned now?"

"They're watching you. Satellite imagery. I witnessed it myself when I met with Minister Cheng. They're concerned about your Uyghur ties, more specifically."

"Phones?"

"That was not mentioned. However, if they haven't been tapped by your government, then I'm sure mine has taken care of that."

"Quite." He tossed back his shot of gin.

"Do they know I was there? In Xinjiang?"

"I can't be sure. I had already left days prior and I didn't receive any messages to that effect while you were away. And we might have another situation on our hands." Greiner placed his hands in his pockets. "A former CIA intelligence officer, now inter-agency liaison at Langley, has reached out to me."

"And why would that be cause for concern?"

"Whatever surveillance he'd obtained captured me entering the offices of Dalian on more than one occasion. He recognized me from my time as an operative in Cairo. We were there together for a short time, and wanted to know what my connection was to you."

"He knows who you are?" Yang poured himself another shot.

"Yes. He also knows that rumor has it I'm for sale."

"What did you tell him about our partnership?"

"That we were business acquaintances and I'd done some consulting for you. And that I've been helping you navigate through the growing regulations being waged against international corporations in light of the Chinese sanctions."

"Was this man named Trevor Axell?"

"Yes. How did you know?"

"Oh, I'm very familiar with Agent Axell and not at all surprised he's been keeping a close eye on me—and by default—you. While I've not had direct contact with the man, or his team, which was the source of our current predicament, I've done favors for individuals who wanted the agent to go away quietly. In fact, the man who asked for such a favor was recently murdered on the courthouse steps."

"Deputy Secretary Turner?"

"Hmm. This is problematic for me. And you. Agent Axell has proven himself a man of action and I have a feeling he is not acting as a liaison, but that he is, in fact, monitoring me. I have yet to find where he and his team are operating, which has been a source of concern."

"I can take care of him. There is no way he can discover the arrangement set forth between us," Greiner continued. "Several safeguards are in place for that."

"I don't wish for any harm to come to Agent Axell. There has been enough blood spilled for a cause rooted in the mind of Lei Jian. I should have stopped him when I saw what was happening. But I didn't want to jeopardize the Movement or my goals in any way. And as it turns out, he brought us together, which has spurred renewed hope for the objective. However, I also do not wish for him to manage a closer look at me or the people I work with. So, Mr. Greiner, in addition to your other duties, you will need to ensure Agent Axell stays as far away from Dalian as humanly possible. For both our sakes. I trust you can handle the task?"

"Of course. That won't be a problem."

"Good."

Outside of CIA Director Handley's office, Axell loitered in the hall. His 9 am appointment had slipped to 9:30 and his patience was running thin. A situation had arisen that required the director's attention and he'd begun to feel slighted by the delay.

"Agent Axell, I apologize for the wait. Please come in." The director stood in his doorway. "Hold my calls, please, Mark, would you?"

"Of course, sir."

Axell followed the director into his office. "Thank you for seeing me on short notice, sir."

"I figured it must be important. Have a seat." He closed the door and walked toward his desk. "This is about Dalian?"

"Yes, sir. Among other things, but primarily Dalian."

"Go ahead."

"As you know from our last briefing, the team has been working on identifying the source of the money tied to whoever our American investor is who now holds majority shares in Dalian."

"Right. And have you unmasked this individual?"

"Not yet, sir. No. However, I have discovered the true identity of an associate of Shen Yang's. One who I believe is helping him skirt the sanctions and SEC regs."

"Who is this person?"

"A former acquaintance who goes by the name of Matthew Greiner, but who I knew to be Casper Janz. Someone I became familiar with back in 2001 at the Cairo Station. I managed to set up a meeting with him last night after I figured out who he was from the surveillance video we have of the Dalian offices. He's one of us, sir. He's CIA. Former CIA by all accounts."

"CIA? Who's he working for and why are we just finding this out?"

"Well, sir, that's the thing. After speaking with him, I can't decide if he's operating with or against us. He recently returned from Beijing and he informed me he's been told to help keep Yang on a short leash."

"Let me get this straight. One of our former officers is taking orders from someone in Beijing?"

"It appears so."

"But you don't know who that is?"

"Not yet. I'm working on that. My immediate concern is that he's offered his services to Yang for what I can only imagine must be a good deal of money. My team discovered he worked for a company called Synergy Dynamics and was awarded a lucrative government contract back in 2014. I have to assume his former position allowed him to pull some strings to get the deal. My best guess is that he's doing the same thing for Yang. Greasing palms and helping Yang with SEC filings and whatever else he needs to keep Dalian in compliance. I haven't ruled out that he could also be behind the purchase of stock. The team is working hard to find any other filings on behalf of Greiner that could suggest the formation of a dummy corporation that fronted the cash for the purchase.

"Now, as far as I know, he's no longer with the agency, and it appears he's been going by the alias Matthew Greiner since at least 2010. But why? He's no longer CIA, why the alias? Unless he's doing something he shouldn't be doing. Which is why I'm here. If I could just get more intel on him, I can place him in this puzzle and we can figure out if he's a threat. Sir, this could be the lead essential to shutting down Dalian—for good."

"I'll need to spend some time on this, Agent Axell. If he's former CIA, it's going to get hairy. I'll get what I can and let you know."

"In the meantime, I do have people who owe me favors in Beijing. I'd like permission to check in with them and see if I can find out why Matthew Greiner, or who I know to be Casper Janz, went to Beijing to begin with."

"Permission granted. Get out there and find out who this guy knows and who he's talking to in Beijing. I'll let you know what I find out."

———

Axell was already on his way to the airport when he made the call. "I'll be back in a few days. Keep doing what you're doing and I'll let you know what I find as soon as I get back."

Lacy listened on the other end, seemingly confused by this quick change of plans. "What about Greiner?"

"You know what the plan is. Keep searching for dummy corporations that are tied to Greiner. He was part of SynDyn. Maybe now is the time for you to dig deeper into your lead. There could be clients of SynDyn that are fronts. Your friend Bruce might have answers. I gotta go, Lacy. Don't worry, everything will be fine."

"Um yeah, okay. I'll let the guys know."

"You're in charge. Goodbye." Axell ended the call. He knew she would have questions, they all would, but there were things they couldn't yet be made aware of. Like Greiner's true identity, or the fact that he knew the man well once upon a time. He had to know the whole story behind Greiner, or rather, Janz, especially as it related to Beijing. That alone made him dangerous. He'd given her authorization to dig into SynDyn and hoped that would keep them busy until his return. And who knew what they might find? He valued their work, especially Lacy's. The woman had a mind of her own, and while it was one of the reasons he admired her so much, it was also the main reason why he worried about her.

CHAPTER
NINE

THE SMELL of fresh brew and the warmth as Aaron held the mug between his hands offered comfort. "Thanks for having me over. You're sure it's not too late?"

"Not at all. We didn't get a chance to talk after I got the call from Trevor. Will's been busy with Agent Fraser and the WFO, and I'm starting to feel like it's just us two against the world right now. Besides, it's nice to have the company. I appreciate you stopping by."

"Are you worried about him? Axell, I mean? You know he can handle himself."

"I know. Trevor can certainly take care of himself. It's not that. You know how he dismissed our lead with Bruce Quintero from Argus?"

"Yeah."

"Well, he said that while he's gone, we should be working on finding other companies linked to SynDyn that might also tie back to Greiner."

"Good. Bout time. I knew you had something there. I was surprised he wanted us to put that on hold."

"I'm sure he had reason at the time. But I think something must've changed. Anyway, I'm not looking a gift horse in the mouth, so you and I can go back to Bruce and maybe make a visit to SynDyn ourselves in the interim."

"Absolutely."

She sipped on her coffee, appearing to carefully consider her next words. "Do you think Trevor might know something we don't? Seems strange he would just up and leave, to Beijing of all places."

"When you put it that way, it's possible. You know how he is. But I wouldn't put too much stock in it. If he finds something, he'll tell us."

"I guess so. And there's the whole thing about where he was during the shooting. He was supposed to be with Will and me, but he didn't show until after Turner was hit. And you weren't there either."

Aaron studied her for a moment. "What are you saying, Lace? I told you where I was."

"I know. I know you did. I'm sorry."

"Why don't you tell me what's on your mind?"

"Nothing. It's nothing, honestly. I'm sorry I brought it up."

"Well, see now, that's the thing. You did bring it up. Lacy, do you really think Axell had a part in Turner's death? And that I did too?"

She shed her gaze to the steaming mug in her hands. "I think Trevor was in a lot of pain when Keith was killed. Then the Meek-ses. You remember how he was with Sajwani?"

"I do."

"Then you know he's capable of, well, murder."

"That's not fair. Sajwani would've killed us. You know that. What Axell did was protect us. That in no way compares to the idea he could go off half-cocked and murder Wendell Turner."

"You know what? You're absolutely right. Of course he didn't. And I know you wouldn't keep anything from me. I'm sorry. I guess I still sometimes feel as though I'm out here on a ledge all by myself. Like the day at the dedication ceremony. I just know how easy it would be to become what we're trying to defeat. I've thought about it. Many times, in fact. I know Trevor's looking out for me—for us."

Aaron reached for her hand on the counter. "We all look out for each other."

"Right. Glad we settled that. So, tomorrow, we'll go back to Bruce and ask if he can get us an in with SynDyn."

"You might've been right about Bruce. You said he seemed nervous. Maybe we should go in on our own. Hold that—I should go in on my own. You're too recognizable. I'll pretend to apply for a job or something. Ask to use the bathroom and have a look around."

"What do you mean? How is that going to help?"

"Come on, Lace, give me some credit here. I just need to take a look at their systems. No one's going to volunteer information. We're going to have to take it."

"You're probably right. If Greiner was tangled up in that company, who knows what it's like inside there? You do that. I'll talk to Bruce. I don't know. I just have a feeling he knows something."

"Then it's settled." He began to rise. "Thanks for the coffee. I should probably head back."

"Already?" She looked outside. "Looks like it's starting to snow. Why don't you stay? I have the guest room all set up. We can watch some cheesy movie on TV. Come on. It'll be fun. We could use the downtime."

Aaron regarded her with surprise and not a little trepidation. "Well, sure, I guess so."

"Good. I wouldn't mind the company, you know? Unless you've got work or something."

"No. No. I'd love to hang out. Watch some crappy TV. Hey, you got any beer?"

"Do I have beer?" She pulled open the fridge and gestured toward the plentiful stock. "Of course I do." She grabbed a bottle of beer and a Diet Coke for herself and headed back into the living room.

Aaron followed her to the sofa, where they both took a seat. He watched her flip through the channels in search of something. He couldn't have cared less what it was. He was just happy to be with her and that she wanted him around.

"Oh, I haven't seen this in forever." She turned to him. "This came out when we were back at school, remember?"

He viewed the television for a moment and couldn't place the movie. He had no idea what it was, but Lacy knew. "Oh yeah, sure. I remember this." He closed his eyes just for a moment, reveling in her touch as she rested her head against his shoulder.

"Hey now. You'd better not fall asleep. This just started." She nudged him.

"I'm not falling asleep." He took a drink and kicked off his shoes, placing his feet on the coffee table.

She looked at him for a moment and soon followed. "Perfect. Thanks for this. It's nice having a friend around."

"Yes—it is."

———

With the rise of the morning sun, Lacy was already in the kitchen making sack lunches for the kids. She was just about to shout at them to hurry when they both trotted down the stairs. "There you two are. I was just about to come looking for you. You both brush your teeth?"

"Yes, Mom," Olivia replied.

Jackson only nodded.

"I've asked Celeste to take you guys to school, okay? I have to go straight to work this morning and Uncle Aaron is asleep in the guest room, so I need to make sure he gets up too."

"Uncle Aaron's here?" Jackson asked.

"He is, but he's still..." Before she could finish the sentence, Aaron appeared.

"I'm awake. Kind of hard to sleep in this house with you two trouncing around upstairs like a herd of elephants."

They both ran to him.

"Uncle Aaron!" Olivia called out before jumping into his open arms. "You said you would teach me how to break into computers and stuff, remember? When are you going to do that, huh?"

Aaron glanced at Lacy, who appeared miffed, as evidenced by her folded arms. "I'm not going to teach her how to break into computers."

"You're not?" Olivia's brow furrowed. "But you promised."

"Ixnay on the omputercay," he whispered.

"Huh?"

"Never mind." Aaron stood and cleared his throat. "Any coffee left?"

Lacy still wore a stern expression but poured him a cup. "Here you go. We'll talk about this later."

"Thanks." With a sheepish grin, Aaron sipped on the coffee.

"Okay, who's ready for school?" Celeste clapped her hands as she entered the kitchen. "Hello, Aaron. Good to see you."

"Good morning. You too, Celeste."

"And how did you sleep?"

"Very well, thank you."

"Right, then. Let's get out of here, kiddos. Don't want to be late."

"Thanks, Celeste. I shouldn't be late tonight."

"Just let me know if things change. Say goodbye to your mom, guys, and hop in the car. We need to skedaddle."

Lacy waited until they left through the kitchen door to the garage. "Okay, then. I'd better get dressed. You know where the towels are? Be ready in twenty."

"Sounds good."

Lacy made her way upstairs and into her bedroom. Last night had been a pleasant reprieve, one she knew couldn't happen again. Not unless she made sure Aaron knew where she stood. She'd seen it in his eyes last night. The way he looked at her. The way he placed his arm around her as they sat on the couch.

She held a towel against her face and stepped out of the shower, and on closing her eyes for a moment, felt Jay's touch on her damp skin. "I miss you so much." But the moment faded and Lacy again opened her eyes. She was alone.

————

"Bout time you showed up." Aaron swiveled in his chair. "Been here for ten minutes already."

"You have not." Lacy approached. "No way did you beat me by ten minutes. Although you were driving like a bat out of hell."

"Says you. Anyway, should we lay out a plan?"

Lacy set her things down on her desk and walked back toward him. "Like we talked about last night, I'll stop by Bruce Quintero's house and if you want to have a look around SynDyn, then I'll leave that up to you. But be careful. Don't get caught."

"Please. What do you take me for? An amateur?"

"Just—be careful."

"I will. You do the same." Aaron pulled his coat off the back of his chair.

"You're leaving now?"

"Why not? The sooner I get there, the sooner I can get back and get down to business."

"Yeah. Okay. I'll head out too, then."

———

The day was clear upon Lacy's return to Bruce Quintero's home. She assumed he would not be as happy to see her as he was on her first visit. She approached the steps of his townhome and rang the bell. Several moments passed and she wondered if he wasn't home or he was and didn't want to answer. She tried again. This time, footfalls sounded on the other side of the door and it opened.

"Lacy? Hi. What are you doing here?"

"Hi, Bruce. I'm sorry to bother you again. It's just me this time. Could I—could I come in?"

He peered beyond her, checking the sidewalk and streets.

"It's just me, Bruce."

"Yeah, okay." He opened the door farther. "Come on in."

"Thanks." Lacy took off her coat and folded it over her arm.

"Why are you here?" He headed into the living room. "Weren't you able to reach out to SynDyn and get the answers you needed? Have a seat."

"Thank you." She waited for him to sit down. "I have a friend who's checking things out over there, actually. I just had a couple things, you know, just to clear my head of these ideas that Jay might've been involved with SynDyn."

"Lacy, like I said, he didn't have anything to do with them. We didn't hang out much, Jay and me. The occasional golf game, but that was really about it."

"Yeah. Of course. So, do you know the kind of work SynDyn did?"

"Sure. Government IT work. Didn't I mention that before?"

"Right. I think you did. Yeah. So was it for the military? Or State or something like that?"

"You know, I can't remember, actually. It was a few years ago. And I was just the account manager and made sure Argus was doing what it was supposed to do. I really didn't get involved in SynDyn apart from that."

Lacy noticed his hands again. He was nervous. "Bruce, do you think Matthew Greiner maybe wasn't working in SynDyn's best interest?"

"Matthew Greiner? What do you mean? He got them the government contracts. Seems like he did them a huge favor. I got to tell you, Lacy, I'm not sure what you want from me. I haven't dealt with Greiner in what, like three years? I don't know anything other than what I've already told you. Is there a question you wanted to ask? Because forgive me, but I don't want to sit here and keep guessing what it is you're looking for."

"Okay. I'll be honest with you. It appears as though Matthew Greiner has committed fraud. And it looks to have happened around the time he worked for SynDyn."

"Fraud? You're a data analyst. Why would you be working on a fraud investigation?"

"Because I do more than just that, Bruce. I can't tell you anything beyond that. So I just need you to trust me. Last time I was here, you seemed a little anxious when I mentioned SynDyn. Why was that?"

Bruce's eyes darted back and forth. "Look, I don't want to get into any trouble."

"You won't, okay? I'm not here to make problems for you."

"These guys—SynDyn—they ran things differently. Matthew

Greiner, my contact, well, I knew something was off when I signed him."

"How? What was off?"

"I mean, like you know, a background check. Argus runs background checks on anything relating to government work. They were contracted with the Pentagon. And from what I understood, a contract was pending with the State Department too."

The hair on Lacy's neck stood on end.

"I don't know for what. It required clearance. But anyway, because it was government work, we have to know who we're dealing with, you know? To protect Argus. We had to make sure we weren't dealing with spies or something like that. I know that sounds crazy, but..."

"It doesn't. I remember the policy on security clearance work."

"Okay. So then I put in the request for a background check. Next thing I know, Greiner's threatening me."

"What?"

"He threatened me. Said I needed to sign off on the deal, forget about the background check, and just do it."

"Did you tell Scott?"

"I needed the commission, Lacy. I—I didn't know what to do. I was afraid. I just figured, you know, it's just a job. Not worth getting hurt."

"No. Of course not. So you signed off. Did you happen to see a background check on him?"

"No. I canceled it. No one ever ran it. He said he would know if we did. And he would at the very least get me fired. I didn't want to know what else he might do."

"I understand."

"All I can think is that this guy was maybe getting kickbacks from someone in government. I don't know. I really don't."

"It's okay. This is enough."

"Are you going to have him arrested?"

"I won't. No. That's not what I do. And I won't bring you into this. I promise you. You have nothing to worry about."

"Thank you. Thank you, Lacy. But just know, Jay was a good man. A good person to work with. He did nothing wrong, from what I know."

———

"Welcome to Synergy Dynamics. How may I help you?" A bright-eyed young woman smiled as Aaron approached.

"Hi. I was hoping I could submit my resume?" Aaron had a quality about him. He was a computer guy, no doubt, but there was something in his eyes—sincerity. Genuine sincerity. Women picked up on that. And when they did, he usually got his way.

"What position were you looking for, sir?"

"Programmer." It was a shot in the dark, but he figured everyone needed a good programmer, even if he had no real idea what this company did.

"Okay. Sure. I'll take it for you."

"You know." He leaned over the desk just a little, the sparkle in his eyes gleaming. "I don't suppose there's anyone here I could maybe talk to about the position? Just a few quick questions to see if I might be a good fit?"

"Well, that would be like an interview, right? I think they'd want to call and schedule something like that with you."

"Sure. Sure. Well, you know, this would be more like an introduction. If at all possible, I'd love to hand over my resume to the person doing the hiring. Just so I could lend a face to the name."

"I'll have to check. You can have a seat over there and I'll make the call."

"I don't mean to be a pain, but do you have a restroom I could use while I wait?"

"Of course. And you're not being a pain. It's down the hall and to the right."

"You're too kind. Thank you so much. I'll be right back." Aaron walked along the corridor and spotted the bathroom, but that wasn't where he wanted to go. Earlier, he rushed to the office ahead of Lacy for a reason. And that was to get the schematics for the SynDyn building. Child's play. He knew exactly where the servers were kept but knew they'd be under lock and key. That didn't matter, though. All he needed was to see them. The servers, for him, were as distinguishable as an Android and an iPhone. Determining the type was all he needed. And now, he also knew the type of software they used. The kind receptionist was very helpful with that information. Her monitor displayed a screen-saver. And when he leaned over, he got a good look at the copyright information and webmaster beneath the SynDyn logo. He could work with that.

But for now, he had to get upstairs. He stepped onto a waiting elevator and pressed the third-floor button. No security key necessary for that floor, luckily. That would've meant the end of this little adventure. Unless by chance he did garner a meeting with an IT director, which was highly doubtful.

Upon reaching the floor, he walked down the hall, passing by staff who seemed to care little whether he belonged there. The server room was just ahead and, as expected, it required a keypad entry code. No matter. The windows, which were partially obscured, still offered enough for him to capture on video.

The hall was clear for the moment. It was now or never. Aaron retrieved his cell phone and aimed it at the window, videotaping as much as he could of the room. The number of servers, the size, and shape. It was all he needed.

In the lobby, he returned to the front desk. "Sorry I took so long. Guess I was a little nervous."

The receptionist crinkled her nose. "Mr. Yi is busy, I'm afraid, and doesn't have time to meet. He did ask that you leave your resume with me."

"Perfect. Thank you for checking. I do appreciate it. Have a good day."

———

Lacy returned ahead of Aaron and heard him enter through the back of the building. "Finally. I've been dying to tell you what happened."

"Same here." He dropped his carrier bag on his desk. "You first."

"Bruce was threatened by Matthew Greiner over Argus' standard background check. SynDyn also had a contract pending with the State Department."

His mouth agape, Aaron replied, "No."

"Yes. I don't know if there's anything there on that front, but I do know now that Greiner is not who he says he is." She filled him in on the rest of the story, waiting for a response. "So?"

"Wasn't as much as I'd hoped for, but better than nothing."

"What do you mean? We know this person is hiding something. And that would explain why we haven't been able to find anything on him prior to 2010. He's connected with State and possibly others. I think this is a big find. And I'll tell you, Bruce came across other subs signed on with them to do work. I've got a list of companies. We might find a front right here."

"That's what we need. Right there. That list. You did good, Lacy."

"I'm glad my work meets with your approval."

"That's not what I meant. I just wasn't sure if Bruce had anything, that's all. But he did. And it'll prove useful."

"So tell me about your morning?"

He pulled his cell phone from his pants pocket and plugged it into his laptop. "I got video of their server room. It was secured, so no way in."

"How on earth?"

"I'm good. What can I say?" He clicked on the video. "It could be clearer, but I think I can work with this. And, I know what software they use. At least some of it. And that'll be all I'll need."

"You really think you can get in with this?"

"Uh—yeah."

"Okay. You get in and we'll start with this list of companies. I'll bet you we'll find Greiner on one of them."

"I hope you're right."

CHAPTER
TEN

RED, the symbol of good luck, already featured prominently in the streets of Beijing as the Chinese New Year approached. Banners advertising the impending celebrations fluttered in the breeze as Axell traveled through the city. The rare clear day was likely a result of the winds casting away the smog over the mountain range.

His first stop was to be at the US embassy to see an old friend. Located in the Chaoyang district, and near his hotel, Axell made his way inside the compound. "Afternoon. I'm here to see Hank Abrams. Trevor Axell. Langley." He displayed his CIA credentials. "He's expecting me."

"I'll let him know you're here, Mr. Axell. Please have a seat."

Axell stepped away but didn't sit down, knowing it would only be for a moment. Abrams was nothing if not punctual.

"Agent Axell, good to see you again."

"Hank, now come on. You know I don't do any of that field-ops stuff anymore. It's just Trevor now." He shook Abrams' hand.

"Sure. Follow me. We'll talk in my office." He started toward the rear of the building. "They keep us USAID folks tucked away in the back. Hope you don't mind."

"Ah, the red-headed stepchildren." Axell laughed. "Been there, my friend."

"Right through here." Abrams held the door. "Have a seat. I'm sure you must be tired after your flight."

"I've been sitting down for hours, although I did have a nice walk through the city streets. When do the New Year celebrations start? I noticed quite a few banners."

"Mid-February. They all close up shop for about a week and the party goes on. It's an incredible sight. Sorry you'll miss it. Unless you plan on staying that long?"

"Oh no. I'm afraid this is an abbreviated visit." Axell sat down.

"Well then, let's hear it. What's going on? Must be important for you to come all the way here. Who authorized the trip?"

"Director Handley."

"I see."

"Yeah." Axell adjusted his shirt, brushing the sleeves to smooth them over. "Listen, I was hoping you could help me get some information."

"I figured that much. What do you need to know? Resources have been stretched here lately, what with our North Korean 'friends' causing us a lot of heartburn. I don't have many ears around town."

"What can you tell me about a visit from a Matthew Greiner? I knew him as Casper Janz, but it seems he's taken on a new identity and I need to know why."

Abrams' face screwed up before he turned to his computer. "Let me see what I can find in here. You say, Matthew Greiner?"

"He was here last week. I know he met with someone in the MSS. I just need to know with who and why."

"MSS? Well, shit, that's something I should be aware of."

"You have someone on the inside? Someone who's keeping an eye out for us over here."

Abrams regarded Axell. "How long have we known each other?"

"A long time."

"A long time is right. So you know I'll find out who Greiner's been talking to. Or Janz or whatever the hell name he's going by." Abrams picked up the phone. "I need an outside line—secure please." He raised his index finger to Axell, indicating the need for a momentary delay. "*Nǐ hǎo.*" (hello)

Axell listened as Abrams spoke Chinese and understood nothing of the conversation. The Chinese language was made up of many dialects, the most prominent one being Mandarin, and Axell didn't know that either. There were over 1 billion people in China. Perhaps he should consider learning the language if he wishes to continue in his line of work.

Abrams ended the call and returned his attention to Axell. "Sorry about that. Yeah, Greiner was here. Made the visit under that name and met with a man in Bureau 17, inside the Ministry."

"What's Bureau 17?"

"Officially? It's the Enterprises Division."

"And unofficially?"

"Businesses controlled by the Party as a front. Mostly for criminal organizations, but some political groups and shell companies too."

"You get the name of the man he met with?"

"An officer by the name of Cheng. According to my friend, the two met up prior for dinner or drinks, but then Greiner was admitted inside the MSS on the following day."

"What intel can I get on Cheng? I need to know who he is and why he's dealing with Greiner. And whether he knows Greiner's real identity."

"Well, now you're asking for favors I'm not sure I can pull off."

"What about a meeting? Can you get me a meeting with him?"

Abrams considered the request. "It won't be easy. Can you get your people to draft a legend for you? Get the bona fides in place quickly?"

"It'll take at least twenty-four hours. But yeah, I can make that happen."

"Good. Get back to me when you have it set up and I'll make the call. I'd focus on garnering partnerships and US corporations. It'll be the best way for you to get inside. And, Axell, you've been out of the game for a while. You sure you're up for this?"

"It hasn't been that long. I think I can handle a meeting. I just need to know who this man is. If Janz, or Greiner, is helping the MSS with a front for Dalian, then I'll know what I'm up against." He began to rise. "I'm at the Hilton. I'll be in touch."

———

Only a few people in Axell's circle were qualified to create the necessary identity on short notice that would pass muster. But there was one person who'd already proven himself several times over. Hunter would be up to the task, and with the resources they currently possessed, Axell had no doubt he could get something in place quickly.

On his return to the hotel, he noted the time. It was 4:30 in the morning back home. The time difference was a killer and Axell had been up for some thirty-six hours as it was. But this couldn't wait.

"You answered. Sounds like I woke you." Axell stood on the balcony of his hotel room.

"You did. Doesn't matter. I need to get up anyway." He paused for a moment. "Oh shit. It's 4:30 in the morning. What the hell time is it there?"

"4:30 in the afternoon. I just got back from meeting a friend of mine at the embassy. I need you to jump on something, like yesterday."

"Shocker. What is it?"

Axell directed him on how to go about getting past records and credentials entered into the personnel database, and how to generate identification to reflect his new fictitious position.

"No shit? I get to make up a background for you? What are you working on, man?"

"It's a long story, but I need this faster than you can say 'when.' You catch my drift?"

"Yeah, I catch your drift, daddy-o."

"What?"

"Nothing. I got it."

"How soon can you do this?"

"I'll head out now and open up the shop."

"Good. How's everything else going? You guys getting anywhere on Greiner?"

"Actually, sort of, yeah. Lacy and I did some digging around. I went to SynDyn and surveyed their ops systems. She went for another visit with Bruce Quintero and discovered he was intimidated by Greiner when he requested the background information. I'm still working on getting into SynDyn's systems to access their personnel files and a list of subcontractors Lacy got hold of. I'll put that on the back burner, though, so I can get this other stuff out to you."

Axell turned toward a window and peered through it. "Look, don't go off half-cocked and start talking to people. What you have is good. But wait for me. I'll be back in a few days. Keep digging, that's fine. But I don't want the two of you on your own talking to anyone else without me getting a chance to find out who they are."

"Why? I thought that was our job?"

"It is, but right now, let me just say that I think Greiner isn't someone we want to screw around with, okay? Just please—just do as I say. Understood?"

"Understood."

"Get to work and call me if you need anything at all. I'll help you through it if need be. But I think you got this."

"Yeah, I got this. Bye."

Axell dropped his phone in his shirt pocket. "Shit." He sat down on the edge of the bed. They were getting closer to Greiner, which was exactly what they were supposed to do. He just didn't think it would be so soon. He needed to get a handle on what Greiner was doing before they got too far and found out he'd been keeping the truth about Greiner from them. But he knew Lacy. And if she suspected something was off, there would be no stopping her. Axell would have to work fast.

———

The call arrived in the small hours of the night. Axell pushed up from the bed, followed by a labored groan and crackling knees. "Hunter. What've you got?" Axell wasn't a stocky man, like Caison. Instead, as he stood in the shadows, moonlight glowing around the drawn curtains, his lean build was acutely defined. He scratched along his flat stomach, waiting for an answer. "You do realize it's 2 am here, right?"

"Sorry. You said to call you as soon as I was finished. And I'm finished."

"Well damn, son, that was fast. You sure everything's up to snuff?"

"I'm sure. I ran the checks. I had Lacy run the checks. Everything came back as it should. I just emailed you an image of an ID. I didn't get a badge or anything made. I didn't think I could get you one in time."

"That's fine." He sat down at the small table and opened up his laptop. "I see your emails here." He began to review the information. "This is excellent work, Hunter. I'm impressed. You know, you could do this for a living." His voice cracked with a half-asleep chuckle. "This will do for what I need."

"No problem, man. Glad I could help. I have to say, it was pretty cool getting to make up shit about you. Anything else you need?"

"No. I'm good. I'll get in touch with one of you after I do what I came here to do. I'm hoping to be on a flight back by tomorrow. We'll see what comes up."

"Copy that—sorry, just always wanted to say that. Talk to you later. Be careful, Axell. We're all anxious for you to come back home so we can do what we're here to do."

"I'll explain everything when I get back. Don't worry. This will all make sense soon enough. I'm out."

———

Hunter pulled the phone away from his ear. "He's out."

"No explanation?" Lacy crossed her legs as she sat at her desk.

"Nope. None. You didn't really expect one, did you? Come on, it's Axell, for Christ's sake. He doesn't tell us anything until he fully understands what's going on."

"I know. I just wish I knew why he told us to hold off. I have to say, Aaron, I still think he's hiding something. Ever since we got that surveillance footage of Greiner, he's been hush-hush. And that whole Turner situation."

"Lacy, stop. Give the guy the benefit of the doubt, would you? It's Axell. Whatever he's got going on, he's not telling us for a very good reason. I think you know that." Aaron checked the time. "Hey, is Caison coming in today? It's almost three o'clock. I thought we would've heard from him by now."

"As far as I know, he's still helping out WFO with the Turner shooting. I'll put in a call and see what's going on. We still have plenty to do on our end. Have you made progress on SynDyn's systems?"

"I got in. I just have to find the right files."

Lacy made the call. "Hey, it's me. Are you coming into the shop today? Aaron and I are here working. He just finished up some stuff Trevor had him working on. We need to fill you in on what's been happening."

"Sorry. I know I've been out of pocket. Yeah. I'll be in. Give me thirty minutes and we can catch up."

"Sounds good. See you then." Lacy ended the call. "He'll be here shortly. Sounds like they've been running him ragged."

Several minutes passed, and then Aaron came upon something. "Lace, you got to check this out."

"What is it? What'd you find?" She approached him.

Aaron turned his screen for Lacy to get a better view.

She peered at the image, which showed Matthew Greiner in a group photo. "What the hell? What is this? When was it taken?"

"More importantly, this isn't from his personnel file. I haven't found it yet. I reached out to a guy last night and had him look into a few things."

"A guy?"

"His name isn't important. Just know it's someone who works in the grey when it comes to the dark web."

"Aaron, we shouldn't have this."

"We shouldn't have a lot of things, but that's never stopped us before. It looks like he served in Desert Storm. Iraq, Kuwait. Shit, I don't know for sure. But what I do know, is that his name isn't Matthew Greiner. It's Casper Janz." He pointed to names listed on the side of the image. "Darker hair, younger, but that's him."

"What the hell did we just stumble on, Aaron?"

"You got me. But this man isn't who we think he is."

"Hey. I made it, finally." Will approached the bullpen. "What's that you guys are looking at?"

"Welcome back." Lacy stood. "How's it going on the Turner investigation?"

"Same shit, different day." He sighed. "We still have no leads. Fraser's running forensics on the bullet found in Turner, but nothing's come back yet. We have nailed down exactly where the shooter was."

"That's right. The building across the street," Lacy replied.

"Trajectory put the shot at about 100 yards away and to the west. So we figured the shooter took the shot from the second-floor balcony and waited for just the right moment. We were right. Found the room today. There was a small indentation on the balcony railing denoting the weight of the weapon that had a hell of a kickback and carved out the notch on the railing."

"Where was the security? Didn't they clear the area before bringing him in?" Aaron asked.

"They did. Guess they missed that floor of that building."

"Sounds like you're not so sure about that," Lacy replied.

"Yeah, well. I have my theories. Just haven't shared them with anyone."

She considered his words, his demeanor, and their previous discussions on the matter. "Well, we're glad you're here. We've got a lot to talk about. Take a look at what Aaron just found."

Will peered at the screen. "What's this?" Leaning over Aaron's shoulder, he studied the photo. "Is that him? Matthew Greiner?"

"We think so. But check out the name over here. Casper Janz."

"How did you get this?" Will waved his hand. "Never mind. What does Axell have to say about this? What does he want us to do?"

"He doesn't know yet. Aaron just got this. Axell's working on something. He didn't say. Just asked Aaron to get him set up with a fake background."

Will turned to Aaron. "You gave him a legend? Why?"

"That's what you guys call it? That's cool," Aaron replied. "Um, yeah, anyway, he said he needed it for some meeting he's got later today—tomorrow? I don't know. But it had to be thorough and legit. So I gave him a new ID. He said it was good."

"But we have no idea who he's meeting with or why?" Will continued.

Lacy shook her head. "He hasn't told us much, to be honest, but said he'd clear it all up on his return."

"I guess we'll just have to trust him. In the meantime, what else can we find on this guy? This Casper Janz?" Will asked.

"Look, when I talked to Axell earlier, I told him we were digging around for information on Greiner."

"And?"

"He told us to back off until he returns. He doesn't want us talking to anyone. Said we could do our research, but not to approach anyone."

"I can tell you, looking at this photo." Will studied it a moment longer. "This was during Desert Storm. Airforce."

"How do you know?" Aaron asked.

"See that patch. What does it say?" He pointed to the arm patch on Greiner in the photo.

"Operation Desert Storm. Airforce."

"Yep. And he's intelligence." He again pointed to the screen. "Air Force Intelligence Command."

"Right. Didn't see that," Aaron replied. "I assume that means he did recon or something?"

"I'm not entirely sure, but I did work alongside one of those guys in Afghanistan."

"What did you do over there anyway?" Aaron continued.

"Army captain. Company commander of a supply unit. We moved supplies around. Not very exciting, is it?"

"I wouldn't say that," Lacy added. "Your job was to find safe passage for the goods and that wouldn't have been easy when most supply units were hit with IEDs and insurgents attempting to cut off supplies going to troops."

"You seem to know a lot about it," Will replied.

"A little. I imagine you worked with an intelligence officer when it came to finding routes and learning what routes had become too dangerous to traverse."

"Yeah. I did." He appeared flattered by her knowledge and admiration. "They did the intelligence gathering. It was a stepping stone for civilian life in a lot of cases."

"You mean like they went on to become CIA or FBI?" Aaron asked.

"Something like that, yeah." He looked again at the images. "So, we've got someone who could be on the inside. I think Axell should know about this right away."

CHAPTER
ELEVEN

THE HILTON HOTEL lobby was busy with weekend visitors and tourists. It was Friday morning and Axell's friend secured the meeting with Cheng. He made his way through the lobby and hailed a cab outside. Upon stepping into the back seat of the small Nissan, he began, "The Ministry, please."

There was no need for further explanation. Everyone knew the location of the ministry, at least the one in Tiananmen Square, not the clandestine site no one was supposed to know about, except for everyone in the intelligence community. This was where the meeting would be held with the man in Bureau 17.

Axell checked his credentials one last time. Abrams, from the embassy, sent him to a place that would get him the printed badge. Many years had passed since he'd been required to conduct this type of operation. He was recruited by Camden Meeks in the early nineties, fresh out of college. His first assignment was Russia, shortly after the Soviet-Afghan war, and during the Afghan civil war that followed. His function—monitor the insurgency and terrorist attacks in Chechnya after the fall of the Soviet Union. To this day, Axell regrets not following through with his opportunity to take out Osama bin Laden when he had the chance. A man who, at the time, was an emerging figure in the new jihadist movement. A man the CIA helped create. Not that Axell could have predicted what would become of him. His order was to stand down—and he did. Still, that was a long time ago in another world. And right now, Axell needed to focus. Get into the building. Make sure his ID checked out, and get in to meet the man who was working with Casper Janz.

———

Axell was escorted to a front desk by armed guards at the entrance. "I have a meeting with Mr. Cheng." He retrieved his badge. "James Fitzgerald. USAID." He waited while the guard verified his ID, and for the first time in a long while, his hands felt clammy. Axell was out of practice and hoped his façade didn't betray him.

It wasn't until the guard made the call that Axell began to relax. Hunter had done it. He'd created the bona fides and so far, they'd passed inspection.

"Someone will escort you to his office in just a moment, Mr. Fitzgerald."

Axell nodded with confidence and began to breathe again.

Within minutes, Axell was on his way to see Cheng and understand the relationship he had with Casper Janz. The crimson carpet and dark wood-paneled walls felt tunnel-like thanks to the arched sky-lit ceiling. Axell fell in behind the guard who led the way through the maze of corridors, eventually leading to Cheng's office. He opened the door and announced Mr. Fitzgerald's arrival in their native language.

"Mr. Fitzgerald, please come in."

Axell entered the room while the guard closed the door on his way out. "Thank you for meeting with me, Mr. Cheng."

"I'm happy to oblige our friends in the USAID. Mr. Abrams is a good man." He offered his hand.

"He is, sir. Thank you."

Cheng returned to his desk and hoisted his trousers before sitting down. "So, Mr. Fitzgerald, what is it that I can do for you today?"

"Given the current climate between our two nations, I'd like to discuss a possible joint venture in an effort to heal past wounds and reestablish the economic ties we once shared."

"Well, that could prove quite difficult considering the restrictions your government has placed on mine regarding investment in US corporations."

"I believe I might have a solution that would be in both of our interests."

"I'm listening."

"As you know, the Dalian Company, based in Virginia, has been the source of great controversy since it sold off the majority share to an American investor." Axell tried to gauge a reaction, but Cheng remained deadpan. "I would like to suggest Beijing offer backing in another US venture here in your country. In fact, as you require US businesses to partner with a Chinese investor, we would like to partner with Dalian, at their headquarters here, on this same venture. This will show both the United States and China that the two countries are willing to work on rebuilding the relationships. And what better way to do so than to choose Dalian as a partner?"

Axell had done his research, studying the trade wars with the US, and most recently, the sanctions. His hope was that Cheng would jump at the chance to tell his premier and president that the US wanted to move past the sanctions and rebuild. He needed Cheng to accept the proposition so Axell could understand the extent of the ties he had with Shen Yang and Casper Janz.

"You offer an interesting proposition, Mr. Fitzgerald. And I am surprised your government has authorized you to speak on the issue. You must be a very important figure."

"I wouldn't go that far. I would simply say that I have been authorized to present such a deal and have worked with those who hold higher positions and want to keep their distance, as it were, in the event the deal doesn't pan out."

"I see. And do you have a plan in writing that I may take to my superiors, should we move forward?"

"I will have one sent to you this afternoon." Axell had no such plan but figured his friend in USAID could provide something on short notice. Something verifiable.

"Very well." He rose and again offered his hand. "I appreciate you coming in and presenting. I will be in touch. How long will you remain in Beijing?"

"As long as you need me to."

"An extended stay won't be required. From this point forward, I can discuss this with Mr. Abrams. No point in keeping you here longer than necessary."

Axell stood. "Of course. Is there someone at the Dalian Company here who could facilitate our coordination efforts in the US?"

The man eyed Axell for a moment. "Let me make a few calls first. Then we can discuss future meetings."

"Thank you, Mr. Cheng. I sincerely appreciate your time." He returned the handshake. "I'm staying at the Hilton not far from here in the event you'd like to discuss anything else. Or perhaps I could invite you to dinner this evening?"

"I'll have my assistant get with you if my schedule is clear. I'm afraid I don't know what's on my agenda for today as of yet." He began to escort Axell to the door. "Thank you again, Mr. Fitzgerald. I look forward to working with you in the future."

As Axell left Cheng's office, he returned to his desk and picked up the phone. "I need you to follow Mr. Fitzgerald back to his hotel and keep an eye on him for the time being. Keep me informed of his whereabouts while in Beijing."

———

Axell returned to his hotel room and immediately pulled off his tie before pouring a well-deserved drink. Disappointed, he'd hoped Cheng would take the bait and start dropping names, ideally Yang and Janz, but no mention of either. Meaning he hadn't trusted what Axell was presenting, or planned on vetting him before disclosing anything that might come back to haunt him. The latter was likely the case and now all Axell could do was bide his time.

His bona fides would withstand some scrutiny, but it wasn't intended to be a long-term solution. And if the truth came out, Axell would need to get the hell out of Dodge. If Janz was working with Cheng, as evidence seemed to point, he would also be able to identify Axell in a heartbeat.

For a moment, he believed he'd risked too much for so little. No new information. No confirmation Dalian was bought and paid for by the Ministry's shell companies, presumably operated by Janz.

"Damn it. There has to be another way in." He pressed his hand against the frame of the sliding glass door and peered out over the city. "I either just motivated him on the deal or prompted him to put me under surveillance."

He was certain Dalian was being fronted by the Chinese government. And had been of this mindset when Lei Jian was in the picture, though they denied he was anything except a rogue agent. What he now knew of Bureau 17, they had to have set up a shell company or had a US investor in their pocket. These were the only ways Dalian could remain in the US. That Yang could remain in the US. But what was Janz's motivation behind mentioning his association with Beijing when they met at the bar? Specifically, telling him they were keeping Yang on a short leash?

An unexpected guest knocked on the door and sounded off alarm bells for Axell as he reached for his gun, which was no longer on his waist. He, of course, couldn't travel with his weapon and had nothing in his reach to defend himself. Axell walked to the door and peered through the security lens. He didn't recognize the individual and waited.

"Trevor Axell, I believe you know Camden Meeks. You need to let me in now."

He pulled back. "What the hell?" The mention of Camden Meeks suggested whoever this was knew him. And, this person was an American.

"I know you were at the Ministry. We need to talk—now."

"Who are you?"

"You're aware of Honey Badger?"

Honey Badger? Axell hadn't heard that term in a long time. It was an operation back a few years ago when CIA agents operating in Beijing were disappearing. Between 2010 and 2012, it was believed China executed some eighteen-plus CIA spies. Honey Badger was the operation initiated to find the mole inside the clandestine organization who offered up its agents for execution. And while Axell was aware of current operatives working here now, this man was not one he knew, but he opened the door anyway.

"We need to talk, Agent Axell. You've ruffled some very important feathers and I need to know why." He entered the room and stood in the middle of it, arms folded at his chest. "By the way, I am sorry about Meeks."

"Thank you. I'd ask how you knew him, but it appears we must travel in some of the same circles. Did I piss off one of the higher-ups? To be honest, I had no idea how long I'd be here. The deal was for me to get in and get out. I didn't think it would be a problem for you."

"I'm one of the few of us left here, Agent Axell. And it's been a challenge rebuilding our sources. I'm here because you might've raised a red flag with someone in the Ministry. One of our colleagues reached out to me. We can't afford for you to jeopardize our efforts here."

"That wasn't my intent. I'm here regarding Shen Yang and a man who goes by Matthew Greiner, but who I know to be Casper Janz, former CIA. I believe he's working with the MSS."

"We're aware of Janz. We followed him on his last visit here to Beijing a week or so ago. He had dinner with Mr. Cheng of Bureau 17."

"I believe he's helping to conceal the identity of the American investor who allowed the Dalian Company to maintain its operations in the US, regardless of the sanctions. Or, he is the investor," Axell said.

"You have anything to drink around here? I guess I should introduce myself. I'm Caleb Shaw."

"Got some whiskey over there." Axell walked to the side table and poured them both a shot. "Here."

"Thanks." He knocked back the shot. "Look, we all know these sanctions are complete bullshit. They'll fall by the wayside as more US jobs are lost and the economy continues to tank. The US can't afford for China to keep dumping its Treasury stocks."

"China can't afford it either. Their currency has already taken a nose-dive."

"It has, but they'll continue to manipulate its value. Listen, Axell, whatever you're trying to prove, it can't be done here. You have to go home."

"Not until I get answers. It's my job to find the source of the money and I will."

"Your job?"

"That's right."

"And when you find this investor, what then?"

"Then we get Dalian the hell out of our country."

Shaw pursed his lips. "That will never be allowed to happen."

"Care to enlighten me as to why?"

"Because Yang is too important. To our government and this one. They're watching him."

Axell set his glass down and considered Shaw. "Why?"

"We have an agreement with Beijing for us to keep tabs on Yang because of his ties to the Uyghur Separatist Movement."

"And what are we getting out of this deal?"

"A behind-the-scenes effort to ease sanctions so China will stop unloading stock. An agreement that will reduce our trade deficit by allowing more US imports into the country."

"Jesus." Axell poured another shot. "More back door deals. This is bullshit. I was tasked with keeping foreign entities in check, preventing the kind of manipulation you're talking about. The administration wants all its bases covered in the event of another attack. It's not just radical terrorist groups anymore."

"I get that, but there's so much more at play than you can imagine."

"Then why haven't I been briefed?"

Shaw walked closer to Axell. "I made a few calls. I know your team. I know what you've all done for our country." He shook his head. "But you need to be looking elsewhere for the real reason you're here."

———

CIA Agent Martin Delgado, former adversary turned friend, seemed surprised to find Lacy Merrick standing in his doorway in the early morning hour. "Merrick." He stood from his chair. "Very nice to see you again. How are you?"

Lacy entered his office, greeting him with a wide smile. "Doing well, thank you. It's good to see you too, Martin. How have you been?"

"Good. Good. Come in and have a seat. So, to what do I owe the pleasure of your company?"

"Sorry to just drop by, but I have good reason and, well, I was hoping to keep my visit off the books."

"Okay. Tell me what's going on."

"You aren't working on anything right now?" she asked.

"Not yet, no. They're considering me for a couple of things, but you know, classified and all that."

"Sure." The smile she wore faded. "Trevor's in Beijing. Due to fly back this morning, I believe. Our time."

"Oh? What's he doing there?"

"It's a long story but I didn't really come here to talk about that. I came here to ask you about something else. Someone else, more specifically."

Delgado leaned back in his chair and waited for her to continue.

"I figured since Trevor is out of pocket at the moment, I could get some advice from you regarding a matter I know you're familiar with. I'd like to talk to you about Wendell Turner."

"He was murdered on the courthouse steps several days ago."

"Right. The reason I ask is when they brought me in—after the speech. I suggested the president order an investigation into the State Department. Because, as you know, there was a strong possibility Turner might not have acted alone, what with his expediting Sajwani's visa. We never quite figured out the reason for that."

"Right. From what I understand, the investigation is still ongoing. So forgive me when I ask, what's the problem?"

"I can't figure out why Turner would've been assassinated moments before he was due to testify in court regarding the allegations of treason. And to be honest, we've heard nothing regarding the status of the State Department investigation."

"These are two separate issues. And you're with the Bureau. Why aren't you asking them these questions? What can I do that you can't? Not to mention the fact that I'm CIA. Not my jurisdiction."

She eyed him. "Really? You're going to use that?"

"Fair point, but that doesn't change the fact that I couldn't begin to know what investigations the Bureau is running and if any of them involve the State Department. Now, as far as the Turner case, well." He shook his head. "Could've been any nut job off the street. What he did, or rather, covered up pissed off a lot of people. There's a lot of animosity toward not just the Chinese government, but our own for their lack of oversight. Lack of concern about what was happening in the current administration. The president has a lot of making up to do toward the American people. I wouldn't be surprised if some idiot took that shot at Turner and got lucky." He studied her for a moment. "Lacy, why don't you tell me why you're really here? You've got plenty of resources to get answers to the questions you're asking me right now. What is it that you want me to do?"

"You were close to Camden Meeks."

Grief masked his face. "Yes. I was."

"And you know we searched for evidence that pointed to Turner. You and I both know he played a hand in his death."

"Right."

"There's someone I was hoping you could look into for me. We've found a name, a short history, but we're stuck. Nothing else at our disposal anyway. At this point, I need to know if he had any knowledge of or knew anyone connected to Meeks. I'd like to find out if he had any connection at all to the deputy secretary. This could also lead us in another direction, but for now, I'd like to know if he might have had Turner in his sights."

"Give me a name. I'll see what I can do."

"I think he might be one of yours. I know he's not FBI. I checked that myself. His name is Casper Janz. He's currently going by the alias Matthew Greiner. And right now, he appears to be Shen Yang's right-hand man."

"Of Dalian?"

"Yes. And since you were embedded with Yang for a long time, I thought you might know of him."

"Name doesn't ring a bell. He must've come on later. But like I said, I'll see what I can do." He regarded her with concern. "Is there a reason you're not asking Axell to do this?"

"As I said, he's in Beijing and there's not much he can do for us from there. And, I'd like to have something for him on his return." She spun the lie with ease. Axell all but ordered them not to talk to anyone regarding Janz until his return. But there were times when the itch needed to be scratched. This was one of those times.

"Okay, then. I'll get back to you if and when I find anything."

"Thank you, Martin. And, you know, maybe don't mention I was here."

"Whatever you say."

CHAPTER
TWELVE

THE REQUEST CAME DOWN from the Cyber Division's department head. Regional Supervisor Lacy Merrick must submit her team's analysis regarding the increase in anti-Asian websites that had seen an uptick in internet traffic. And the steps necessary to remove said websites. It was a fine line between First Amendment rights and actual, viable threats to other people. And lines had already been crossed.

The concern was that groups had emerged that had the propensity and funding to plan retaliation efforts for the Fairfax mall attack last summer. Her region had yet to submit its report, thanks in part to the time Lacy had spent with the task force and her own covert efforts to get to the bottom of nagging concerns that lingered in the back of her mind. Concerns she was reluctant to share with the rest of the task force. Namely, her boss.

"Hey, Lacy?" Michelle stood in her doorway. "You have a minute?"

She glanced away from her computer. "Sure. Come in."

"You got that request from SSA Banks?"

"I did. I'm working on it now. I just had to write the summary of the team's results. I'll have it on her desk by the end of today."

"Okay. Good." Michelle appeared reticent. "Look, I understand you've been through a lot recently. More than most of us, that's for sure."

Lacy interrupted before Michelle could continue. "I know what you're about to say. And I won't disagree. I've been slacking off on my duties here, what with Brian leaving. I need to find a replacement for him. And I need to stay on top of these troubling events that seem to be developing in the wake of the sanctions."

"I'm not going to lie, Lacy. You have been distracted. Is there anything at all I can do to help?"

"No. Thank you, Michelle. This is on me. I'll get it worked out. I promise you. I know my job is a reflection on you too and I won't let you down."

"We've got a very disconcerting problem brewing and we're all scrambling for answers. No one wants an attack on the Asian community. We need all hands on deck to make sure that doesn't happen."

"I understand."

"Okay." She turned to leave but stopped short. "I can help you find a replacement for Brian if need be. In fact, I'll send you some promising resumes I've had on my hands for a while."

"I'd appreciate that. Thank you." Lacy watched Michelle leave, knowing she was letting her down. Not getting to the source of the task force's problem, which was finding the money behind Dalian Company. She was letting everyone down, including herself.

Lacy returned to her report, putting on the final touches before sending it up the chain when she spotted Will enter her office.

"Afternoon."

"Hi. What are you doing here? Figured you'd be out with the WFO, with Fraser, still working on the Turner shooting."

"I was with him this morning. Nothing new on their end. Still working on ballistics."

"I'm sorry to hear that. It'd be nice to actually reach an end to one of the many problems we're dealing with at the moment. I'm starting to feel like we're running in circles, you know?"

"I know." He sat down. "Axell left me a message. He's on his way home. Should be here late tonight."

"Oh yeah?" She checked her phone. "Damn. Looks like I missed his call."

"He wants to meet with us on his return to the shop. He said he'd be there around 10 pm."

"Sure. I can be there. Must be important if it can't wait until tomorrow."

"Couldn't tell you. He didn't say much over the phone. But I assume it must be."

"Hey, can I ask you something?"

"Of course."

"Are you starting to feel like you're being pulled in too many directions? Like there isn't enough time in the day and that we aren't moving ahead the way we should be?"

"Sometimes. Why? You feeling like that?"

"I'm falling behind. Michelle was in here earlier. I was supposed to turn in a report. Haven't done it yet. And with everything going on in the media, and the protests against seemingly every Chinese company in the country, she was right to push. There's no room for error here. No room for slacking off either. What if I miss something? Like I missed the mall attack?"

"You didn't miss the mall attack, Lacy. You did everything you were supposed to do in those initial days and weeks before everything went south and we were running for our lives."

She smiled. "Yeah. How could I forget? I don't know. I just don't feel like we're getting ahead."

"I know you don't. But if it were easy..."

"Yeah, yeah. Everybody would be doing it."

"Listen." Will glanced at the time. "Why don't you finish up your work? It's what, 5:00 now? Finish that up and you and I will go grab a drink and maybe a bite to eat before we start our second job."

"I'll tell you what. I'll finish this up, but then I need to run home and see the kids. How about we meet around seven?"

"I can live with that." He stood up. "I'll see you later."

"Bye." Lacy returned to her work. If she didn't get that report out, she might no longer have to worry about working here anymore. And who knew how long this task force would last? Probably about as long as the sanctions. To her, it didn't seem like any of this would last much longer because the American people were losing jobs and the dollar was wasting away to nothing. She'd pulled at the thread and the entire country was falling apart before her very eyes. Just like Turner said it would.

———

With a fresh set of clothes and her straight, brunette hair resting against her shoulders, Lacy walked into the restaurant and spotted Will already seated at a table.

He stood on her approach. "You look nice." He glanced at his own attire, which had been exactly the same as earlier in the day. "I feel like a slob now."

"Don't. I wanted to change. You look just fine."

"A ringing endorsement, if I ever heard one." He pulled out her chair.

"You know what I meant."

"I took the liberty of ordering you a glass of red. I hope that's okay."

"Perfect." She picked up the glass and took a sip. "Boy, I needed this. Don't suppose you heard from Aaron? I haven't talked to him since yesterday." She perused the menu.

"I did, actually. He says he's working to get more information on our Casper Janz before meeting with Axell tonight."

She hadn't yet heard back from Delgado, which was cause for concern. Either he was getting push-back, or there was nothing to find. Neither was a good result. "Now I feel bad he's missing out on dinner."

"He'll be fine. He's a grown man who can manage to find something to eat."

She picked up on his blunt tone. "Are you upset with him or something?"

"No. Not at all. I'm just saying that sometimes you treat him like a kid. And he's our age."

"I don't."

"Lacy, you do. I know you two have been friends a long time, but you treat him like he's your little brother. Which I'm sure he appreciates, considering."

"Considering what?"

"Nothing. What are you going to order?"

She had no desire to address his comment. "Salmon. I'll have the salmon."

"Sounds good. Me too." He set down his menu and held her gaze.

"What?"

"Nothing. I was just thinking," Will replied.

"About?"

"Well, about your kind words yesterday when we were talking about my military service. And how much you knew about it."

"To be honest, I've come across a lot of vets working for the Bureau. As I'm sure you have too. And I respect the hell out of each and every one of you for the sacrifices you've made for this country."

"Thank you. I don't often talk about it—my time in Afghanistan. I did a shorter stint in Iraq, but when the insurgency happened again, I was back to facilitate the movement of supplies. You know, I wanted to be on the bomb squad."

"Really?"

"Yep. Sure did. But I didn't have the right training. I could've gotten it, I suppose, but I did the whole ROTC thing in high school and college and was recruited as an officer as a result. And I guess, well, I guess I just decided the responsibility of supervising was enough. I should've done more."

"You do realize how much you've done with the Bureau, right? If I hadn't met you, I don't know if I would've pursued any of this."

"Yes, you would have. Of that, I have no doubt."

In the hours that flew by, the food was gone, and so was the wine. Lacy was glad for the reprieve, but it was time to face the music, which was Axell's return.

"There's no way we can show up buzzed like this," Will began. "Axell will have our heads on a platter."

"I'm not drunk. Well, maybe a little. Guess we'll be taking a cab there, huh?"

"I'd say so." He signed the bill.

"Thanks for dinner. You didn't have to pay."

"I know that, but I wanted to. Come on, we'd better get going."

"I'll text Aaron and let him know we're on our way. He's probably already there."

"Probably," Will said as he helped Lacy out of her chair. "You know, he's a good man. Flawed though he may be. He is dedicated to the team and to you."

"As if any of us are perfect." She followed him outside. "Holy hell, it's cold out here. I left my coat in the car."

"Here." Will placed his coat over her shoulders and hailed a cab.

———

Will held the door as Lacy entered the shop. Ten o'clock on the nose.

Axell noted their arrival with some reservations. "Thanks for coming down. You two look like you've been out enjoying yourselves."

Lacy greeted him with a warm embrace. "I'm glad you're home, Trevor."

"Have you been drinking?" Aaron asked her.

"Will and I had dinner and I had a couple glasses of wine."

"My fault. I think we both needed to blow off some steam and I ordered the wine."

"I think we deserved it, to be honest," Lacy continued. "What with the country falling apart."

Axell regarded her once again before turning his attention to the others. "So it does appear our friend Matthew Greiner is working in some capacity with Beijing."

"You mean Casper Janz?" Aaron said. "We were able to track down more information about him while you were away. Turns out the guy was in the armed forces and I was able to get hold of some records."

"And what else did you discover?" Axell glanced at Aaron and Lacy. "I know you two did some investigating of your own."

"We did," Lacy replied. "I wanted to follow up on Bruce Quintero. And I was right to. So was Aaron. He got into Greiner's personnel file, even if it didn't yield all we had hoped. And then he managed to discover the military service. That's when we put two and two together."

"You two did your job. And I need to remember that is exactly why you're both here. I'm sorry if I made it seem not to be the case. So what else did you find?"

"Apart from the fact that Greiner, or Janz, used intimidation tactics on Bruce. Threatened him if he ran the background check. And of course, discovered his alias. We were hoping you could shed some more light on your return," Aaron replied.

Lacy noted Axell's demeanor. As if he was already well aware of this information. And it was probably the wine, but she had to speak up. "Look, Trevor. There's something else I have to tell you. I went to see Martin Delgado this morning. I asked him to look into Casper Janz for us after Aaron uncovered his alias. And with you away, I thought Martin could offer up something new for us. And I need to ask you, is Janz CIA?"

"How would he know? We only just got the name," Aaron replied.

Axell paused for too long.

"Axell?" Aaron pressed him. "What's going on?"

With a heavy sigh, Axell finally spoke. "I wish you hadn't involved Delgado. Especially when we don't know what we're dealing with. Which was why I went to Beijing in the first place. What did he have to say?"

It seemed the entire team realized Axell hadn't answered her question. Lacy continued anyway. "Nothing yet. I don't know if he's had any luck. I'm sorry. I know I should've waited. But do you know who he is?"

"Patience never was your strong suit. But then, it's not mine either. And you know what?" He cast his eyes on the team. "I owe you guys the truth. I knew who he was before I left. Not long before, but I knew. And in the interest of safety, I didn't want to say anything until I figured out what part he played. Who else might be involved. Mostly because I wasn't sure who or what to believe. But now that I've confirmed my suspicions, it's time I let you in on the details."

Axell carried on and told them about how he knew Janz back in Cairo and his unexpected visitor in Beijing who had offered a vague message.

Regardless of his reasons, Lacy felt betrayed. "You should have told us, Trevor. What do we have if we can't even trust each other?"

"You want to talk about trust? You went to Delgado rather than talk to me."

"You weren't here."

Will stepped in. "It doesn't do any of us any good to argue about this." He turned to Axell. "I get why you kept this to yourself. Honestly, I probably would have too. And except for the fact that Aaron and Lacy have been running in circles as a result, you did what you thought was in our best interest. But the question remains, if everyone suspects Yang of terrorist ties, why is he still here?"

With regret written on his face, Axell continued, "With the intel I have at the moment, consensus seems to be that with all eyes on Yang, it would be easier to spot if he was planning something either here or in China. The subway station bombing a few weeks ago? Beijing suspects Yang was involved in the planning of that attack. There have been several other smaller attacks they believe the Separatist Movement to have been a part of. But are unsure if Yang was too."

"Why would Beijing have wanted Lei Jian to become involved with Dalian Company to begin with then? To what advantage did that serve?" Lacy worked to dismiss the frustration she felt at Trevor's actions. But if she was being honest with herself, she was keeping something from him too. There was another reason why she went to Delgado. And it was something she would not divulge. Not now or maybe ever. Not unless her suspicions rang true.

"Ultimately? Because they wanted the market. They wanted to subvert the US economy. And in the process, it seems Yang wanted something else. And so here we are," Trevor replied.

"In the beginning, Jian was Beijing's puppet, plain and simple," Will added.

"That's what we've been led to believe. Look, I can't postulate on the reasoning behind anything the MSS does. All I can tell you now is that I believe the reason we haven't found this so-called US investor is that we aren't meant to find him. There's a strong possibility we're being played. And before you hurl more questions at me, I don't know why or how, but there's a reason why we've been virtually at a standstill since the beginning."

"What do we do about this?" Will asked. "If what you two are saying is true, then this reaches far beyond anything we ever suspected. Far beyond the State Department."

"This could go all the way up to the president," Aaron said.

"There could be another explanation," Axell continued. "Like I mentioned, the agent who came to my hotel room essentially warned me that Yang was far more important than anything we might be working on. And the only way for us to find out is to bring Janz into the fold."

"What? No way. He's a spy. You said so yourself," Aaron replied.

"I've known him, from a distance, but I know what he's capable of doing. What he's done. And I do believe that he's being handled by someone on our side. It's that someone we need to find."

CHAPTER
THIRTEEN

THE PARKING LOT of the restaurant was empty, except for the two cars that had been temporarily abandoned, but whose owners had now returned. Her head down, Lacy minded her steps in the thin blanket of snow on the asphalt as they walked toward their cars.

"Are you okay?" Will asked

"To drive? Oh yeah."

"No, I mean about the meeting. What Axell said?"

She stopped short of her driver's side door and turned to Will. "No. I'm not okay. Not with what he did, keeping the truth from us, and not about the idea that we've been sidelined on purpose. If it's true—that this whole time we were just placated and made to be distracted from what was really happening." She shook her head. "Then nothing we've done will have made a damn bit of difference."

"That's not true. And aside from Axell withholding Janz's identity from us, which by the way, I think he was right to do." He held up his hands in defense. "He was, Lacy. He was. Janz is dangerous. Everything Axell told us about him? He was right to try to find out for sure what was happening and who he was working for. And as far as everything we've done—you've done—it has meant something. People know now, Lacy. That was the whole point. That the government was held accountable."

"Accountability? No. I don't think so. More lies and manipulation. More corruption. And for what? So a few powerful people at the top can become even more powerful?"

"You don't believe that, do you?"

"I don't know what to believe right now, Will. I thought they wanted us to help keep tabs on those who weren't playing by the rules. But it seems no one is playing by the rules, except for us. Two hundred thirty-five people died in the mall attack, including my husband. Countless others were horribly injured. We lost a good friend. For what? Where does it end?"

Will pulled her close. "Please don't give up. I don't think I could take that. There's more to this and that's what we need to find out. Axell's being cautious and rightly so. He wants to protect us, more than anything, I think."

She pulled back and held his gaze. "And what about our theory? Where was he that morning, Will? Where the hell was he? First, he keeps this from us. What if we're right about Turner? Especially in light of Janz's identity. Former CIA? Maybe Axell knew something else and didn't tell us."

"You can't think like that. Not about Axell. Come on. You know him better than that. We both do. It has obviously crossed my mind, but frankly, after tonight, I'm thinking we're the ones off base on that idea. He's been worried about us. I don't think he'd risk taking out Turner. Not if he already knew what Janz was."

"There's just one other thing I have to know."

"And that is?"

She wore a dismal smile. "How can you stay so positive in the face of such adversity?"

"What choice do I have? I won't give up. Not on our team, not on this country, and more importantly, not on you. I won't watch you throw in the towel. I think it would break my heart." He tucked her hair behind her ear and placed his hand on her cheek. His eyes never left hers, even as they swelled with tears.

"I'm tired. I need to go home." Lacy turned away from him and opened her car door, wiping away a stray tear as it streamed down her cheek. "Good night, Will. I'll see you tomorrow." She slipped into the driver's seat and pressed the ignition.

Will closed her door and stepped away. She watched him shrink in the rearview before turning on the car radio. A news broadcast was on. It was 12:30 in the morning when she heard the breaking bulletin.

"A Chinese Cultural Center was burned to the ground earlier tonight in Richmond. The four-alarm blaze brought firefighters from the Richmond Fire Department and surrounding communities to get the fire under control. Current reports indicate no one was inside, but authorities caution that they cannot confirm this until emergency services are allowed inside the charred remains, which could still be some time. The mayor of Richmond advised residents to keep calm and stay home. Reminding the citizens that the community must come together and not be allowed to rip itself apart in the wake of strained relations between China and the US."

Lacy turned off the radio as a flood of tears fell from her eyes.

———

The house alarm beeped as Lacy entered through the garage side door and into the kitchen. She keyed the code and the beeping stopped. The house was dark with everyone asleep at the late hour. Lacy slipped off her shoes and padded along the travertine floor toward the foyer, eventually making her way upstairs. She pushed open Olivia's door and spotted her tucked under the covers. With a smile, she pulled it closed again and walked across the hall to check on Jack, who was fully covered and began to wonder if she should turn up the heat. Her own skin seemed to be numb to anything, any feeling at all, but it was her children with whom she shared this concern.

Lacy walked into her bedroom and switched on the lamp that rested on a side table where her laptop lay. She'd received an email from Martin Delgado during the meeting but failed to make mention of it. For reasons currently unknown to her, she was reticent to completely open up about her concerns with the team. Even standing in front of Will. The honesty his eyes portrayed as they stood freezing in the parking lot. She still withheld her true feelings. Was it out of caution or fear that she would discover something about one of them? Something that would shatter any remaining illusions of goodness left in this world? After all they'd been through, it was an unfair assessment on her part. But a piece of her heart had already been ripped away and she had to protect what remained.

As she opened her laptop, Lacy viewed the email from Agent Delgado. It contained the information she'd requested on Casper Janz, but not without a warning from Delgado.

In the email, he revealed Trevor had been honest in his rendering of how he came to know Janz. They had both been in Cairo, but Janz, only in passing. Delgado advised her not to take matters into her own hands when it came to Janz. That he was a ruthless man and his involvement in the torturing of prisoners held without proof meant he would toe the line of whoever he was taking orders from. Good or bad. And right now, it seemed Lacy couldn't be sure whose side he was on. For that, she and the team would need to fall back on Trevor. But nothing about Janz's relationship with Camden Meeks. Or that there had even been one. "Maybe Will was right."

She sat back from her monitor and studied the email, the one she'd been afraid to show her team. Right now, she was the one behaving like a traitor. What gnawed at her still was not knowing Trevor's whereabouts the morning Turner was killed. She had to know. If he'd done it, why? Did he know more than he was letting on?

It was too late to think about it anymore tonight. It was past one in the morning. Tomorrow will bring more answers. It had to because, right now, Lacy could think of nothing else but the potential betrayal at the hands of her president, and hidden agendas from the man she held in the highest regard.

———

Axell studied the front of Janz's townhouse as he sat in his parked car a few hundred feet away. He'd procured the address thanks to Aaron Hunter, a man who had gained his full respect. And in the hours between midnight and dawn, he waited, planning for the moment of his arrival. The only way he could understand the part Janz was playing in this was to confront him. Not in some seedy bar with cryptic words, but in the dark of night, the cold barrel of his gun pressed against the head of this man who held the answers Axell desired. He saw that same desire imbued in Lacy's eyes. The others were patient. Caison and Hunter didn't really want the truth. They thought they did, but it was only Lacy who needed it so much it was beginning to tear her apart. Axell lay witness to the fact this very evening. She'd revealed too much to him. He would get her the answers because he needed them too. And maybe then he could tell her everything he'd wanted to say. This woman was making him do things he never would've done before. From Day One, it had been that way. He held no notions that Lacy could ever have romantic feelings for him, in fact, it was the one feeling he didn't possess for her either. This was something else. Something deeper. She had been wounded many times over. And like the man he always knew he was, he would get her what she needed. After all, she was like a daughter to him. Only Lacy hadn't disavowed him the way his real daughter had.

Axell stepped out of his car, clinging to the shrubbery that fronted the road and acted as a barrier to the residents situated close to the street. He walked within the shadows until reaching the home. He didn't know if Janz was inside, but in the event he wasn't, he would at least have the opportunity to search for something that might expose his objectives. Agent Shaw was right to warn him in Beijing. Now the time had come to understand where Janz's loyalties lay.

The only way to get in was through the front. The home was attached to another property on the right, and on the left was a fenced area thick with tall, screening shrubs. He wasn't about to go through there where he couldn't be sure what he would encounter. A logical assumption was that Janz had the house well-secured. Given his known associates, it was to be expected. So how had Axell planned on entering this mini-Fort Knox? Simple.

Several devices were available on the internet that could defeat garage door openers' rolling codes. Luckily, Axell worked for the CIA, and getting his hands on a device slightly more sophisticated wasn't hard to do. The trick would still be what was inside, but getting into the garage would be child's play. And inside of 8.7 seconds, the door rolled open, revealing Janz's Mercedes. Good news. He was home.

Axell withdrew his gun and made his way to the garage entry door—locked, with a deadbolt. This wasn't much more of a problem considering the age of the home and, by the looks of the lock, it was the pin and tumbler style most homes had. He retrieved his bump key, a specially made key that could penetrate and unlock most of these styles. If the CIA was good at anything, it was getting inside people's homes or as they call it, a black-bag job. Though a US citizen wasn't usually the target demographic. Nor was former CIA.

Without a trace of forced intrusion, he disengaged the dead-bolt and quietly turned the handle under the assumption that once he was inside, an alarm would beep until shut off, or without a code, would sound loudly throughout the home. Axell had less than a minute from the time the beeping began until the time the alarm activated. He would ascend the stairs, assuming Janz had already been roused by the noise and was likely holding a gun at the door. At which time, Axell would make his presence known. Janz would either shoot him through the door, a likely possibility or inquire as to his presence. It was a crapshoot.

The beep sounded in a low "I'm warning you" sort of way. The time had come for Axell to make his way up the staircase. However, it seemed Janz had other plans.

"What the hell are you doing here?"

Axell whipped around on his heel, gun aimed at the voice behind him. "Well, this is unexpected."

The men held each other within point-blank range.

"I said, what the hell are you doing here, Axell?"

"I need answers. And I knew you wouldn't fall for the note on the windshield trick again. Though I had considered it."

"Fuck you. You're in my house. I could shoot you and no one would blink an eye."

"You could. But so could I. What are you willing to bet I hit you first?"

Janz paused, appearing to consider who was the better shot.

Within seconds, he held both hands up, gun aimed at the ceiling. "Fine."

"Okay, then. We can get down to business." Axell kept an eye glued to the man's gun even while he'd begun to lower his own. "Can we talk now? Officer to officer. After you turn off the alarm, of course."

Janz ejected the cartridge, placed his weapon on a nearby table, and keyed in his alarm code. "Have a seat." Janz walked into the kitchen and pulled out a chair. "You want a coffee?"

"Sure." Axell followed him after placing his own weapon out of reach. "Sorry it had to be like this. I'll be honest with you, Casper, I can't tell which side you're on. I had to take precautions."

"I'm on the winning side."

Axell nodded. "Pretty much what I thought. So not much different than Cairo, then, huh?"

"What the hell do you know about Cairo? You didn't have to go through the shit I did. At least I was getting intel. What were you doing? Kissing the station chief's ass? Looking for a way to get out of that desert hell hole?"

"I think we remember that time a little differently."

Janz placed a mug in front of him before taking a seat opposite at the table.

"Thanks." He sipped on the coffee. "Are you playing both sides, then?"

Janz laughed. "Both sides? Of what?"

"Look, we can pussyfoot around this until daylight, but I'm not leaving here until I get some answers."

Janz grinned. "Who are you talking to at the Agency?"

"No one. Not about this." Failing to mention that Handley authorized his trip to Beijing was vital because Axell couldn't rule out anyone's potential involvement at this point.

"What about you heading to Beijing? I have friends there, you know. They were all up in arms when you showed up to meet with Cheng in Bureau 17. What? You think they wouldn't figure out who you really were? I told them to back off. You're welcome, by the way."

"Was it you who sent Agent Shaw to see me at my hotel?"

"No. I don't know Shaw. Not personally. I know CIA has operatives there again, but I stay out of their way and they stay out of mine."

"Who's Dalian's US investor, Casper? That's all I want to know." It wasn't, but he had to start somewhere. "You tell me who it is and we're done here."

"You can't believe that's what this is about? My work with Yang? The MSS?"

"If not, then what? Why don't you shed some light on this situation for me?"

"Look, I can get you the investor, but it won't matter. The deal was done legally, within the sanction's regs."

"Who would want to keep Yang here? And keep Dalian functioning. Have you seen the news? You know what's been happening in this country, right? Tonight? The Cultural Center? This country is about to blow. Just like Egypt did during the Arab Spring. Only it'll be so much worse."

Janz studied Axell. "Malcom Ford. That's who you're looking for. It's his money."

"He's the Dalian investor?"

"Yes. Look, Axell. Regardless of what you might think of me, and what I've chosen to do with my skill set, we were on the same team once. And I need you to listen to me when I say you and your team need to end things here. You're on your own if you choose to pursue Ford or any of his associates. And especially Yang."

"How far up the food chain does this go?"

"Honestly? I don't know. I do what I'm told and that's that. I do what I have to do to stay alive. And I suggest you and your people do the same. Things are going on that neither of us knows or fully understands. Give Ford a cursory look. You'll see that I'm right. Nothing out of the ordinary. They are exceptionally good."

"Then why couldn't we find him? We found you."

"I'm not the one who matters in this game. That, you need to understand. I don't matter and neither do you. And Lacy Merrick? The woman who started this?"

"She didn't start this."

"No. You're right. She just shoved it in the public's face and created the situation we're in now."

"Sounds like this would've come to a head regardless," Axell continued.

"In time. But I'd hoped to do my part and get Yang on the ropes. That's what they want."

"That's what who wants?"

The window behind Janz shattered and the ear-piercing crash forced Axell to jump. A bullet sliced into Janz's head. "Jesus!" Axell rolled out of the chair and onto the floor when the flurry of gunfire raged.

He low-crawled through the house to get his gun and continued through the back exit. The shots ceased and the sound of car alarms and dogs barking replaced the noise. He had no idea who was after him, but he suspected Janz had been under surveillance and his house bugged. Now, as he stood outside in the dark, his eyes struggling to adjust to the scant light, Axell had to find a way out. He didn't know who was there or if he was outnumbered. Going through to the front of the house was high risk and he preferred to take calculated risks. But he would not have that luxury this time.

Sirens sounded in the distance. A neighbor must've called the police. "Thank God." Axell knew the man or men would flee the scene and then he could make his way out the front and toward his car. But he would have to do so without being seen by the approaching cop cars or anyone else.

He stepped carefully through the backyard, getting tangled up in the shrubs he'd already tried to avoid once. And for this very reason. The thorny branches poked through his long sleeves and jacket. "Should've worn my leather coat." He pressed on until making his way to the fence where he could examine the street. "Shit!" Cops were already there, but no sign of anyone else. The gunmen were gone.

He waited for the police to kick their way into the townhouse before he hopped the fence and high-tailed it to his car. He reached the street, where he spotted officers still huddled at the home's entrance while others were inside, flashlights shining. It looked like spotlights on a stage, swaying back and forth.

The remote on his car made the lights flash as Axell stepped inside. "Damn it." It seemed he was far enough down the road not to be noticed. Still, he pulled away, leaving his headlights off until he was far enough from the scene. Axell retrieved his cell phone. "Meet me at the shop. Now!"

CHAPTER
FOURTEEN

DAWN BROKE through the clouds when Lacy arrived at the very place she'd left only a few short hours earlier. But the urgency in Trevor's voice had forced an abrupt awakening and she left the house leaving only a note for Celeste.

She pushed through the rear entrance and into the grey-lit halls to the voices in the bullpen. The rest of the team was already inside. "Sorry. Got here as fast as I could. What happened?"

Axell was pale and his face glistened with sweat. "Casper Janz is dead. I was with him when shots were fired into his house. They must've had him under surveillance."

"Oh my God. Are you okay?" Lacy rushed nearer.

"I'm fine. I got out undetected. Thank you all for coming down. I know it's early."

"What does this mean, Axell?" Will was the first to ask the question all seemed plagued by. "Who do you think did this?"

"And more importantly," Aaron began, "are we in danger now?"

Lacy noted his concern and turned her attention to Axell. "Was it Yang's people?"

"I wish I could answer all your questions. Right now, I have far more questions than answers myself and that's a very bad position for us to be in." He began to pace the room. "My gut tells me this was not Yang."

"Then who?" Lacy continued. "Our people?"

"What do you mean, our people?" Aaron asked her.

"I mean, our government. You said yourself, Trevor, Janz was former CIA. Is it possible he's still engaged? Or playing ball with someone in the administration."

"State?" Aaron asked.

"Possibly. That's where I would suggest we look," Will replied. "But the moment we start getting more intel on Janz, he's taken out?"

"There's one other thing," Axell began. "I know who the investor is. Just before they got him, he gave me a name. Malcolm Ford."

"Maybe you should've started with that." Aaron approached his workstation and opened his laptop. "What else do we know about him?"

"Nothing, except Janz insisted that the transaction was perfectly legal. That we wouldn't find any wrongdoing on his part. And—that we shouldn't look too deep."

"Then why has it been so difficult to find him?" Lacy asked. "This could get us a step closer." She'd all but forgotten about her earlier animosity. Axell had been in real danger and it frightened her.

"Look, I just had bullets whizzing by my head. You'll forgive me if I lack a willingness to sit here and stare at a computer screen until we find something on Ford. Or nothing, as the case might be. My main concern right now is to find out who wanted Janz dead and why. I can only assume it was because he was talking to me. If it was Yang, then I could deal with that. If it was someone else, on our side of the fence, then I see this as a problem that could put us in jeopardy."

"We should see Mobley and tell him what's happening. This isn't like before. We're here because of him and Director Handley. Trevor? What about getting a meeting with both of them? They have to be made aware. Now that we know Malcolm Ford is the investor, that gives us a jump start. Let those guys put a team together to find out who killed Janz. We can't do this on our own again. We don't have to do this on our own again. That was the whole point of this task force, right?"

"Lacy's right, Axell," Aaron began. "We have the backing of the intelligence community this time. How can we draw on that support to get some answers?"

"I'll visit Handley. He'll need to know about Janz," Axell began. "Caison, you and Lacy should get with Mobley. Tell him what we know so far about Ford and Janz. Get a recommendation from him. Let's get down to business. We'll reconvene here later today."

"What can I do?" Aaron asked.

"Get anything and everything you can on Malcolm Ford."

"Will do."

———

With the uncertainty of who fired the shots into the home of Casper Janz and the possibility of CIA involvement, Axell would deliver his remarks to the CIA director with careful calculation. His briefing would include the request for additional resources: surveillance, analysts, and help from Agent Shaw in Beijing, who was already very familiar with the situation. In fact, Axell was reluctant to reveal the name of the investor until he knew more about him.

"Thank you for seeing me, Director Handley. I know it's early." Axell tendered a greeting.

"Of course. I don't have much time, so let's get down to brass tacks. Your call mentioned the loss of one of our own."

"That's right, sir. Former CIA Officer Casper Janz, who it seems was operating under the name of Matthew Greiner and who we believe was Yang's right-hand man."

"The same individual you suspected of dealing with the MSS? The reason you went to Beijing in the first place. Only now, he's dead. And you suspect Yang's people?"

"I can't say with any certainty that's the case yet, sir. My team and I are working on it. And the reason I'm here is to request additional resources. We're a four-man operation and in need of help from an operative I met with in Beijing in addition to a top analyst who can jump in with both feet. There's no time for red tape in this situation, sir. We need to act now."

"Get in the proper request and I'll expedite it."

"Thank you, sir." Axell pushed off his chair to leave.

"Has Mobley been briefed?"

"He has, sir. I need to get back to the shop and come up with a game plan for my team."

"Axell, do you believe your life or the lives of your team are in danger?"

"I have no idea."

———

Aaron diligently worked on obtaining intel on Malcolm Ford when Will and Lacy returned to the shop. "Good. You're back. How did Mobley take the news?"

"Not well, but he's authorized additional resources," Will replied. "Axell's not back yet?"

"I am." He appeared from the rear entrance. "I heard the tail end of your conversation. I'm about to send in the request for satellite surveillance and an analyst to back up anything Hunter might need on Ford. The director said he'd process it ASAP."

"What did he say about Janz? About losing him?"

"Nothing. Not to me, anyway. Until we know who's behind Janz's death, the need to tread lightly around those outside our team is paramount. I know we have help, but the four of us here? We need to depend on each other right now." Axell turned to Aaron. "Any luck on Malcolm Ford?"

"I did find something of interest. Come take a look." Aaron turned around his monitor. "A shell company. Out of Luxembourg. I had to dig pretty deep inside the SEC, but I found his name in a filing and discovered the PLC's managing partner was Malcolm Ford. What's interesting here is that the company sells shares privately, not on the exchange."

"Why would that matter?" Lacy asked.

"Well, I'm no expert in business structure, but from what I read, they would've sold shares to raise capital. Maybe enough to purchase Dalian stock. I don't know."

"I could ask someone in White Collar," Will began. "Gain a better understanding of the structure."

"Okay. So we know who this guy is. The name of his company. Now we need to know the source of the funds. I'd like to know where we can find him too."

"What do we do about Janz's death? Do we need to be concerned here, Trevor?"

"Lacy, no one knows about the task force apart from the president and the directors. No one else knows any of us are a part of it. Janz was spilling intel, and he got killed for it. Now, if he was under surveillance, which seems the most probable scenario, they would find out it was me he was talking to. And I'll take precautions. However, I don't believe any of you are in danger. If we get intel to suggest otherwise, we have the resources to do what we need to do to protect ourselves. I'm going to get a team to sweep the house. If Janz was bugged, we'll know and we'll know who was doing it."

———

Shen Yang stood, his back turned to the unexpected guest who had arrived unannounced, and gazed out over the garden of his lavish estate from his home office window.

"We've suffered exposure at the hands of your friend, Mr. Matthew Greiner, who is no longer with us as of 5 am D.C. time."

"Witnesses?" Yang said, still turned.

"One. Trevor Axell, CIA. Earlier this morning, I received a call from one of our operatives inside the agency. He informed me a meeting had taken place with the CIA director. Agent Axell requested additional resources."

Yang finally turned. "I will take it from here. Thank you." He waited for the man to leave before picking up his phone. "I trust you've been made aware of the situation?" Yang sat down in his chair. "I felt it necessary to inform you that we will need to take precautionary measures to ensure no evidence is found in the home of Matthew Greiner. I'll need all files deleted. Personal and otherwise. Can you confirm that will happen?" He waited for the reply on the other end of the line. "It will need to be sooner rather than later, or we risk discovery of our arrangement. And you'll inform your people?" He waited again. "Very well. Goodbye, sir."

"Goodbye, Mr. Yang." The secretary stood in a ray of gray morning light and opened his refrigerator door, its bright bulb stinging his tired eyes. Inside was the water he now craved, and on closing the door again, he drank almost the entire bottle in one fell swoop. This wasn't supposed to happen. He'd only just been made aware of this debacle and so Yang's call was to be expected. He thought they had enough on Janz that he would remain loyal, which was why he was chosen. But he hadn't diverted Agent Axell's attention, and in fact, appeared to have offered evidence that could destroy everything. Now Janz was gone. The facilitator. And Trevor Axell knew things.

The problem now was how to keep Axell from getting to Yang. He needed Yang and vice versa. They'd come so far and had accomplished a great many things he thought impossible. China was still dumping stock and their currency was tanking. The sanctions were working, even if it was beginning to tear apart the country. Sacrifices still needed to be made. And had been made. The devastation of the mall attack was still fresh on the minds of the American people.

He picked up his phone again and made the call. "We're going to have to give him up. They're too close." He waited on the line. "Given what's happened, I doubt he'll get a word in before they kill him. If it has to be that way, then we'll deal with it. We have much of the plan in place already. And he has people inside Xinjiang who are aware. We'll have to use that to our advantage. Nothing has to change." He tipped the few drops of water left into his mouth. "No. Once he's gone, I'm confident it will end there. We'll just sit back and wait. Don't make a move. Just let it happen." He ended the call and started back up the stairs.

CHAPTER
FIFTEEN

TWENTY-THREE MILLION, give or take a million or two. That was the number of Muslims in China, the majority of which resided in the Xinjiang region and were of Uyghur descent. This equated to roughly two percent of the entire population. A notable minority. One which the Chinese government had been grappling with in its efforts to control the population's growing extremist views. A consequence of their own harsh actions.

This was Yang's home. This was Yang's belief. And as he sat in his American home, with his Han Chinese wife, he knew that the bold alliance he helped form put them both in grave danger. The closer he came to completing the objective, the riskier it was for him to even leave his home, let alone visit his homeland.

What started as a joint effort to bring an end to, as he saw it, the complete extermination of his people through eradicating their religion appeared to have become beneficial to only one side. And that side was not his.

Now, the man who had been a trusted liaison, ensuring the money flowed and the inquiries were squelched, was gone. Dead. And Yang was on his own. He'd helped them get rid of

Lei Jian. A man who, for all intents and purposes, had become drunk with his own perceived power. He'd helped keep the Dalian Company running, avoiding the tough US sanctions. And now he'd begun to feel his friends were no longer his allies. That perhaps they no longer wanted the same things. Or was it that they never wanted the same thing to begin with? Had Yang been so consumed with the objective that he failed to see its faults?

Trevor Axell was going to be a problem, one he hadn't counted on and certainly not one he believed was his problem to solve. Would Yang have to renege on his agreement? And if so, what would the ramifications of such an act have on his people?

He walked downstairs as the sunlight soared in the sky. The time had come to confront those who had put him here.

————

Aaron rubbed his eyes and rolled back in his desk chair. The information he'd uncovered and its consequences were still sinking in. Inside his apartment, timidity climbed up his spine. He eyed his front door— it was locked. He stood from his chair and walked to the middle of the room, standing still, eyes cast in every direction. Soon he began checking all the windows of his third-floor unit. All were secured.

He reached for his phone, hand hovering over the call button, and hesitated. Since working inside the Agency, Aaron learned how easy it was to listen to anyone, anywhere. And with the evidence he'd just come across, it wasn't worth the risk.

The car keys sat on the small breakfast bar. Aaron snatched them up along with his coat and laptop and was out the door. The question became, who would he turn to first? Axell, out of a sense of duty, or Lacy, out of a sense of loyalty. Both would need to know and his heart told him to turn to the woman. It would of course be Lacy. No one mattered to him as much as she did.

Within minutes, he found himself standing at her front door, hunched over in the freezing rain that was beginning to turn to hail in the building storm.

Lacy opened the door before he had a chance to knock. "I saw you pull up. What are you doing here? Are you okay?" Her concern for him appeared in her worried eyes. "Come in before you freeze to death out there."

"Thanks. I had to talk to you and I just wasn't sure if I could call." He shed his drenched coat, hung it on the rack, and walked into the kitchen. "I need to show you something."

Lacy followed him, glancing up at the staircase, hoping the kids wouldn't come down.

"Are the kids asleep?" he asked.

"Yes. I was just making sure no lights were on, that I hadn't awakened them." She walked toward the coffee maker and started a pot. "Let me get you something hot to drink."

Aaron set up his laptop. "Thanks. That's some storm out there tonight."

"It is. This must be important for you to come out in this weather. It couldn't wait until tomorrow?"

"No. I don't think so."

She returned with two mugs in her hands, placing one in front of him. "Here."

He sipped on the warm drink. "Sit down. This is going to take some time."

Lacy appeared even more concerned. "What did you find, Aaron? What's happening? Have you told Trevor?"

"I came straight here. I thought you should know first. Then we can figure out what to do." He directed an anxious eye to her. "It's always been you and me, right, Lace?"

"Of course, it has. Aaron, you're starting to scare me."

He turned the laptop toward her. "Axell forwarded me a contact at the Treasury Department's FinCen and I emailed him earlier today after you all came back from speaking with the directors."

"FinCen is the Financial Crimes Network, right?"

"Right. They have an international Financial Intelligence Unit. This guy is in that unit. They track international organized crimes, money laundering activities—things like that to help combat the financing of terrorist organizations. And there are like a bunch of other of these units worldwide. All share the information, right?"

"Got it. Go on."

"So anyway, he sent me this reply. Basically, just giving me some whitewashed version of how things ran over there and if I wanted something, I needed to fill out umpteen forms. You know, all that bureaucratic shit that I loathe."

"Great. So he was a big help, then."

"More than he thought, that's for sure." Aaron smirked. "I had an email address. I had a link to the forms to fill out and well, you know, I just did what I do best, right?"

"Of course you did. What did you find, Aaron? It's late. You'll have to spare me the hacker lingo."

"Sure. Yeah. Okay, so with some tricks I learned at the agency and additional clearance I got from Axell because of the meeting, I got into the database where their forms are filed. A 314a request was filed by the DOJ on Shen Yang. The request allows FinCen to contact international financial institutions regarding companies or people who may be involved in money laundering or terrorist activities. The request helps them locate accounts and transactions of the suspected person or company."

Lacy nodded, appearing to grow impatient by Aaron's over-explanation to which he was often prone.

"I'll get to my point." He picked up on her frustration. "The request filed on behalf of the Department of Justice was an effort to trace any transactions between Yang and the MSS through one of their many shell companies set up as fronts. I came across a name I know you're familiar with. Synergy Dynamics."

Lacy peered at the screen, which displayed the form. "Syn-Dyn. I knew there must be more to it than Bruce let on."

"Lacy, this could mean that SynDyn is a shell company the MSS created to shield money going to Dalian. And Matthew Greiner, aka Casper Janz, worked for them. For a while, anyway."

"But why shield the money? So far, Dalian's done everything by the book."

"Have they? Lei Jian worked to help crush Dalian's competitors, which included Nova Investments and, of course, its parent company, Liwa Properties. Maybe this goes back much further than we ever believed."

"But you're saying that this FinCen is meant to help find money going to terrorist organizations. And SynDyn could be a front to get money to Yang. Does that mean the Treasury Department knows about Yang's associations with the Movement? And did they know before the attack?"

"This form was filed very soon after the sanctions. Meaning the DOJ already suspected Yang of funneling money to terrorists."

"And yet let him continue to run Dalian. Unless this was something that they intended to use against him at some point in time."

"What we have now is proof, Lacy. This establishes ties to Dalian, Yang, SynDyn, and suspected terrorist groups. And SynDyn's former frontman, who is now dead. This appears to have been put on the back burner. And like you say, maybe it was intended for use against him down the road. Now I just need to find out how Malcolm Ford fits into this."

"Casper Janz, or rather, Matthew Greiner left SynDyn to work more closely with Yang. Maybe Ford is the new frontman. Keeping the money going into Dalian."

"This muddies the waters, Lacy. At least as far as Janz is concerned. This guy bounces around between SynDyn and Dalian. Who is paying him? Who is he really working for?"

She peered through her kitchen window. "I really don't know. Former CIA turned Chinese operative? We'll need to let the guys know about this. It's important. But you know, it's late. None of us have had any sleep. Least of all Trevor. Why don't you crash here? Storm looks to be hitting pretty hard right now. We'll head out to the shop first thing in the morning. Gives us a few hours' rest anyway. I won't be able to stay long, though. I've still got a job to do at the Bureau. I'm on thin ice as it is."

"This is starting to get very complicated—and possibly danger-ous, Lacy. Why can't you just leave the Bureau? This going back and forth, it can't be what's best right now."

"I don't want to leave, first and foremost. I'm happy there. But I don't know how long I can do this either. If I let my duties slip and something happens. You've been watching the news, right? You see what's going on out there?"

He nodded.

"How long before we get a home-grown attack? I can't let that happen, Aaron."

"I know. None of us can."

———

Axell stood outside the home of Casper Janz. A sideways rain pelted his face while he secured the buttons on his overcoat. He'd been told the job was done. The sweep was complete. And that they'd found nothing.

He entered the home where another agent stood watch. "Where's Hicks?" He'd called on the man who'd helped him bug the Meeks' home because he knew he could be trusted, insisting that he run the sweep.

"In the kitchen."

Axell made his way through the entrance, amid other agents donning headgear and instruments that would locate recording devices. "You found nothing?" He continued his approach.

"Axell. You didn't need to come down here," Hicks replied.

"The hell I didn't. You cannot seriously tell me there were no devices in this house?"

"Look, I know this isn't what you expected, but my guys know what they're doing. And I thought you had the same confidence in me."

"I do. I apologize." He examined the home in disbelief.

"It's possible someone beat us to it," Hicks continued. "They knew we were coming and cleaned the place out."

The kid had a point. "Whoever fired at Janz knew I got away, and probably came back to clear out. Nothing left behind to trace or listen to. So we've got a big fat zero here? Nothing that will help us figure out who wanted Janz dead?"

"Axell, I respect the hell out of you, you know that. I wouldn't have offered my services before if I didn't. And because Colburn vouched for you. You want to discover who took out Casper Janz, best bet is to look at who gave him his backstop, right? Whoever that was stood the most to lose if his cover was blown in my humble opinion. It's a start anyway."

"Thank you, Hicks. You're a smart kid. I appreciate you coming out here in this shit weather and doing this. And, I'll take your idea into consideration. We have to start somewhere. I was just hoping we'd find something here."

"That would have made things easier. But since when are our jobs easy?"

Axell patted him on the back. "Go on. Your team should pack up and get out of here before the streets start flooding. I'll close up here."

"Want to take a look around?" Hicks asked.

"Might as well. Got nothing to lose."

"No, sir. Good night, Axell."

Axell waited for several more minutes for the team to pack up. And as he stood in the now-empty house, his mind flew at lightning speed in search of answers. So many open ends remained and now Janz was gone. A man who had been working for Yang for some time, which was concern enough for Axell. "What am I missing?"

And as he stood inside the home with only a few lights burning, he considered the idea that perhaps he wasn't alone. That they could well be watching him now. "You're starting to sound like Merrick." It was hard to miss Lacy's propensity for paranoia. Maybe she was right to feel that way—probably was right. But he couldn't let his own feelings turn. It was reckless and dangerous. No. They didn't want Janz to talk and killed him when they thought he might reveal something important.

He knew about Ford now. That was a start. But what else was there? What was so important that they killed a former CIA officer? Not that these people, whoever these people were, hadn't done it before. After all, Colburn was dead. He'd suspected it had been Yang's people and still believed that but had no evidence to offer up. And with Turner gone too. People in the know were dropping like flies.

It occurred to him in that moment that if Hicks was right, and the place had been cleared out before they'd arrived, there could be some evidence to that effect. Axell walked upstairs and began searching the home for files, papers, and anything that would help him piece this together. He'd hoped that his file and whoever authorized his cover, or backstop as Hicks called it, would be here somewhere. Sometimes, only one or two people would know of an agent's cover, and if something happened and the agent was exposed, the file would be destroyed. The agent disowned. Happened all the time. It was part of the job. So he again wondered if Janz had kept his true identity hidden somewhere in this house. Papers that would prove Matthew Greiner wasn't real, and in that, he hoped he might find his handler.

———

In the quiet of his room and the black of night, Will's cell phone illuminated and droned on his bedside table. He reached for it and immediately answered. "Caison here."

"It's Fraser. I'm outside. Can I come in?"

Will sat up, his feet flat on the floor. "What? You're here?"

"Yeah, man. Can you let me in or what? It's raining like hell out here."

"I'll be right down." He ended the call and pulled on jogging pants and a t-shirt that were wadded up on the floor next to his bed. The first thought was that Lacy was in trouble or danger, or a combination thereof. Agent Adam Fraser worked in the Washington Field Office in D.C. And Will's team at Headquarters was asked to assist in the Turner investigation to rule out a terror attack, or retaliation, as the case might have been. But for him to show up now, unannounced and in the middle of the night, brought to mind that she had been hurt or worse. Why this occurred to him, he couldn't be sure. Maybe it was because she was still a federal employee and worked for the Bureau and Head-quarters didn't generally get involved in city murders. Still, his mind could wander all night with terrible thoughts. Right now, he needed to see Fraser for himself.

He buzzed to let him in through the foyer downstairs and now spotted Fraser walking quickly toward him.

"Hey, man, I'm sorry it's so late. We need to talk."

"Yeah, okay. Come in." He closed the door after Fraser entered. "You want something to drink?"

"Water, thanks."

Will padded into the kitchen and grabbed two bottles of water. "You picked a hell of a night to show up."

"You're telling me. It's like friggin Armageddon out there with that rain." Fraser opened the bottle and tossed back half of it in about ten seconds. "Listen, you know how we got that surveillance footage from the building across the street with the suspected shooter?"

"Yeah. I thought it wasn't good enough to give us a positive ID."

"It wasn't. But," he raised an index finger for emphasis, "I just reviewed additional footage from the ATM across the street. Seems our guy walked by there on his way to and from the scene."

"And?"

"We aren't one hundred percent certain, but markers match your recent vic, Casper Janz."

"What? No. That can't be. I'm sure he was in Beijing at the time. Or had come back. Shit, I can't remember now. I'd have to ask Axell." Will knitted his brow. "Really? I mean, are you pretty damn sure?"

"Similar build. Similar height. And to be honest with you man, who the hell else could it have been? Janz makes the most sense.

Targeting Wendell Turner because he might say something about Yang. It's plausible, right?"

"Yeah. I guess it is. The guy's dead now. We'll never know if it was him or not."

"That's not entirely true. I've got a team scouring the rest of the area for any additional surveillance, so I can track where he came from and when. We got cameras all over the place downtown. We'll find him on another one. I'm sure of it."

"So if it's him, then what?"

"I say it gives us reason to bring in Yang, don't you think? The guy worked for him, after all. CIA and all that. He was in Beijing. I mean, shit, how much more intel do you need to put two and two together?" Fraser studied Will. "Why don't you look happy about this?"

"It's good news. Something's better than nothing."

"That's what I thought. And I figured, given all we been through, you'd want to be the first to know. Hell, I haven't even told my ASAC yet. I came straight here. But I feel like an asshole now."

"No, man. I just need to get my head around this." Will walked back into the kitchen. "Sit down. I'll get us a drink and we can chew on this some more. Because if what you think is true, then we need to get Axell involved. He met with the guy. Knew his real identity."

"Okay. I'm not sure I get your point here."

"Because. Look, I just need to be sure Axell's not tangled up in this somehow."

"Why the hell would you think that?"

"A little bird whispered something in my ear that I can't seem to shake."

CHAPTER
SIXTEEN

THE SECRETARY of state found himself inside the Oval Office more regularly in the past few months than at any time since his appointment. And today's visit was prompted by the phone call he'd received in the early hours of the morning. With mounting worries, he waited for the president to excuse his chief of staff before beginning, "I appreciate you clearing your schedule for me, Mr. President."

"Of course. I understand you have some growing concerns about our situation with Dalian."

"Yes, sir. Concerns—to say the least."

The president took his seat on the sofa across from the secretary. "Then, by all means, fill me in."

"I was briefed by the CIA and FBI directors that additional resources were requested by the task force as a result of their recent unmasking of Casper Janz, who was acquainted with Agent Axell in a previous life. And who, incidentally, was murdered yesterday in the early hours of the morning."

"Janz was murdered?"

"He was."

"And he knew Agent Axell?" The president didn't wait for a reply. "Why am I only now hearing about this? Do you have any idea what this could mean?"

"I'm sorry for any delay in getting to you, however, I felt it necessary to be briefed by the directors and understand where the task force is headed with this latest development."

"And what is your assessment now? This could expose all we've put in place."

"Yes, sir. That's why I came as soon as I had viable options to present to you." The secretary retrieved a folder tucked inside his laptop bag. "We've made it possible for the discovery of additional surveillance footage in regard to the Turner investigation. That footage, as I was informed, was shown to an agent at the Washington Field Office who has direct contact with a task force operative. Now, we think it will be enough to change the course of the investigation, pointing it toward Janz and possibly derail further inquiries into him. This will buy us some time."

"How much time?"

"I can't say for sure. A few days, possibly."

"Then we'll need to be ready. Is Yang under protection at the moment?"

"Not by us. By his own people, yes. I believe he will be safe until we can get him back to Beijing to prepare. I can keep Agent Axell and his team occupied in the short term. He ordered a sweep of Janz's house but found nothing. I confirmed that myself."

"I certainly hope so. It was a careless oversight on the director's behalf not to realize Axell had personally known Janz. If it had been discovered sooner, we would likely be having a very different discussion right now."

"I agree with you. And I believe the diversion will be effective —in the short term."

"Fine. Do what you need to do but keep on the schedule. And

keep Yang in line. Remind him of his ultimate goal. You say jump, he'd better ask how high." The president stood.

"Understood, sir."

———

Axell was the last to arrive. He marched inside toward the others who were viewing the additional surveillance footage Fraser had discovered. "Is this it?"

Lacy turned to him. "CCTV from near the courthouse at the ATM. Yes. Here, I got you some coffee." She handed him the cup.

"Thanks. It was a late night for all of us, by the sounds of it." He sipped on it while watching the images on the screen. "Caison, Fraser dropped this by last night?"

"He came by my house around 1 am after he viewed it himself, and handed it off to a few of his team. I got my hands on a copy of it first thing this morning. He's pretty confident that man is Matthew Greiner, AKA Casper Janz."

Axell leaned in for a closer look. "Any confirmation from facial recognition?"

"No. He's running it through this morning. Still tough to see a face, but look at the build. Matches Janz. And, who else would have the motivation to take out Turner?"

"Yeah, well, Janz is dead."

Lacy regarded Axell with some unease. "If it is Janz, wouldn't it be a good thing to know for sure? He worked for Yang. Fingers would start to point at Yang himself." She hopped off the corner of Aaron's desk. "I wanted to wait for you to arrive before bringing this up, but Aaron came across something last night too that could solidify our case against Dalian and Yang." She looked at him and nodded. "This was your find."

"Right." Aaron began to relay the information about SynDyn

and Yang and the one variable that seemed to tie everything together, Casper Janz. "Sounds like Janz might have had his hand in a whole lot of different pies."

"The only way that would've happened was if he had help from someone behind the scenes." Axell eyed the team. "It's time we move forward with the goals of this task force. And that is to follow the money to Dalian and Malcolm Ford. This footage doesn't help us out with either of those things, unfortunately. I'm not saying it doesn't matter. It does. But I think what Aaron discovered, that's where we should be looking right now."

Lacy held Axell's gaze. "This all links to the one thing we're working on, and that's Dalian Company. One way or another. You can't dispute that."

"I'm not disputing it. A former CIA agent was gunned down right in front of me and I have no idea why or who did it. I don't know if I'm being watched or if any of you are. I apologize if I seem curt, but we can't afford to divert from our goal and I feel as though that's all that's been happening. Diversion after diversion and we're losing sight of our target." He stopped for a moment and appeared to temper his response. "Hunter, what you've got is good. Better than good. But, have you found Ford? Does he work for SynDyn? Who is he?"

"I was inside FinCen and discovered the form filed on SynDyn. I haven't seen any transactions regarding money going from Ford-slash-SynDyn to Dalian. I'll keep working on it."

"Okay. Caison, I need you to do some recon at Yang's house. I need to know who's coming and going. I want you there tonight. Get a team together and get it done. You already said you have the additional resources from Mobley—use them."

"Yes, sir."

"Lacy, I need you to come with me." He already began to walk away. "Now."

She eyed her partners and set her coffee down. "Guess I'd better go." Lacy was embarrassed and angered by the way Axell had spoken to her. He might have been her superior, but that didn't mean she shouldn't be respected. This was not Trevor Axell. Something had him rattled.

As they made their way into the parking lot, Lacy began, "You mind telling me what that was about back there?"

He opened the car door and slipped inside, waiting for her to join him. "Things are going on here that I think are meant to distract us and I need to know why and who the order came from."

"We're all trying to do our jobs, Trevor. The way you were with the guys and me, particularly me—it wasn't right."

He pulled onto the street. "I'm sorry, Lacy. I'm just starting to feel like someone's dangling a carrot in front of us. Janz was killed and I'm not seeing a whole hell of a lot of concern on the part of my bosses. We found nothing in his home. And now this CCTV footage magically surfaces." He glanced at her. "This isn't adding up for me."

"All signs point to Janz working for the enemy—for Yang. Former front man for SynDyn, right-hand to Yang, ensuring the flow of money from this Malcolm Ford."

"That's what they're making it seem like. But I'm not so sure. That's why I wanted you to come with me this morning. We're going to see a friend who you'll remember. She might be able to shed light on this rabbit hole we're in."

"Then I'll take this opportunity to ask a question since it's just us. Are you pissed I talked to Agent Delgado the other day?"

"No. Well, maybe a little. Look, I know I've been cagey. I know I kept pertinent information from you and the team. I did it because I thought it was in your best interest. Right or wrong, I just want to protect my team and do what we're supposed to be doing. But now, I feel as though there are outside influences. Like someone's working against us."

"I went to him because I was concerned too, about something else."

He eyed her briefly before peering back again at the road ahead. "Why don't you tell me what's on your mind, Lacy? I know something's bothering you. And I don't think for one minute you'd have gone to Delgado without knowing exactly the purpose for your visit."

"This surveillance footage that's suddenly appeared. Everyone seems to think the man resembles Casper Janz. But I'm not so sure." She swallowed down the lump in her throat. "Trevor, I have to ask—because I know what losing Keith did to you. That morning, the morning Turner was killed—you were supposed to meet us ahead of time before the trial started. And you showed up after Turner was shot. I have to know—where were you? Where was Aaron?"

"Do you think I killed him?"

"I'm just asking where you were. Cell signals were down. Aaron said he was home. I believe him. But that doesn't mean he couldn't have been a backup for you. I'm sorry. I'm probably way out of line, but you get a feeling something's not right. Well, so do I."

"I had every reason to kill him. That's for damn sure."

"You still believe he had a part in the Meeks' death. And Keith's too?"

"Come on, Lacy. You're not that naïve. Not after all you've been through."

"You're right. I'm not. Because I see you're deflecting right now. Reason or not, Turner is dead."

"I was in a meeting. It ran long. And as far as Hunter is concerned, you know him better than I do. I guess you'll have to decide if you trust him. And me, for that matter." He turned right into a strip plaza. "We're meeting her in there. The coffee shop."

It wasn't enough. Not nearly enough. But other pressing matters needed addressing. Lacy wanted to believe him and was afraid not to.

Axell pulled open the door and held it for Lacy to enter. The quiet coffee shop was outside of D.C. where there were fewer concerns of prying eyes. Axell had traversed the route well enough to shake any tails they might have had and felt confident they were alone.

"Thank you for meeting us, Elizabeth." Axell offered his hand. "You remember Lacy Merrick."

"It's very nice to see you again," Lacy replied.

"Pleasure. Please sit down. I took the liberty of ordering you both coffees. I didn't know how you took them, but there's sugar and creamer over there."

"Thank you. This is fine." Axell took a drink. "You know why I asked you here?"

"I do." After taking a sip, she continued. "I share your concern after Janz's murder. I believe this creates a good many complications I don't think the higher-ups intended on."

"Higher-ups?" Lacy asked.

"Let me ask you something, Lacy. Since you've joined this covert task force, which by the way, I'm not even supposed to know about but through some mutual friends, I've learned of recently. How much help have you been given by those in charge?"

"You mean the directors?"

"Yes. Partly. But also the administration. It was my understanding the president wanted regular briefings."

"That was my understanding too and I honestly have no idea how involved he's been."

"For a man who wishes to understand why the attack happened and how best to prevent another, he seems a little out of touch, wouldn't you say?"

"As I said, I'm not privy to that information. I just try to do my job, which also still involves my work at the Bureau."

She smirked. "Exactly my point. Why are you not on this task force full-time? Why is it so secretive, even inside the intelligence community itself?"

"I don't think I can answer that. Except to say I believed our safety was a top concern for the president. No one was to know what we were working on in the event China or other foreign governments attempted a similar act."

"Safety." She sipped again on her coffee.

"What can you tell us, Elizabeth?" Axell pressed on.

She retrieved a flash drive from her coat pocket and slid it across the table toward Axell. "Take a look. I think you'll find something interesting here."

Axell picked it up and began studying it. "What's on here? Forgive me, but I don't have time for the cloak-and-dagger routine. We've had enough of that lately."

"Surveillance from Janz's home. You know, the home you searched and found nothing? I'm trying to help you and your team, Trevor. Things are happening in Beijing and they're stemming from here. I'm doing this because our operatives in Beijing need your help as much as you need mine." She began to rise. "Take a look at what's on there. I'll be in touch soon."

———

The sound of the back door shutting hard against the frame reverberated through the office.

"They're back." Aaron pulled away from his computer and

looked at Will. "Axell's going to be pissed I haven't come up with anything new."

"Don't worry about it, man. I think he's just under pressure right now. We all are. You're doing the best you can. That's all any of us can do."

"I guess." Aaron spotted the two emerge from the hall, but before he could say anything, Axell approached him.

"We need to know what's on here." He handed Aaron the thumb drive.

"Where did you get this?"

"D.C. Station Chief Elizabeth Ward. You remember her?"

"I do." Aaron inserted the drive and waited for the files to load. "What the hell is this?"

"Casper Janz's home, by the looks of it." Axell pulled in closer. "Can you project that to the monitors up there?"

"Hang on." Aaron pressed a button and the video flashed on the two large monitors mounted on the wall. "The images are a little distorted now, but it looks okay. Not the best quality I've ever seen."

"Doesn't matter. I just want to see something." Axell folded his arms and walked toward the monitors.

"I thought the sweep was a bust?" Will asked.

"For us it was. Guess someone else hit the mother lode."

They all watched with intense scrutiny, but so far, the only thing on the screen was Janz coming and going through different parts of his house.

"Hey, we got audio on this thing?" Axell was growing impatient.

"It's turned up. He's alone and not saying anything," Aaron replied.

Several minutes in and nothing. Janz sitting on his couch watching television was about the extent of it.

Will cast an anxious eye to Lacy, appearing to wonder what was so important.

"Lights." Axell pointed to the monitor. "Headlights just passed in front of the window." Thirty seconds passed. "Someone's there. Did you hear the knock?"

In a split second, everyone's eyes fixed firmly on the screen as they watched Janz get off his couch and walk toward the front door. He pulled it open.

"Holy shit." Axell whipped his head toward the other three, who seemed to catch on to what he'd just seen.

"It's the director," Axell began. "Director Handley."

"Oh shit," Will said.

They continued to listen as Janz let him into his house. The two walked back into the living room.

"Turn it up!" Axell said.

With the volume at full, the men on the video began speaking.

"He's been watching you closely," Handley said.

"I know. I've been careful. I promise you," Janz replied.

"If Axell gets one whiff of what we're up to, it's over. You understand that, right?"

"I understand. I'll be sure he stays a few steps behind. It's worked so far. You just keep to your end of the deal and I'll keep to mine. I know he went to Beijing, but he won't get anything there."

"He'd better not. We're much too close and can't afford for him to figure out your part in this. Just see to it you keep ahead of him. He's good. And so is his team."

Lacy's mouth hung slightly ajar at the troubling scene. "What the hell? Trevor, what is he talking about?"

"Son of a bitch. I suspected it—but now—seeing it right there." Axell looked to his team. "Shaw warned me something was going down. But I don't think even he knew for sure."

"How did Ward get this?" Will asked.

"She's high on the food chain. Must've gotten word from Shaw and started looking into it. Janz was working with Handley on something. And the moment he even hinted at letting me in on it, he was shot dead."

"By Handley?" Lacy pressed on.

"That's the million-dollar question of the day."

CHAPTER
SEVENTEEN

THE DEPTH of the betrayal seemed to know no bounds. But this? The CIA director himself? This seemed incomprehensible.

"My God," Lacy began. "Is this why Camden Meeks was killed? And Keith?" She watched Trevor's face grow red with anger. "We're outnumbered. This is never going to be over. We can't win this."

Axell shook his head, his gaze aimed at his feet. "We're being played. Each and every one of us." He eyed the three people who'd been through so much with him. "If the Agency is behind this, something big is about to happen. That's why Janz was killed. He was talking to me and they couldn't afford that. Shaw warned me. Asked me to think about what we were doing and why. Why it's been so hard for us to get a leg up on tracking Janz, or Greiner, or whatever the hell you want to call him."

"If Janz was working for Handley, we have to assume Yang was in on it too, don't we?" Aaron asked.

"Honestly, I couldn't tell you. We have Janz-slash-Greiner who worked for SynDyn. Gets chummy with Yang, gets chummy with the MMS, then what? He turns on them?" Will added.

"I don't think so. I think the director must've had something on Janz and threatened him with it. There's no other reason Janz would've given up the money train. Handley knew what Janz was like. Knew he sold his services and was ready to throw the book at him, unless of course, he did this one thing for him. And that thing could've been to help Yang keep Dalian out of our sights. But for what reason?" Axell replied. "Hide the video. Make sure no one finds it. I don't care what you do. Don't let anyone else near it, you understand me?"

"Yeah," Aaron replied.

"I'm also going to need you to work outside the lines, Hunter. Can you do that?"

"You know I can. I just need access. I'll stay hidden."

"Good. You're going to need to find all financial accounts tied to Yang. Not just Dalian. Yang, himself. If the CIA is giving him money, via Janz or Malcolm Ford or anyone else, I need you to find it. Got it?"

He nodded.

"We've been running in circles and that ends now. Something else is at play and I think the only way to get answers is to see Yang."

"No way, Axell. Not after this. Not after Janz was killed," Will said. "You go and see him and you won't make it home. No matter what we've just seen. I can't believe the director is helping Yang. It just doesn't make sense. There has to be another way to get answers."

"What if we talk to Mobley?" Lacy asked. "Show him the video."

"We can't be sure if he's involved too," Axell continued. "It's too risky. There's no doubt in my mind that we're on our own, once again. I'll hold off on Yang—for now. Agent Shaw is our only other option. I might be able to get word to him via Elizabeth."

Lacy studied her colleagues before continuing. "If this goes as high up the ladder as it appears, we'll be silenced before we get close enough to find out."

———

Armed with this new and troubling information, the time had come for Axell to meet again with Elizabeth and try to get word to Agent Shaw in Beijing.

"I'm going with you." Lacy grabbed her bag. "There's nothing else for me to do here, Trevor. I can be of use."

Axell looked to Caison. "Get back to HQ and talk to SSA Kelly. But make sure it's in reference to Turner. See if he's authorized surveillance on Yang or anyone in his employ. Don't let him know about the task force or what you think is going on. It's just got to be us on this, for now, understood?"

"Ten-four."

"We'll reconvene here later today. Everyone keep your heads down. Hunter, if you get any clue you've been compromised, destroy everything. Including the video."

"Got it." He looked to Lacy with growing concern. "Stay in touch."

Lacy followed Axell outside and both entered his car. She waited for him to pull onto the road. "Listen, I'm sorry about what I said earlier, about Turner. We're supposed to be a team. None of this probably matters in light of everything, but I just wanted you to know that."

He peered at her briefly. "I don't hold it against you, but you and me? We need to keep trusting one another. And from this point forward, we work together, just like we have been for the past several months. We keep open the lines of communication.

And if there's something you want to know, ask. I don't ever want you to be afraid to ask me anything."

"Okay."

"I asked Elizabeth to meet us here." Axell pulled alongside the curb and cut the engine.

Lacy noticed that the line of buildings ahead appeared to be offices and tucked between two of them was a small café. "In there?" She gestured to the café with the green awning that hung over a patio, though it appeared near-empty.

"Yep." He stepped outside and approached the sidewalk.

Lacy joined him and the two walked the twenty or so paces to the café. "I don't see her car. Is she here yet?"

"Yes. She just texted me. She's inside." Axell pulled open the door and waited for Lacy to enter.

"Did she close the place just for us?" she asked as she entered the empty café having only spotted one employee behind the counter.

"As a matter of fact, I did." Elizabeth approached and offered her hand. "I'm glad to see you again so soon. Just wish it was under different circumstances." She turned on her heel and walked toward the back of the room. "A friend of mine owns the place. Please, have a seat."

Lacy was the first to sit, followed by Axell.

"Either of you want a coffee? Something to eat? They've got the best bagels in town."

"I'm fine, thank you," Lacy replied.

"Same here."

"Okay, then." Elizabeth sat across from them. "I'm sure you were surprised at the video. Same as me."

"That would be an understatement," Axell replied.

"I passed along the message you requested to Agent Shaw." She eyed both of them. "He'll continue to monitor the increased activity inside the Movement. As we all discussed months ago, we knew this could be a concern. And it appears that that concern has grown exponentially. They've seen an uptick in chatter in the region and Shaw and his team have worked to figure out what they're planning. He believes a bomb that exploded in a subway station more than a week ago was the work of the Movement. And most likely, Yang was involved."

"Any chance you know where Shaw is right now? I need to speak to him," Axell replied.

"He figured that would be the case. For right now, all I can tell you is that he believes CIA is funding Yang's operations in Uyghur. Based on what he and the few key operatives have discovered, Handley has people loyal to him. Operatives who agree with what he wants to do."

"And that is?" Axell continued.

"To fund the Separatist Movement with Yang at the helm."

"He wants to destabilize the region with attacks in Beijing," Lacy said.

Elizabeth touched the tip of her nose. "What better way to retaliate for the mall attack?"

———

Mehmut dropped the front room curtain and made his way to the door. "He's here."

His associate quickly joined him, "Open it."

"*Salom, men kiramanmi?*" (Hello, may I come in?). With a briefcase in hand, the guest entered.

"I speak English," Mehmut replied.

"Thank you. My apologies, but my Turkic is rusty." He peered over his shoulder and another waited at the car. With a nod, his partner stayed behind.

"You have what was requested?"

"Of course. May I?" He set the briefcase on a kitchen table that appeared ready to collapse under the weight. With a click of the lock, it opened. "As promised, three million US dollars."

"And the rest?"

"When we've received confirmation the deal has been made, you'll receive the other half and the hardware."

"Hardware?" His associate appeared confused.

"Weapons," Mehmut replied. "I will inform Shen Yang when the necessary arrangements are finalized as well. In the meantime, I cannot travel to Beijing without arms."

"Of course not. My associate outside has what you will need in the interim. You understand this cannot be delayed any longer. The time is now for the trial run and as I understand it, Mr. Yang is also aware of our new timeline."

"He is." Mehmut closed the briefcase and carried it to the living room. "The first phase will be to disrupt the broadcast, replacing it with our morning prayer. When that is shut down, and it will be, the people will take to the streets. Removing the banners, dismantling the Party's statues and symbols that I'm sure you noticed on your arrival. This will be the beginning."

"And after that?"

"I will go to Beijing for the transfer and finalize the planning."

"How long will it take?"

"We will likely be under surveillance; however, with Mr. Yang's connections, we should complete the planning in time for the proposed date," Mehmut continued.

The man began to leave but was stopped short.

"Why are you doing this?" Mehmut asked. "To what benefit will the CIA get for allowing the Movement free rein?"

He turned on his heel. "Make no mistake. This money does not allow you free rein. That said, the United States believes in freedom of religion. The Party has all but extinguished your beliefs in this region. That cannot stand."

He began to nod. "A very noble effort on behalf of the Americans. Thank you."

"Goodbye, and good luck." The man opened the door and walked toward his car. His partner was already keying the engine, waiting for him to enter.

The men inside peered out again as they watched the CIA agents drive away.

In Turkic, Mehmut's colleague asked, "How do you know we can trust them?"

"I don't. I trust Yang. He knows what the United States is after and he has agreed because it will benefit us here."

"I hope you are right."

CHAPTER
EIGHTEEN

WHAT HAD BEEN a mission to bring justice to the Dalian company and have them ousted from the US had appeared to become something much more sinister. A covert attempt at destabilization of the world's second-largest economic and third-largest military superpower—China.

Lacy and Axell returned to their state-of-the-art facility, which was intended to monitor Dalian and other companies but was now something else. Axell would now use its resources against the very people who had authorized the resources in the first place.

"We can't let this happen, Lacy." Axell pushed his way through the rear entrance. "What Shaw said? I just can't wrap my head around it."

"I don't know how we stop it. There are very powerful people willing to go to any lengths for what now seems to be retribution for the attack."

"Yes. Retribution. That's what this is. But the question remains, is the president aware? This will bring war if it comes to light the US assisted and in fact funded the Uyghurs in committing terrorist attacks in China."

They arrived in the bullpen area where Aaron continued working at his desk.

"You find anything on Ford yet?" Axell approached him.

"What's wrong? Something happened. I can see it in your face." He turned to Lacy. "What is it?"

"Did you find money tied to Yang?" Axell asked in a forceful tone.

"We've got two things happening right now," Aaron began. "First of all, I discovered funds from a variety of shell companies dumping right into several personal accounts of Yang's set up in London, New York, and Panama. This must've been the reason the DOJ filed the FinCen forms. They were already aware."

"And of course, sat on it. But London and New York?" Lacy said.

"That was my reaction. Not your typical hiding place for money, until I figured out why. The larger banking systems appear to be in the money laundering business too. They're willing to pay the huge fines imposed by the DOJ and others because they make two or three times more money than that by allowing the cartels to launder and looking the other way at a host of other suspicious transactions."

"Cartels, terrorists. Guess it doesn't matter to them," Axell continued. "So Yang's getting money from presumably shell companies set up by who? The US or China?"

"I'm still working on the origins. The money's been bounced around between so many different companies, including SynDyn."

"Okay, so he's got all this money. Did you find evidence he's sending it overseas? Beijing or any other province? That will tell us where they plan on taking their stand," Axell said.

"Taking their stand?" Aaron replied.

"We knew early on that Yang had possible ties to the Uyghur

Separatist Movement," Lacy began. "Well, wherever he's getting the money, he'll be using it to fund potential terror attacks. Likely in Beijing, but we haven't gotten that far yet."

"And what Lacy's leaving out is the fact that it appears funding could be coming from the US. Maybe from our elusive Malcolm Ford. And most likely from our own CIA. Who knows? They could be one and the same."

"What? We're funding Yang's terrorist ties?"

"That's what we need for you to prove, but that's the prevailing theory," Lacy replied.

"For God's sake. Why?"

"Retribution is our best guess," Axell continued. "CIA Director Handley, as we spotted in the video, was working with Janz. He in turn was working with Yang. We now believe Janz was a middleman helping Yang clean the money and sending it overseas. And yet keeping the MSS intentionally out of the loop. His ties to the Chinese government were likely the reason Handley recruited him for this task. Elizabeth and Shaw both indicated that the US, or just Director Handley, wants to bring about a destabilization effort to throw the Chinese economy and anything else it can into chaos."

Aaron appeared stunned by the revelation. "How can we possibly go up against something this big? Why have us here to begin with?"

"Distraction," Lacy said. "We uncovered the truth once before; they don't want us to do it again." She surveyed the room. "Where's Will?"

"Still at HQ, I think," Aaron replied.

"Find where Yang is sending the money," Axell said.

"What happens after that?"

"It'll be time for me to take another trip. Shaw and I will have to uncover their plan of attack."

"You're not going back there, Trevor. You can't. After what we just found out? Are you kidding me? You won't last a day in Beijing if they find you. Handley has his own operatives working for him there too," Lacy said.

"They won't find me."

"Then I'm coming with you."

"Oh no. I don't think so."

"You're not going alone, that's for damn sure. I can help. You know I can."

"Then we should all go," Aaron said. "I can be your eyes and ears. Lacy and I can track the funds from the banks there. In fact, it might be easier to find the sources that way. And since you and Caison are trained for the field, he can be your spotter."

"Where did you learn all this, Hunter?"

"Hey, I did work inside Langley for a while. I picked up a thing or two there."

"We can stop whatever's coming before it's too late," Lacy said.

"Fine. I'll have to ask Elizabeth to help us get expedited tourist visas. We can't go under our real names either. It'll take a few days at least to get the paperwork sorted and new passports issued. In the meantime, Lacy, get with Caison. Tell him the plan and make whatever arrangements you need to make to get the time off and take care of your kids. Do you think Vogel will be a problem?"

"Not at all. She'll cover for me."

"Good. I'd prefer if Caison not tell SSA Kelly. I can't be sure Director Mobley's hands are clean in this. So maybe I'll just reach out to Caison and tell him what to say to Kelly. Don't talk to anyone else about this. You all know the drill. As soon as I get what we need, I'll let you know. Keep your heads down until then."

———

Elizabeth stood on the balcony of her apartment and spotted the arrival of Trevor Axell, a man she knew would return. She'd counted on it.

A knock on the door sounded and she snubbed the butt of her cigarette in the nearby ashtray. Inside, she made her way to the door. "You're lucky you caught me. I was just about to leave for the airport."

"Really? Where are you off to?" Axell walked in.

"New York. The work never stops piling on."

"You knew I'd come back, didn't you?"

"I hoped you would." Elizabeth closed the door. "You ready for a drink now?"

"Absolutely." Axell shed his coat and sat down on the sofa in the well-appointed apartment. "I've got a contact at the Chinese embassy. But before I talk to him, I need to know if he can still be trusted."

"I assume you're referring to Chi?"

"I figured he must still be on CIA payroll."

"He is. Yes, he can be trusted. Then you'll be going to meet with Shaw?"

"Yes. My team is coming too."

"What? No. That's not possible. Shaw's not expecting all of you and I don't know if he'll be able to keep them safe in the event things go bad."

"He won't need to. They're more than capable of handling themselves, in case you don't remember. And I need them. We've been sidelined, Elizabeth. Not only that, we've been lied to, once again, by our government. They won't sit this out and neither will I, which is, of course, why I'm here. Can you coordinate with Chi to expedite our visas, or should I?"

"Under assumed names?"

Axell nodded.

"It's a risky move, Trevor. One that might catch the eye of those we're trying to circumvent."

"It is, but we can find out things quickly if we have boots on the ground. Hunter is as good a hacker as anyone I've seen. He'll find the money. Lacy can track down the banks—get inside. Caison and I will run the field with Shaw."

"It won't be that easy. They control everything. Internet, media, and their cyber-security measures are at least on par with our own. Maybe better."

"My people are good at what they do. This is not up for negotiation."

"Fair enough. I'll make the call. Chi will do what is asked of him."

"How long?"

"Days." She tossed back her drink. "Why don't you stay for a while? I can catch the next flight. And there's nothing we can do right now. It'll have to wait until the embassy opens in a few hours."

Axell noted the look in her eyes. "How did we get to this point, Elizabeth? After the administration offered up transparency, here we are again."

"I wish I had an answer for you, Trevor. I don't. Except to say we have to assume Director Handley, and who knows how many others, maybe the president too, wanted a military response to the attack, once your people revealed the facts. Congress would never have let that happen. It would've been a lose-lose scenario. We're already in an economic freefall."

"So are they."

"Yes." She placed her hand on his chest. "I've stopped trying to figure out what goes on in the minds of men."

"Are you sure about that?" He held her gaze before pressing his lips against hers.

———

Lacy opened the door. "Thanks for coming over."

"Absolutely." Will walked inside and placed his coat on the rack.

"Have you eaten?" She headed into the kitchen.

"No, actually. I'm starving. I've been with my team all day."

"Anything new on that front?" Lacy pulled out lunchmeat and cheese and began to make him a sandwich.

"Not yet. Ballistics came through, but we can't tie a weapon to anyone. I'm starting to think SSA Kelly is becoming single-minded on the issue. Unwilling to identify outside causes. Since they got that new video, he's convinced it was Casper Janz and has almost convinced the WFO's ASAC too."

"It doesn't exactly sound like him to box himself in like that."

"No. From what I know of him, it does feel out of character. But I can't pinpoint the reason."

"Maybe he's being led to believe it was Janz, led by people he trusts and respects." She pushed the plate toward him with a sandwich and some chips. "I hope this is okay. Kids ate up all the dinner Celeste fixed tonight."

"Perfect, thank you. I wouldn't mind a beer, though, if you've got one."

"Sure do." Lacy retrieved two bottles of beer from the fridge. "Here you go." As she popped open hers, she continued, "Do you think this is also an intentional diversion?"

"The Turner investigation? Seems a little far-fetched, but at this point, anything's possible, isn't it?"

She bit her tongue, declining to bring up their previous discussions of the possibility that it had been Trevor. She'd already questioned him and he denied it. She would have to leave it at that or risk damaging their relationship to the point it could not be repaired. Lacy wasn't willing to do that for a man like Turner. "Guess it's going to take a back seat for us anyway. Did you get Kelly's authorization to leave?"

"I did. I told him I was going back home because of an illness in the family."

"You did?"

"What else could I say? I couldn't afford for him to question any other reason. The man knows I don't take vacation."

"I suppose. What if he checks?"

"He won't."

"You sound pretty confident. I hope you're right. Axell said it would be a few days. I got approval from Vogel. Of course, I was mum to the real reason, but she suspected something was up. She always does. I hate lying to her, especially after all she's done for me."

"What did you tell her?"

"That I was taking the kids to see my parents."

"Seems legitimate."

"I called them and gave them a heads-up. Although I think they wished I was coming home. Last time I saw them was when they flew in for Jay's funeral. I've seen Jay's parents more than I have my own."

"They do live here."

"That they do." She placed the bottle of beer against her lips before continuing. "I don't think I can continue on this way."

With a half-full mouth, he replied, "What do you mean?"

"The Bureau. I don't think I can do both anymore. Although I can't be sure this task force won't be completely dismantled on our return." She chuckled. "Maybe I'd better wait until this next crisis is over."

"You know what, Lacy? I'm starting to think that they're never going to be over. There will always be another crisis around the corner. What I find difficult to swallow is the sheer underhanded corruption. It's wearing me down and making me feel as though we'll never get ahead of it."

"Same here. If Trevor and Agent Shaw are right, what's the point, you know? Why go to Beijing and fight a battle that no one wants us to win?"

Jackson appeared in the kitchen's entrance. "I brushed my teeth, Mommy." His hair was wet and his pajamas clung to his tiny frame.

"Did you forget to dry off with the towel after your bath?"

He looked down. "No."

She laughed. "Okay. Is Celeste still upstairs?"

"Yep." He turned to Will. "Hi, Mr. Caison. How are you doing?"

"Very well, Jack. Thanks for asking."

"Where's Uncle Aaron?" He looked to Lacy again.

"He's not here, sweetheart." Lacy set down her beer. "Come on. How about I let you watch one cartoon before bed? I need to talk to Mr. Caison for a little while longer. Will that be okay?"

"Uh-huh." Jack turned and began to walk again toward the stairs. "Goodnight, Mr. Caison."

"Goodnight, Jack." Will watched as Lacy ushered her young son up the stairs. And as he cast his gaze around the home, his eyes landed on a photograph of the entire family, including Jay. He smiled.

Within a few minutes, Lacy returned. "Sorry about that. I put on the TV for them. It'll keep them occupied for a little while."

"How are they doing? Really?"

"Better. Not one hundred percent but getting closer every day. We all are."

"That's good to hear. You know, Jack looks so much like Jay. I see you in Olivia, but Jack," Will shook his head. "Spitting image."

"I know. I'm glad, though." She turned her sights to the photograph.

"What will you do if you leave the Bureau?" Will asked.

"I have no idea. I never thought it would ever happen. Of course, so many things have happened I never thought possible." She turned on her heel. "You want to sit down in the living room? It's a little more comfortable." She peered over her shoulder at him. "You still hungry? I can get you something else."

"No. No, I'm fine. Thanks for the sandwich. It really hit the spot."

"Good. I'm glad." As she made her way to the couch, Lacy switched on the television as a news broadcast began. "Oh no."

"What is it?" Will followed behind and glanced at the T.V. "Where the hell is that?"

"North Carolina."

"For God's sake," he replied.

A protest that had turned ugly was being broadcast while journalists and camera people rushed to get closer to the action. The breaking news headline that appeared at the bottom of the screen revealed what was happening. "Peaceful Protest Turns Violent."

Lacy lowered herself onto the couch. "When is this going to end?"

Will joined her. "I don't know. At this rate, I feel like they'll start using internment camps just like they did for Japanese-Americans during World War II."

"No. It won't get that bad. It can't."

They both watched as a city was burning. People running for cover.

"The president has to do something about this. Innocent people are being convicted of simply being of Asian descent. Most aren't even Chinese," Will said.

"I think the president may have already made his decision."

She turned to him. "And if it's what I think it is, then we're all going to suffer for it."

Will placed his arm over her shoulder and pulled her close. "We're going to do what we've always done, Lacy, and that is to get the truth to the American people. To the world. For better or worse, that's what we're here for. Corruption, lies, manipulation. It has to end somewhere."

"And you think it will end with us?"

"Maybe not, but if we don't try, then who will?"

CHAPTER
NINETEEN

THE DAY HAD ARRIVED. Visas issued. Flights booked. The first-class trip on the CIA's dime, whether they knew it or not, thanks to Elizabeth, would be the only first-class flight Lacy had ever taken. While this was a bonus, it hardly made up for the dire circumstances and the risks of heading into China as agents of a foreign, now hostile government.

This was a fact she did not share with the kids, who remained with Celeste. And while she didn't have the same sense of fear as before, she was not so naïve to assume there would not be danger. It was something she'd come to accept in her new line of work. And her dedication to Trevor and the rest of the team compelled her to act and not be left behind while they took all the risks. It was who she had become. Good or bad. The woman she was—married to Jay Merrick—and who held an honorable, albeit safe job—was no longer. But who she would be after this was a mystery, even to her.

"There you are. I was worried you'd been caught up at security." Aaron approached just inside the passenger-only area behind the gate entrance. "You catch sight of Axell or Caison?"

"No. Not yet. You sure they're not already here?" She peered into the long corridor. "They're probably in a bar. Come on."

Aaron followed. "How'd it go with the kids? I wanted to stop by this morning to say goodbye, but I ran out of time. I got some last-minute info on the banks."

"You did? Best not to discuss it here. But this morning was fine. Kids were okay. Better than I expected, actually. They would've enjoyed seeing you, though." She continued along the busy gangway when the announcement came. "Oh, that's us." And as she spotted the bar nearest their gate, she also spotted their colleagues. "And guess who it is?" She looked at Will. "I figured you two would be in a bar. Not that I blame you. I would've if I'd gotten out of the house sooner. It's only 9 am, but a Bloody Mary sounds fantastic right about now."

"You'll have a chance to order one on the plane." Axell patted her shoulder. "Come on. We'll be boarding first."

"How'd you manage to get us in the good seats?" Aaron asked him.

"Elizabeth's got access to more money than Bill Gates' net worth. Wasn't really a problem."

"Ah, our tax dollars hard at work," Aaron replied. "Not that I'm complaining."

They boarded the plane, stowing away their hand luggage and sitting down in the reclining seats, complete with televisions and privacy walls.

"Get settled in. This is going to be a long flight," Axell positioned himself in his recliner.

"Hey, Axell, I wanted to tell you what I found late last night," Aaron began.

"Not here. Wait until we arrive."

"Yeah, okay." Aaron took his seat.

Will was next to Lacy in his own private pod and pulled down the partition between the two. "You doing okay? The kids and everything?"

She smiled. "Yeah. Everything's fine."

———————

The 14-hour flight was over. The captain made the announcement and they had begun their descent into Beijing Capital International Airport. Lacy was pleasantly surprised to discover she'd slept through a fair bit of the flight. While the boys had managed more sleep, to no one's surprise, she was glad to have passed some of the time.

Will began to stir. "Hey. Did you sleep?"

"I did. Not as much as you, though. We're here. Playtime's over." Lacy reached for her makeup bag and headed into the restroom to freshen up.

"She all right?" Axell leaned over his seat toward Will.

"Seems like it."

"Good. We'll get checked in. Stay below the radar, because I guarantee we'll have eyes on us almost as soon as we land."

"Whose? Who knows we're here besides Shaw?"

"Other CIA operatives, I'm sure. It's just the way it goes here. Don't worry. Our cover will get us by for a day, maybe two, before any MSS shows up for us."

"Seriously?" Aaron interrupted.

"No. Stop worrying so much. We'll be fine. We'll get in touch with Shaw after we check in."

Lacy returned to the men talking among themselves. "Everything all right?"

"Never better," Axell replied.

The first to deplane, Axell took the lead and Lacy was sandwiched between Aaron and Will.

"Just stay behind me. I want to see who's out there waiting for us first," Axell said.

"Fine by me," Aaron replied.

Axell peered over his shoulder. "Figures you'd say that." He revealed a half-cocked smile.

———

Axell dropped the window curtains and pulled away from the view of the hotel's entrance. "He's coming up now." For confirmation, he checked his phone where a text had appeared on an encrypted app.

Their hotel was in the middle of the Dongcheng district, which was thick with tourists. It was the perfect place situated near Tiananmen and en route to the Forbidden City, the 180-acre grounds that housed the Palace Museum, and was one of the most popular attractions in the world.

The knock sounded and Axell approached. He glanced at the others, who appeared as though holding their breath in anticipation of what would come next. Upon opening the door, he greeted the agent. "Shaw, please come in. We've been waiting for you."

"Thanks, Axell. I trust your flight was acceptable?" He walked toward Lacy. "Mrs. Merrick, it's a pleasure to finally meet you. You're an inspiration."

"You're very kind. Pleasure to meet you too, Agent Shaw. This is Aaron Hunter, our cyber-expert, and FBI Counterterrorism Agent Will Caison."

"Gentlemen. It's a pleasure. I'm glad you're all on board. Axell's spoken highly of all of you." He turned to Axell. "I understand you have additional information regarding accounts tied to Yang?"

"We do. Hunter, why don't you go over what you found?"

"Thanks. So I was tasked with uncovering the financing Yang's received for what we now believe will be used to fund his interests in the Uyghur region. And I discovered a source just prior to our departure and wanted to bring it to light now." He peered at Axell.

"Go on," Axell replied.

"Yang's been receiving money from both sides of the coin, so to speak. On the one hand, the MSS has been shifting monies from various shell companies that eventually landed in a few of Yang's personal accounts. This was done, presumably, in an effort to help him move forward in the US by continuing to grow the Dalian Company and invest in other Chinese interests in America during the sanctions. Additionally, Yang appears to be receiving money from the CIA in what we now believe is an effort to destabilize the Uyghur region and fund Yang's terrorist ties."

"This, I already knew," Shaw said. "So tell me something I don't know, Hunter."

"Okay. We insisted on accompanying Axell because we believe we will be able to identify the organizations on the receiving end of Yang's blood money. In doing so, forwarding that information on to you so that you, Axell, and the rest of your team can infiltrate these organizations and determine if and when an attack might happen."

"We are all on the same page," Shaw began. "And we appreciate your willingness to assist us in this operation." He looked to Axell. "This was the primary reason I came to you. We can help each other. Because what I can tell you is that we are alone in this endeavor. Except for a few of my team, no one knows you're here. It will be up to all of us to locate the groups, assess their plans, and stop them before it's too late."

"Aaron and I can start by handing over the banking information of the accounts he's discovered to date. We will, however, need access to these institutions in order for us to get into their systems. This can't be accomplished remotely."

"You want to go to the banks themselves and hack into their systems?" Shaw asked.

"Yes. It's the only way."

"And you knew about this?" He asked Axell.

"Yes. If anyone can do it, these two can. I have no doubt. And while they're getting that information, Caison and I will travel to the Uyghur region with you and meet with your people."

"I can live with that. However, I would like to post one of my team with your people here. They know where MSS has eyes, which is everywhere. And I'll bring another with us to the region. He's worked the area for some time and has the right contacts."

"It's late now." Axell checked the time. "We'll leave at first light?"

"Yes. I'll be in the lobby. My guy will stay posted here after our departure to ensure the safety of Hunter and Merrick. And I'll take your list of suspected banks. I've got an asset who can assist you with server access, but it'll be up to you two from there." Shaw paused and observed the people surrounding him. "There are many people who want this country to fall into chaos. After what they did to us—I can't blame them. And my first inclination was for the same thing. However, I believe these people are acting out of emotion and impulse. Not out of reason. Because if reason were to enter into the equation, they would understand that the end result could well be the end of our countries. The chances a Uyghur uprising would succeed are minimal. And if these people were on the ground here, as I am, they would see that. But they aren't. They're operating out of their D.C. offices and don't see the whole picture. The MSS is powerful. And while it could mean disruption for a while, it won't last. They've done a great deal to squelch the

Muslim culture in the region. They're attempting to eradicate an entire religion. Moderates, extremists, Christians, Catholics. They are all the same to the Party. The Republic of China is atheist. And they will do what it takes to keep it that way."

"We all understand what's at stake here." Axell showed him to the door. "We've faced opposition before."

Shaw began to shake his head. "Not like this you haven't. Good night."

————

In a café near the bank Aaron and Lacy intended to hack into to get Yang's personal account, another man appeared.

"You think that's him?" Lacy asked.

They both watched as he approached. The man with black hair, dressed in a black hoodie and skinny jeans, surveyed the café until his eyes landed on the two obvious Americans staring back at him.

"That's him." Aaron held his phone so Lacy could see. "Shaw sent me this image. Looks like the same guy."

The man now stood in front of them at their small table but didn't say a word.

"I'm Aar..."

The man, more like a college kid, interrupted him. "No names." His English was fractured and he pulled out a chair to sit down. "I know who you are."

"Okay." Aaron cast a worried glance at Lacy. "Then you have something for us?"

The kid pulled a mini-SD card from his hoodie pocket, tucking it between his thumb and forefinger as he offered his hand. "You can call me Majian."

Aaron returned the greeting and with the slip of a hand, the exchange was complete.

"The Xiajina bank has many zero days. You'll find what you need on there." He stood up to leave but not before scanning the café once again. With a nod, he walked away.

"What did he mean by zero days?" Lacy asked.

"Software flaws." Aaron slid the mini-SD into this laptop and viewed the files. "It's code—Malware."

Lacy leaned in to whisper. "To gain access?"

"Looks like it. The kid's good. Not many can write code. I can, but…"

Lacy interrupted him. "Not like this."

"No. Not like this." Aaron clicked a few more times. "There are email addresses on here. Probably bank officials. Workers. I'll need to send an email and hope one of them clicks on the Trojan Horse. It'll give us control of the computer. Once we have that, we'll be able to get Yang's account information and find the source of the deposits."

Aaron sent the emails while Lacy never took her eyes off the door or the window in front of them. She knew from experience they were vulnerable sitting here alone. "What can I do to expedite this?"

"Right now? Nothing," Aaron replied. "Once we're in, you're going to have to go inside and talk to someone about opening an account, or something like that."

"That seems like a big risk. There'll be security cameras everywhere. I'll be exposed."

"You're here on a tourist visa. Under a different name. I need you there, Lacy, to watch for anyone acting differently. Concerned. Worried."

"You mean like they just figured out someone's accessed their computers?"

"Exactly."

"And if that happens?"

"Leave. Make up some excuse and get the hell out of there. I'll watch for you to come out. If I see you, I'll shut down and we'll jump ship."

"Yeah. Okay."

"I won't need access for long. Just long enough to get inside the bank's servers and find customer account information."

"How long, Aaron?"

"Minutes. Less than five. I'm confident. This code is good. It won't be easily detected. In fact, I'm not sure I've seen anything quite so sophisticated. Even at Langley."

She stood and grabbed her purse. "Better get this over with."

"Lace, be careful."

"Always." Lacy pushed through the door and emerged onto Wangfujing Street, a famous street known for its shopping. While the area was crowded, she suspected it would be much worse in a couple of weeks for the Chinese New Year. It was hard to miss the upcoming celebration as signs were posted everywhere. It was a sea of red. And the shoppers weren't swayed by the bad weather, either. The smog lodged in her throat, making her want to cough. Lacy had read somewhere that the air was worse here in the winter. She noticed several people wearing masks and wished she'd had one right now. The only plus was that the yellow haze would help disguise her to a degree. It was the only cover she had right now, exposed out here in the middle of Beijing—alone.

The bank was just across the street, however, and she arrived without incident. The warmth and clean air were welcomed as she made her way to a help desk. And while she did not know Mandarin, she figured in such a touristy area that the personnel would hopefully speak English. Her assumption was correct.

"Good morning. How may I help you?" The woman wore a pleasant smile as she spoke.

Good morning. I'm here to speak to someone about opening an account?"

"A personal account?"

"Yes, please."

"One moment." She gestured to a small waiting area. "If you'll take a seat, someone will be with you momentarily."

"Thank you." Lacy returned an equally warm and hopefully unsuspecting smile as she made her way to the chairs. So far, everything seemed perfectly normal. That could mean Aaron was in and no one knew, or he wasn't in yet. He said max five minutes. She checked the time on her phone, just to be sure, and hoped it would take at least that long for someone to come and offer her the help she'd requested. But she would not be so lucky today. Less than one minute. Damn.

"*Nín hǎo.*" (Hello) The gentleman bowed his head. "You are American?"

"Yes, sir."

"Hello. What can I do for you today, madam?"

"I'm interested in opening an account here."

"I see. Are you a resident?"

Lacy casually averted her eyes in attempt to find anything remotely suspicious. "Um, no. I'm just visiting."

"I see. Well, I am sorry to inform you that as of 2015, we are no longer allowed to open accounts to foreigners. I'm so very sorry."

She needed more time and began digging through her purse while trying to spot anyone with raised brows in the vicinity. "But I have my passport." She shoved it in his face.

The man leaned back as she invaded his personal space. "I'm afraid that does not matter, madam. The rules have changed. And

I do wish I could help, but I cannot." He smiled, waiting for her to leave.

Another minute. She began rubbing her chin and peered around the building again. "Is there a manager I can speak with about this? It was my understanding that this would not be a problem."

The man appeared to be growing irritated, but his tone was calm and polite. "He will tell you the same thing, madam. The rules have changed. Please accept my apologies." He offered his hand.

This was it. If she didn't leave now, he would become suspicious. A final look around and Lacy nodded her head. Still, no one seemed overly concerned about much of anything. Perhaps they were in the clear.

"Well, that is very disappointing, but I understand. I appreciate your help." She returned his greeting. "Thank you."

"Enjoy the rest of your day, madam. But please do wear a mask. The air is quite bad today."

"Of course." She began to leave, again stealing looks and again finding nothing. If Aaron wasn't finished now, it was too late. She had to go back.

Outside and back into the cold and dirty air, she walked toward the café. And as she entered and spotted Aaron's face, she knew he'd done it. He wore a demure smile on her approach. "Everything okay?"

"Perfect," he replied. "And you?"

"They don't open accounts for people who don't live here. Guess the rules changed a couple of years ago."

"Good to know." Aaron stood and grabbed his bag. "We should get back."

"That's what I was hoping you'd say."

CHAPTER
TWENTY

IN A CITY of roughly 22 million, Beijing remained permanently congested, the skies almost always tawny. And in a regional airport on the edge of the city, a private jet commissioned with CIA funds waited on the runway. Shrouded in the haze, Axell, Caison, and Shaw approached the plane to Xinjiang.

"Don't worry about it," Shaw said. "They're used to this weather. You'll be there in no time."

Axell glanced at Caison. "See? There's nothing to worry about." He whipped back to Shaw. "Wait. You aren't coming?"

"This is as far as I go, guys. I can't be seen traveling to Xinjiang right now. I've been informed of rumblings among the operatives loyal to Handley. I don't want to jeopardize the mission. I need to make sure I'm seen. I'll stay here and keep an eye on the rest of your team and ensure your flight's anonymity. One of my guys will meet you on arrival. He knows the region and it's his contact you'll be meeting with."

"And you trust him?" Axell said.

"I wouldn't send you if I didn't. Now go on. You'll need to

depart on time. I've got people looking the other way, but only for so long."

"Thank you." Caison started up the stairs.

Axell followed him as both stepped onto the plane. "Not too shabby," he said.

"Right this way, sir." A flight attendant showed Axell to his seat. "And if you'd like to take a seat here, sir." She gestured to Caison.

"Thank you." Caison sat down. "CIA doesn't mind spending taxpayer dollars, does it?"

"Taxpayer dollars?" Axell began. "Partly, but I can assure you, the money seized from war-torn regions, assets, and drug dealers in Mexico keep the CIA more than flush with cash. More than most Americans could imagine."

"What a surprise." Caison peered through the window as they began to roll off the blocks. "Don't suppose you've heard from Aaron or Lacy yet? I'm anxious to know if they got what they needed."

"No. It's still early. They'll contact us when they know something." Axell noticed the worried expression Caison carried on his face. "They'll be fine. Like Shaw said, he's got people looking out for them. They'll be safe."

"I'm sure you're right."

Axell continued to study him. "You know, when you start getting close to someone you work with, it can create a lot of problems."

"Excuse me?"

"You heard me. It's not exactly a secret how you feel about her. Or if it is, then you're terrible at keeping secrets. And the problem is, Hunter feels the same. I know it. Lacy knows it, even if she won't admit it outright."

"I care about her the same way I do you and Hunter."

Axell chuckled. "Oh, I doubt that very much. Just take my word for it, Caison. Don't get attached. And especially to someone who's still in mourning. Lacy's not over the loss of her husband yet. And who knows if she ever really will be."

"I care for her, I'll admit it. But I'm not completely insensitive to where she's at right now. Hell, I wouldn't blame her for never dating another man in her life, given the shit she's been through."

"You wouldn't want her to be alone forever, Caison."

"No. It's just, yeah, I mean, it is too soon. I know that. And the thing with Hunter, well, I don't really know how to address that. They've been friends a long time."

"They have." Axell peered through the window as the wheels lifted from the ground. "Just take a step back and remember the job. Everything else will fall into place when the time is right."

"This job. Who knows what will happen here or back home? If we're successful or not."

"Who knows, man. We just have to do what's right. And this is what's right. No matter what top brass thinks. They're running on revenge. Fear. And who knows what else."

"What if they're right to take this course of action? What if they know more than we do?"

"Then we'll be the ones to pay the price for interfering. But I don't think they are, Caison. The way this whole thing's gone down if something else was going on, something the Chinese were doing, I'd know about it. My friends would know about it. No. I think this is an act of revenge in defense of the American people. On the one hand, I want to do everything in my power to make them pay for what they did, but not at the expense of more American lives."

"And you truly believe that would be the case?"

"I truly do."

———

The plane touched ground on the runway of Terminal 2 at the Ürümqi Diwopu International Airport. The regional airport of Xinjiang was more modern than Will had expected, given the much poorer areas of the province.

"Looks like they've got new construction going on here," Will said.

"From what Shaw indicated, China's pumping a shit ton of money into the economy here. They want to pull people out of poverty and have created a lot of jobs in recent years."

"Doesn't sound so bad."

"Unless you're Muslim. They've also deliberately increased the Han population here, and now there are almost as many of them as there are Muslims in the region. It was a planned migration in an effort to keep the religion from spreading and the Uyghurs from continuing toward more extremist views. They give them jobs and money in exchange for giving up their beliefs."

"My God."

"Oh, you won't find him here. Not ours anyway." Axell retrieved his carrier bag as the captain emerged from the cockpit.

"You have four hours, gentlemen. Then we will go back. With or without you."

"Understood." Axell turned to Caison. "Doesn't give us much time. Better get to work."

They made their way to the airport exit where several taxis waited to take passengers to their destinations.

"I have a feeling we'll need an interpreter," Caison looked around. "Shaw said someone was meeting us."

"I can help you out with that." A man with an American accent approached them. "Shaw sent me. Come on. My car's just over here." He flicked his cigarette to the ground and began walking away, soon noting that the men were not following him. "Everything okay?"

Axell and Caison exchanged an unspoken affirmation.

"Yeah. We're coming," Axell replied.

The man opened his car door and slipped into the driver's seat. He rolled down the window of the passenger side as they continued to wait on the sidewalk. "Well, get in. I won't bite." He reached inside his pocket for proof of identity. "Here, this make you feel better? I'm here because of Shaw, gentlemen. I guarantee you, we are on the same team."

At this, Axell stepped into the passenger seat and Caison slid in the back. "Now that we've got that cleared up. Where are we headed?"

"To meet an asset. A member of the Movement who says she's got some new intel for us." He keyed the ignition and pulled away from the curb. "How was your flight?"

"Fine," Axell replied.

"Sorry, I suppose I should introduce myself properly. I'm Brent Maddox. I've been working this region since a mole ratted out our people and the Chinks executed them. So, a few years now, I guess." He turned to Axell. "I heard about you, Axell. You've been out of commission for a while."

"Not as long as you might think."

"But you work at Langley as some sort of go-between for the Feds and CIA, isn't that right?"

"That's right."

"And that's what you are, am I correct?" He peered through his rear-view mirror at Caison. "You're one of them CTD Feds, right?"

"I am."

"Well then, welcome to the shitpit. Not much different here

than Afghanistan, is it, Agent Caison? Same desert. Different towel-heads."

Will furrowed his brow, wondering how he knew about Afghanistan. Then realized he was CIA. "Yeah. I guess so."

"You might not see it now because we're in the north and it's cold as a witch's titties, but where we're going, down south, it's warm and dry. Even in January, it's still pretty damn hot. But you'll see. Strangest damn thing here. It's like two different worlds. From this city, the capital, you see all these high-rises and nice buildings and shit. But down to the south, it's third-world shit down there."

Caison eyed Axell from his wing mirror and noticed his brow raise ever so slightly.

"So we're meeting with an asset." Axell wanted to change the subject. "How long you been running him?"

"Well, here's the thing about that, he's a she. And I've handled her for the past, what, two years? Since the attack in Beijing the Movement botched."

"Botched?" Axell said.

"Yes, sir. They got them, what like five? Injured lots, though. That was, oh, hang on now, that was in 2013. That's right. Since then, they've conducted half a dozen or more attacks right here in this very region. The capital city and other parts of Xinjiang. I been running her since then. She wanted out and we'll get her out, but now with this shit coming down the pike about Shen Yang, well, I don't think we can let her go just yet."

"Does she know Yang personally?" Caison asked.

Maddox peered into his rearview again. "Personally? Yeah, you could say that. Before ol' Yang got high and mighty and went to earn the big bucks in Beijing, she was his piece, if you know what I mean."

"Yeah, I think I get it."

"And she wants to get him back for leaving her here?" Axell continued.

"Can't speak entirely as to her motivations. She's very well paid for her services, but she was pissed he went to the US of A after he got married to some Han woman he met in Beijing." He glanced at Axell. "Anywho, it's a bit of a drive. Feel free to get some shut-eye if you need to. Jet lag's a bitch."

———

Caison opened his eyes, not realizing he had dozed off, as Maddox pulled onto an unpaved road rife with potholes and large stones that could shred a tire without warning. He sat up and drew Axell's attention by tapping his shoulder. It hadn't appeared Axell managed any sleep. Caison figured it was because of this peculiar man neither of them could quite read, but had put faith in him that he would get them where they needed to go. And back in time.

"I see you've returned to the land of the living," Maddox said. "Good. Because we just arrived. Sorry about the bumpy ride. Most of the streets in this village are shit."

"Where exactly are we?" Axell asked.

"Kashgar. It's the hub of the Movement. Doesn't look like much, I know. But believe me, this is where the action is."

"Is this where Yang comes when he's here?" Caison asked.

"Sure is. And this is where we'll find my lovely leading lady." He peered at both of them. "Bear in mind, this is Muslim territory. And as such, she might be wearing a burqa. Although they're banned in public areas. So, we'll see." He pulled the key from the ignition. "Come on. We've got a lot of work to do and I really hate driving back in the dark around here. You never know who's just around the corner." He stepped out of the car.

"Axell?"

He stopped short of exiting and turned back to Caison. "Yeah?"

"You sure we can trust this guy? We're out in the middle of nowhere."

"We have no choice." Axell stepped out.

Caison surveyed the thinly populated street with many of the homes, little more than shanties. Those who were on the street cast wary gazes upon two of the men who could be mistaken for nothing other than federal agents of the United States. Maddox blended in and Caison wondered if they might blow his cover if the wrong person took notice of their arrival.

They caught up with the quirky agent who'd clearly spent too much time in the communist country. Perhaps this was the reason behind his odd behavior and grossly prejudiced views, even with his obvious lineage. Nonetheless, they had no choice but to see this through. The stakes were high and their team split up. A particularly bad combination in Caison's mind, as the veteran of Middle Eastern wars who'd seen his share of death and destruction.

"Her place is just ahead." Maddox pointed toward a building roughly five hundred feet away. "That crap shack over there."

"And you're sure she's here? How do you contact her?" Axell asked.

"She's not the only asset here I run. She's just the one with the intel we need right now. Plenty of people around here need money and food. I give them what they need, they talk. Simple as that. We will, however, need to cut down this alley. There's a back entrance that's preferable. Believe it or not, some of these people don't like us very much."

"Really? That is surprising," Caison said as he quick-stepped toward them. The soldier in him couldn't help but eye the position of everyone around them. Fortunately, there weren't many. But he'd known well enough when an enemy was approaching.

They were in unfriendly territory. The Communist Party had pressed its foot hard against the necks of these people, banning prayer, banning the teaching of their native language in schools. Instead, the children were taught traditional Chinese—Mandarin. They'd done the best they could do to force what had been a moderate Muslim population into growing extremists as they attempted to snuff out their religion altogether. That would piss anyone off. And in fact, countries had been born as a result of such efforts.

Maddox stepped toward the rear entrance of the shack and knocked on a screen door that hung precariously loose from its hinges.

The woman covered in a burqa opened the door carefully.

"Salom." With his hands at his sides, Maddox avoided eye contact with the woman as he greeted her.

"Come in, quickly."

Her English wasn't half bad.

The men walked in and she peered outside in search of any onlookers before closing the door again and securing the lock. For her to have men, especially men of non-Muslim faith in her home, was risky at best. And she was a widow, making it all the more scandalous and dangerous were the agents to be seen with her.

"Thank you for agreeing to meet us," Maddox began. "I know what you are risking and you will be rewarded for your efforts."

And in that moment, Caison watched this strange man transform into someone else, someone who knew what he was doing. Shaw was right after all—sending them alone with Maddox.

"We know Shen Yang was here a couple of weeks ago," Maddox began. "Do you know who he met with? What they discussed?"

"Who are they?" she asked.

"Friends."

"American friends?"

He nodded. "They're here to help. But I have to know what Yang is planning and when he's planning it."

The woman walked into the kitchen, or what could pass as a kitchen. A small two-burner propane stove, a bar-sized refrigerator, and a rusted sink. She pulled out an audio recorder from the false bottom of a drawer. "Here."

"Have you listened to this?" Maddox asked.

"Yes. I knew of the meeting and planted it before their arrival. I recorded their conversation. They're planning an attack in Beijing. It will be larger than the one in the Tiananmen subway station. Much larger. It will be a bomb."

"In the Square? The subway? Where? When?" Maddox pressed on.

Caison and Axell stood silent and let him do his job.

"The Square. Next month."

"During the celebrations?"

She nodded.

"Jesus." He looked to Axell in disbelief before returning his attention to her. "How many has he recruited?"

"I don't know, but I can find out. He has a lot of money going around. People want to join him for that reason alone. Please, you have to go." She headed toward the back door.

"Where do they meet?" This time, Axell spoke.

"Inside the mosque, or what used to be our mosque. Now it is a propaganda machine for the Party. No prayer allowed."

"Is it guarded?" Maddox continued.

"Sometimes there are guards posted. But this late, I don't think they will be there. There is a basement. You might find more there.

Behind the walls are hollow spaces. They keep plans inside there sometimes."

"Isn't that risky? Meeting there?" Caison asked.

"Everything here is as you say, risky. They go there as a symbolic gesture. To prove to the Party that they can't be controlled. Go now. You must go."

Maddox withdrew his wallet. "Here. Thank you for your time. I'll be in touch again."

"I'm sure you will. If I'm right, I expect more in return for my troubles. The more people he brings here, the harder it will be for me to do as you ask."

"If and when that time comes, I'll make sure you're safe. I'll get you away from here. I promise." Maddox stepped through the door.

Caison and Axell followed and the three made their way back to the vehicle, taking caution in their passage.

As they stepped back inside the car, Caison began, "Are we going to the mosque?"

"Yes. We'll look for anything else they might have left behind."

"What about that?" Axell pointed to the recording device.

"Do you speak Uyghur?" Maddox asked.

"No."

"How about Turkic?"

"Nope," Axell added.

"Neither do I. We'll have to send this out for interpretation ASAP. I'll take care of that."

"So he's planning an attack during the Chinese New Year," Caison began. "How the hell are we going to stop it from happening? Sounds like he's got the funding and the people already in place."

"That's your job. Not mine," Maddox replied.

CHAPTER
TWENTY-ONE

THERE WERE four major state-run banks in China. And the Bank of Beijing, a branch of one of these four that serviced urban areas, was the target of the operation. Yang not only held his personal accounts here but also several of the shell companies on which his name appeared as a shareholder. This made transfers seamless and this was where Aaron and Lacy found the deposits.

This was the reason they chose the hotel. It was in close proximity to the bank's Xiajina location and they could easily slip back inside the hotel had the situation gotten out of hand. Luckily, it hadn't and now Lacy and Aaron sat in their room, analyzing the data, preparing for the return of the rest of the team.

"There's a history of roughly ten million US dollars changing hands between these accounts since the sanctions. I've noted the use of cryptocurrency here as well. Meaning we'll have to work harder to find payees," Aaron said. "However, some accounts, about half, trace back to Malcolm Ford and Casper Janz. As a side note, Janz's accounts are inactive. I couldn't see anything."

"They've erased him. The CIA," Lacy replied.

"Sounds about right. When do you think we'll hear from Caison and Axell?"

"Your guess is as good as mine. Shaw might have an update. He said his team would be near and to go out onto the balcony if we needed him."

"I'd rather wait until Axell comes back. The less attention we have, the better—for now."

———

In a room secured by a steel door and thumbprint-activated keypad for entry, a team of security officers review closed-circuit video of City Commercial Banks and their more than 140 branches across the country. One such location was the Bank of Beijing. The daily monitoring of the central banking system was implemented in 2009 when some of the branches brought in foreign investors and were no longer wholly owned by the state. The People's Bank of China wasn't willing to give up control completely. And the monitoring included facial recognition programs, passport scanners, and other identifying material from anyone and everyone who entered each branch.

"*Duìbùqǐ, xiānshēng?*" (Excuse me, sir?) One of the officers approached his superior. "*Běijīng yínháng fēnháng hóngqí.*" (I have a red flag at a branch of the Bank of Beijing.)

The ranking officer stood and followed the man to his station.

He began to replay the video and stopped when the image froze and zoomed in on the woman's face.

They continued their conversation as the officer explained the woman's behavior, as though she was looking for something. That was when the facial recognition picked up on potential matches to her identity. A message displayed on the screen.

The ranking official studied the screen and grew concerned by the finding. He continued in Mandarin, "Do you have a copy of the passport?"

"No, sir, they did not ask for her passport and she left shortly after this point here." He forwarded the video to the moment Lacy left the bank.

"These names, have you run them through the system?"

"It's running the program now."

Within minutes, her identity was matched and the officer shot upright in his chair. "Wait. Here it is. It's an American woman. Lacy Merrick, from Virginia. Do you know who she is?"

The superior appeared to bear a full understanding of the situation. "I will handle this from here."

————

"It's getting dark," Lacy moved away from the window as the lights of the city shone into their modern but compact suite. "They should've been back by now."

Aaron checked the time. "It's getting close, but there's no need to panic yet. Not in my opinion. You've got three well-trained field agents, one of whom is on familiar grounds. They're fine, Lace. We got what we needed to get. Besides, if you're that concerned, step outside. Get Shaw in here."

"No. You're right. I'm just being paranoid—again."

"It's not like you don't have reason to be. But it's fine. They'll be here soon. And we'll be that much closer."

She returned to the chair next to Aaron. "What if the president did authorize this?"

"Axell thinks he did. I have no reason to doubt him."

"Why would he risk such a thing? It would without a doubt bring mutual annihilation. China hasn't stopped building nukes, regardless of what they say. Everyone in the intelligence community knows that. They have something like 250 nuclear warheads now. Still, how many nukes do you need to destroy a country? Probably nowhere near 250."

"Probably somewhere around two, three? Maybe four? Look, I don't think it would come to that. And if Axell's right and the president is involved, I don't think he truly believes it would come to that either."

"But we don't know. How many Americans have already lost their lives to the mall attack? The other attacks?" Lacy turned her gaze downward. "Everyone wants payback. Hell, I want payback. But this can't be the way."

"I think the president's goal, or whoever's goal this is, is to turn China inward. Force it to handle what could turn out to be a civil war. Weaken it. Economically, politically. Do to them what they tried to do to us."

"And here we are, a handful of people doing what we can to stop that from happening."

"If we don't, there are just too many variables."

A knock on the door caught their attention and Lacy stood. "That could be them." She began her approach.

"Why would they knock? They have a key." Aaron quickly followed her and reached for her arm. "Hang on." He peered through the security lens and returned to Lacy, shaking his head.

"Turn-down service." A man's voice carried into the room.

Aaron pointed toward the balcony and mouthed, "Go outside."

It was the only way to get Shaw's attention, or his men's. She walked softly toward the door, peering over her shoulder to confirm Aaron's position.

The voice sounded again. This time, louder and more urgent. Lacy opened the sliding glass door with quiet precision and stepped outside. She didn't know where to look and hoped Shaw's man was still there and could get word to him quickly. This could be nothing, but it sure felt like something.

The air chilled her skin as she stood on the balcony, no coat, hat, or anything to shield her from the falling temperatures the night brought. She turned back to Aaron, raising her palms upward, relaying that she had no idea if anyone noticed her yet.

He held up his hand and mouthed, "Stay."

Lacy held her position. She wanted to go back inside and get the gun, the one Trevor left for them in case of emergency. This was as close to an emergency as anything.

The man tried again, knocking harder and speaking louder. Enough was enough. Lacy turned outward a final time. "Come on, Shaw. See me." She walked back in and straight toward the gun.

"What are you doing?" Aaron asked with a renewed panic.

"They're going to get in here." She pushed in front of him and aimed the weapon at the door.

When the sound of a card key sliding into the lock reached her ears, she whipped back at Aaron with wide eyes. They had a key. Either they always had it, or in the time they'd spent calling out to them, someone went and got one. Didn't matter. They were coming in. Now.

Lacy turned off the safety and steadied herself. "Go. Aaron, hide."

"Not a chance." He grabbed a paperweight from the desk. "I hope you're a good shot."

The door slowly opened and that was when chaos erupted. Gunfire from the hall.

"Shit." She pushed Aaron back and caught sight of the unknown assailant.

The door flung open, slamming against the wall, and Lacy fired. More shots sounded in the corridor. The man she hit collapsed to the ground. The other two defended themselves against whoever was in the hall firing on them. A moment later, they went down.

Aaron grabbed her arm and pulled her behind the sofa. "Gotta be Shaw out there. Jesus. Who the hell fired on us?"

"I don't know. I don't know, but I think he's dead." Her voice was steady, but fear surged through her.

"Merrick? Hunter? Where are you?"

The two glanced at one another, recognizing the familiar voice entering the room.

"We need to get you two out of here, now!"

"Agent Shaw?" Aaron stood.

"Yes. I saw Merrick on the balcony. Come on. We need to get the hell out of here."

Lacy still held the gun and hadn't realized she was pointing it at Shaw.

"Whoa, whoa, put the gun down. You got the bad guy."

"I'm sorry." She lowered her arm. "Aaron, get the laptop."

"Hurry it along, people." Shaw continued to canvass the hall. "My guy is downstairs. Let's get a move on."

Aaron grabbed his laptop bag. "Okay, okay. I'm ready." He turned to Lacy. "Let's go."

They followed him into the corridor and to the emergency stairwell.

"Guests are going to start spilling out into the halls. Best if we go this way and hopefully avoid security." Shaw jogged down the steps. "Hurry up. You gotta hurry. Police will be here soon if they aren't already. Son of a bitch. How the hell did you end up on their radar?"

Lacy glanced nervously at Aaron but said nothing, only continued down the stairs. Her legs began to burn as she kept pace with Shaw.

They reached the bottom floor and exited into the parking garage where a car idled only feet in front of them.

"Get in." Shaw slipped into the passenger seat. After he ensured they were in, he turned to the driver. "Get us the hell out of here. Out of Beijing." He turned back to Lacy. "They must've picked you up on surveillance and figured out who you were. Damn it! I should've realized. This whole damn city is covered with cameras. Skynet."

"Skynet?" Aaron furrowed his brow. "You mean like in…"

"'I'll be back.' Good old Arnie. Yes. That Skynet. Only here it's the country's public surveillance system."

"But I don't understand. They might've picked me—us up on video, but why would I have mattered to them? My passport would've checked out with a different name."

"It should have, yes. I don't know, Merrick. They've got facial recognition. You must've been on a list and they put two and two together."

"Are the others on their way back yet? Have you heard? We have to warn them," Aaron said.

"They're probably still on the flight back to Beijing." Shaw reached for his cell phone. "I'll text Maddox. Tell him where to go."

"Won't they be able to trace your phone?" Aaron asked.

"Oh yeah, you're the hacker guy. No. This is CIA issue. It's secure. Goes direct to satellite. Not cell towers."

"Where are we going?" Lacy asked.

"Someplace safe. Outside the city. We've got a safe house—a heavily guarded safe house. We'll be fine there until we can figure out how they knew who you were and where you were staying. That hotel was booked under a completely different name. They had to have been following you. Shit, I don't know. We'll figure it out. Right now, we just need to stay on the side streets and get out of here without being noticed."

"Do you think they'll be waiting for our team to land?" Lacy continued.

"Without knowing how they found you, I can't say if they discovered the rest of your team, or mine. They'll be all right. Maddox knows what to do. Best I can do is get word to them of our location. The rest, they'll have to handle."

———

The private jet aimed toward the runway and the landing gear dropped.

Axell retrieved his phone and quickly eyed Caison. "Hey, you get any messages?"

"I don't know." Caison pulled his phone from his pocket and checked. "No. Why?"

"Hey, Maddox, you get a message from Shaw?"

Maddox, who was in the next row up, looked at his phone. "Are you shitten' me? We're about to land!" He walked toward the cockpit and knocked on the door. "Hey, hey, we can't land here. We gotta turn up, man. I mean, like now!"

"Sir, you're going to have to sit down." The flight attendant approached.

"Hell no. You go in there and tell the captain he's got to pull up. We land here and we're as good as dead, you comprende? All of us!"

"What the hell is going on?" Caison stood.

"They had to leave Beijing. Someone came after them. I can only assume it was MSS or someone under their orders," Maddox replied.

"What? How? How the hell did they find them? Are they okay?" Axell said.

"Shaw got them out. Says they're headed to Chengde. It's an hour or so away. There's a safe house."

"Are they looking for us too? They know we're in the air?" Axell continued. "Maddox, how do you know they'll be on the ground waiting here for us?"

"Better to be safe than sorry. They might decide to check every American passport they come across."

"There's no place else to land? Not anywhere close by?" Caison said.

"No. Shit." Maddox pushed his hand through his dark, straight hair that brushed against his shoulders. "I just don't think we can chance it."

"I don't think we have a choice. We have to land."

Maddox picked up his cell phone again. "It's me. I need a car on the private runway asap. We're landing in five minutes." He waited for the person to speak. "There was no time. This needs to happen. Can you do it?" After eyeing Axell, he continued. "Good. Keep it running." He slipped the phone back into his pocket. "They let limos and some private cars, like town cars and shit, on the runway to pick up big-wigs so they don't have to walk far. I gotta guy. He'll meet us on the ground. I'll need you two to get in the car pronto. And do as I say."

"Got it," Axell replied.

Maddox returned to the flight attendant. "Never mind. False alarm."

Within minutes, the wheels touched down and rolled to a stop. Axell peered through the window. "I don't see a car, man."

"He's there. Don't you worry about it. Never let me down before. See, that's what us field officers gotta deal with, you know?

We gotta have each other's backs. Now come on. I'll lead the way."
He drew his weapon.

The flight attendant opened the door as the staircase rolled in front of it. "Thank you for flying..."

"Yeah, yeah. Thanks a bunch, lady." Maddox was the first to exit but not before checking his surroundings. "I see the car. My one o'clock. Let's do this." He descended the steps, gun still aimed at the darkness. That was when the light flashed. "That's him. You see? Now let's jet before the Chinks get here with their tiny revolvers."

Caison followed Axell as they hunched low to avoid detection. "Is this guy serious? I mean, he's Asian, right?"

"He's keeping us safe. That's all that matters right now."

They made it to the car.

"Man, am I glad to see you," Maddox said to the driver.

"Where to, my friend?"

"Chengde. Safe house."

CHAPTER
TWENTY-TWO

ON A NARROW SIDE STREET, cramped, ramshackle housing structures appeared in the darkness. This was where Lacy and Aaron now found themselves. Chengde—northeast of Beijing —in a suburb where less than half a million people resided and whose most popular attraction was the nearby Mountain Resort. The resort was a Qing emperor's summer residence over two hundred years ago and is now an historic site filled with lavish gardens and a palace museum.

But Lacy would not see the beautiful gardens. Instead, she and the rest of her team would search for a way out of the country without being captured, a prospect that seemed to grow fainter by the moment. And all because she walked into the bank to make sure Aaron could do what he needed to do.

Aaron waited on the edge of the chair in the confined living room. His elbows rested on his knees and his hands clasped. "Have you heard from them?"

Shaw turned away from the television. "Not since they landed. They should be here soon."

"Tell me we aren't on the news," Lacy asked.

"Not that I can see so far. That's a good sign."

"Boss, I see the car. I think that's them," Shaw's colleague said.

Shaw walked toward the window and checked for himself. "That's them. Maddox told me what car they'd be in." He appeared relieved. "Okay. Now maybe we can figure out what the hell happened in Beijing and hope those guys got the job done too."

The car pulled alongside the street running perpendicular and Shaw watched as Maddox, Caison, and Axell emerged. "They're coming down the street now." He moved toward the door and unlatched the lock, but not before turning his attention to Lacy. "I've got men on the roof watching them, in case you were wondering."

"Open it," the other agent said as he pulled away from the window.

Shaw pulled it open and stepped aside.

"I never thought I'd be so happy to see your ugly mug." Maddox entered, followed promptly by Caison and Axell.

Shaw closed the door and secured the lock once again. "You had me worried, Maddox. I thought maybe you might've lost your touch."

Lacy approached Will. "They found me. It was me." She embraced him, but only for a moment before turning to Axell. "Shaw's been trying to get answers. We've been here for a couple of hours. I didn't think you were coming back."

"They found you?" Axell said.

"They came knocking down the hotel room door," Aaron began. "Shaw told us what to do to get a signal to him. Lacy got the signal out and grabbed the gun. We just waited for them to bust through."

"They got a key, somehow, and opened the door, but Shaw got the message." Lacy regarded the agent with gratitude. "If he and his team hadn't shown up, we wouldn't be standing here right now, I can tell you that much. They got us out."

"You don't know how they were located?" Axell turned to Shaw. "Were they followed?"

"I don't think so. I think it was CCTV. They have cameras on every square inch of public space in the city. They must've had her picture and got a hit."

"Damn it. Why didn't I think of that before?" Axell rubbed his five o'clock shadow before turning to Lacy. "You can hardly go anywhere at home without being recognized. You're famous for what you did. Guess you're famous here too."

"And what you did to them," Shaw added. "The sanctions." He shook his head. "I didn't think. Son of a bitch. I didn't think and that's the problem."

"Well, I'm here and we're safe. That's all that matters right now."

"I agree," Will began. "But how are we going to get out of here? There's still a job to do."

"First of all, what happened in Xinjiang?" Shaw asked Maddox.

"We know what they're planning." He retrieved the thumb drive. "Got audio on here. They're planning an attack sometime during the New Year celebrations."

"No way. They'd have to be insane to think they could pull that off. Do you have any idea how tight security is around there during that time of year? No fucking way is Yang that stupid."

"You're forgetting who's footing the bill for the idea. They've got access to deep pockets. People can be bought. Especially here," Maddox replied.

"Okay. So if this is the plan, how are we going to stop it?" Lacy eyed the people surrounding her. Not only did she have no idea how they were getting out of the country, but now they were going to have to prevent an attack in Beijing. She believed in their cause, but this? This was the very definition of insanity.

"Evidence," Aaron said. "The only way we stop this is to bring the proof of it home. Proof that the US government is behind the funding. That Yang has been receiving money and the CIA had one of its own working to help him plan it, until he decided to start talking and got himself killed."

"He's right. Aaron traced Yang's accounts, some of them, and found money. What did you say, Aaron?" Lacy turned to him. "Money that bounced around from shell company to shell company with Casper Janz's fingerprints all over it. And it ended up in Yang's personal account."

"That's right. We have to get the evidence back home. Take it to someone who can keep it from getting buried. Take it to Director Mobley."

Axell looked to Shaw. "What are the odds we get this proof back home? And somehow manage to bypass CIA Director Handley in the process? I'm positive he made sure Janz was taken care of. What's to stop him from taking us out too?"

"Absolutely nothing. But it is possible for us to get the evidence into the right hands even without our being there. I just need to get it to someone I trust."

"Is there anyone left you do trust?" Axell continued.

"A few people."

"And how do we get back home?" Will added. "Make sure once it gets in the right hands that it stays in the right hands? We don't know if Director Mobley is taking orders from the CIA. And we don't know if it's the president who's issuing them. Not for fact."

"I hate to be Captain Obvious here," Maddox began, "but you all mind sharing with me how the hell you plan on stopping Yang? We can tell whoever we want till we're blue in the damn face, doesn't mean shit cause Yang's still got the money. Our government put this into motion. Yang won't stop because they say 'Pretty please.' He gets wind they want to pull the plug, I guaran-damn-tee you that he'll disappear along with the millions. This is what he's wanted his whole life. Ain't nothing or nobody gonna stop him."

"The only solution, then, as I see it, is to take Yang out." Caison looked to his colleagues. "Find out when he's coming back here, which I imagine won't be too far off, and take him out of the game. No one so far as I can tell, in his organization has his connections or will have access to the funds to pull it off."

"That means we aren't leaving any time soon. And they're after us. The Chinese Police, probably the MSS. They're after us," Aaron said.

"They're after me. It's me they want," Lacy replied. "From what we know right now, none of you have been compromised. I was careless and that's on me."

"No it isn't, Lace," Aaron said. "I asked you to go into the bank."

"You did what?" Caison furrowed his brow. "Why the hell would you do that? Send her in there without any backup?"

"I needed a lookout. I had to make sure no one started freaking out when I got into their system. I didn't realize."

"Neither did I. This isn't Aaron's fault."

"Look, it's nobody's fault, except mine. This is my territory. It was my responsibility to make sure you stayed safe." Shaw regarded Axell. "I knew about the cameras. Everyone knows about the cameras. They're friggin' everywhere. What I didn't know was that they'd have her in the system. That's something I should've picked up on. Now it's up to me to find a way to get her out."

"We have ample resources, here, Lacy," Axell began. "I have every confidence Shaw can find a solution. In the meantime, you're safe here. We all are. And we need a way to get Yang back in the country. Maddox, what can you do? Can you use his ex to get a message to him?"

"I can do that. That might work. I know who his right-hand man is too. Between the two of them, I can get Yang here. Might take a few days."

"You don't think it's better to, you know, take him out in the US?" Aaron asked.

"Not a chance. It'd be an international incident. And I thought that's what we were trying to avoid," Shaw replied.

"Right."

Maddox clapped his hands. "Alrighty then, let's get this show on the road. I'm outta here." He grabbed his coat. "Shaw, I'll be in touch."

"Same here. Thanks for getting them back safely."

"That's my job." He turned to Axell. "Today was a blast. We'll have to do it again soon."

After he left, Axell turned to Shaw. "I have to ask. Where the hell did you find that guy?"

"Maddox? He was instrumental in Operation Honey Badger. Figured out that the restaurant was bugged. I trust that man with my life. We both lost good friends when that shit went down. Neither of us has forgotten it either."

Axell nodded. "That's good enough for me."

"What's Operation Honey Badger?" Lacy asked with marked hesitation.

"They found our people, our operatives," Shaw began. "Took most of 'em out. Executed them. Some went to prison and are still sitting in some shithole cell today. Somehow, they figured out where we were taking our assets. No one really knows who fucked up. Our intel or if they just got lucky. Anyway, we lost a lot of damn good case officers. It won't happen again."

———

Inside the Oval Office, the president listened while his chief of staff briefed him on the day's agenda. Before he was finished, Secret Service opened the door. "I'm very sorry to interrupt, Mr. President, but Secretary Bainbridge is here to see you. He says it's urgent."

The secretary of state entered. "I sincerely apologize for the interruption, Mr. President, but it's imperative I speak with you." He looked at the chief of staff. "Alone, if that's all right, sir."

"Tom, would you give us a moment, please?"

"Of course." The chief of staff nodded to the secretary and made his way out.

"Thank you, sir."

"Have a seat, Frank. What's happened?"

"Mr. President, I received a call from Ambassador Browning and I'm afraid I have some disturbing news."

"Yes?"

"The Beijing police force has requested assistance from the embassy on locating one of our citizens in their city under false identification."

The president's expression hardened.

"The name on the citizen's passport was Jacqueline Russell. However, the woman was caught on surveillance in a branch of the Bank of Beijing as well as the streets of the city. And on further inspection, they recognized this woman to be Lacy Merrick. They matched it up with the passports of recent arrivals and made the connection."

"How the hell?"

"I don't know why she's there, sir. And especially traveling under forged documents. This is serious, Mr. President, which is why the ambassador called me. Local authorities have been unable to locate her, as of yet."

"For God's sake. What the hell is going on? Traveling under a fake passport? This doesn't make any sense to me."

"It's no surprise she was flagged in their system," the secretary continued. "Their facial recognition program is as good if not better than the FBI's, and given what this woman did, we shouldn't be surprised that they would have identified her. Virtually the entire world knows what she did."

The president slammed his fist on the desk. "Damn it. How did this happen? We need to find her. And there's not a chance in hell she's alone. Get the CIA director in here. Now! He needs to put all available resources into finding not just Merrick, but the rest of their team."

The president stood from his desk as the secretary left. The only one he could trust apart from the secretary was Director Handley. No one else knew what was about to happen. Not the vice president and certainly not any of the cabinet members. He was doing what he needed to do for the American people, for Lacy Merrick herself. And now she was about to destroy it all. If the Chinese captured her, it would be all over the news. They would insist she'd been sent for some nefarious purpose. They would undoubtedly kill her and the others if they were unfortunate enough to be caught.

But he knew Trevor Axell well and knew he would protect Merrick at all costs. Along with the rest of his team. The president couldn't allow the Chinese to capture her and would insist Director Handley put into motion a plan to bring them all home. And the sooner the better. It was only weeks away and this could scare Yang enough to pull out. He couldn't allow that to happen either.

———

It was far too early for the knock on the door to be anything but an omen. Yang had gone dark. No email. No cell phone. Nothing that would tie him to anyone in Xinjiang. The only way to get any word to him was by courier; a member of his staff who had set up secret communications with those working alongside Yang. And any messages received were delivered in person. No paper or electronic trail.

Upon opening the door that revealed a rising sun against a bright blue sky, his courier stood firm.

"My apologies for the early hour, sir."

"Come in." He again cast his gaze outward before closing the door. "What do you have for me?"

I received message from Xinjiang, from Fatima. She has indicated Mehmut could be discussing the plans with individuals not associated with the cause."

"Why would she say that?"

"She spotted him in the café with men from the village. Men who had recently been reprimanded for taking to the streets and calling for prayer."

"Reprimanded? How were they disciplined and by whom?"

"I do not know. She did not know. Only indicated he was discussing a potential end to their suffering. And that they would soon be able to return to the mosques and again answer the call to prayer."

"I need to know, specifically. Did she overhear him speaking of the plan?"

"No. Only what I told you. However, given that she agrees with what you're doing, she does not wish you to fall upon disruptions. Whatever else you might think, she does not wish that on you, sir."

"I need to get word to Mehmut, then. I must know who he's talking to and what he's saying. He's jeopardizing everything by openly speaking about it to anyone. Even if only in vague terms."

"Sir, she has suggested you return as soon as you can to prevent further occurrences. She has indicated he believes he is the one in charge. Not you, sir. He says you are living comfortably in America and why should you wish to make changes to their small village?"

"No. I can't believe he would say that. She must be lying."

"What would be the point in that, sir?" He stepped back. "I'm sorry. It is not my place. You will, of course, do what you need to do. I simply came to relay the message."

"Your point is not lost on me. Thank you for coming. I will attempt to settle this one way or the other." Yang walked toward the door again.

He bowed his head.

"Goodbye." Yang closed the door and standing in his pajamas, the wheels began to spin. The Party already had a heavy presence in the village. If they overheard anything—anything at all, there would be no more Mehmut. He would be dead. And he was not—yet.

With only weeks left, perhaps it was best if he went back to ensure the mission's successful completion. How else could he be certain the plan would survive? He could find a way to get out from under the thumb of the administration, from Handley. No more money was coming. He'd been given the resources. Yes. He would need to personally see this through. All he'd worked for. It was all at stake. He would not see it fail.

CHAPTER
TWENTY-THREE

THE UNRELENTING JET lag refused to allow Lacy to give in to sleep. Now she found herself sitting in the metal kitchen chair, its torn yellow Naugahyde snagging her pants and staring through the tiny opening in the curtains at the rising sun. The others were splayed out on the floor, Shaw on the couch, and all finding sleep just fine.

Lacy had a chance to think about all that had happened as she sat alone in the quiet. Finding herself on the other side of the world, away from her children. Something that had continued to happen despite her best efforts. This was no longer about Jay so she couldn't fall back on that justification. While her family wasn't in danger, her absence was yet another reminder of the woman she'd become. And it was a woman with whom she was no longer acquainted. Why was she really here? To stop some terrorist attack in a country that brought about pain and death to her own beloved country, or to stop a war? Was she so arrogant to believe she wielded that kind of power?

Her goal had always been to protect her country. That was why she joined the FBI. But Lacy was just a civilian, an analyst in the Cyber Division who helped the field agents find the bad guys. She didn't actually find them herself. Not until recently.

Lacy suddenly became very aware of just how out of her depth she really was. And how her kids would be missing her and how she put them second behind this insane act of what anyone else would call heroism. But she was no hero. She wanted people to know their government lied to them. And now they did. Maybe that was what drove her at this moment. More lies and conspiracies, this time to topple the world's second-largest economic superpower. She let slip an incredulous giggle before realizing those around her still slept. It wasn't until she spotted Will's approach did she grasp how loud that must've been.

"Hey," he whispered. "You're up early."

"Couldn't sleep. Did I wake you?"

"No. Not really. Still fighting the jet lag?"

She nodded. "There's coffee." She pointed toward the kitchenette. Lacy watched as he poured himself a cup. Black. No sugar here. Or creamer. Oh well. *Beggars can't be choosers,* she thought.

Will returned and sat down next to her. One sip of the coffee and his nose crinkled.

"I know. It's awful."

He shrugged his shoulders. "Better than nothing, I guess."

"Not much."

A grin spread on his lips. "We'll figure this out, Lacy."

"I know."

"What is it, then? I can see something's bothering you."

Lacy glanced at the floor where Aaron and Trevor still slept. "I don't want to wake them. It's nothing."

He held her gaze. "You sure?"

"Why don't you guys talk a little louder? I don't think the neighbor heard you." Axell sat up and tossed the blanket from his legs.

"Sorry," Lacy whispered.

"We're all awake now." Shaw sat up too. "Just as well. We've got a busy day ahead of us."

At this, Aaron finally stirred. "Man, is it morning already? I don't think I slept two hours."

"Yeah. It's tough getting over the time difference. It'll wear you down." Shaw stood in a long stretch. "Thanks to whoever made the coffee."

"You're welcome," Lacy replied. "But I'd hold off on the thanks. It's not good. Like—at all."

"She's right. It tastes like dirt," Will replied.

"So, what's the plan, Stan?" Axell emerged from the restroom. Hair slicked back with water and appearing more awake than only moments ago.

"I'll contact Maddox to see if he got word to Yang. His network is pretty extensive. It won't have taken long to make it happen. Then we can figure out what we're going to do on our end. We need Yang to return, though. That's the most important thing."

"What about getting Lacy out of here?" Aaron said. "That should be our priority. They're already looking for her."

"I know that. I need to make some calls so I can understand how much effort they're putting into finding her."

"Well, they did try to kill us at our hotel, so I'm guessing it's a decent effort on their part."

"Aaron," Lacy said.

"No. It's fine. He's right. You two got what we needed and there's absolutely no reason either of you should stay. It'll put you both in peril. Now I'm fairly confident I can get you back to Beijing without any trouble. But getting you through the airport will be the hard part."

"Wait a second," Lacy began. "I don't like the idea of leaving Trevor hanging out to dry."

"Um, hello?" Will interrupted.

"There you go." Axell gestured to Caison. "And with Shaw and Maddox—we'll work on Yang. We'll take care of him. Shaw's right. You two should go home. If I'd known any of this was going to happen, there's no way in hell I would've let you come in the first place."

"Let us? You needed us, Trevor," Lacy replied. "Aaron got the goods, but I wasn't exactly sitting on my thumbs."

"I'm sorry. I didn't mean you..."

"Don't worry about it. I'm just tired. Look, I can still be of use. I can act as the diversion you're going to need."

"What do you mean?"

"I mean, instead of us trying to avoid the cops or whoever else is out looking for me, why don't I just go to the American Embassy and turn myself in, so to speak? That should put the brakes on efforts to continue any search, meaning they won't find you either. What are they going to do? Shoot me?" Her attempt at humor fell on deaf ears. "Okay, okay. I just need to get to the embassy. I'll be safe there. Even if they don't let me go home, the embassy won't just turn me over to the Chinese, right?"

"It's unlikely," Shaw replied.

"Unlikely? I think I'd prefer something a little more convincing than 'unlikely,'" Aaron replied.

"Point being is that I take the heat off and you can do what you need to do. They don't have your faces. You guys weren't all over the news for the past few months. No one knows you're here."

"Believe me, Lacy, it won't take long for them to figure it out." Axell approached her. "They'll pull the airline's passenger manifest."

"And they'll find your fake names."

"Yes, with our real faces. These people aren't stupid. They have the same tech we do. Even if they did steal it. They got it and that's all there is to it. So, no. I don't think it's a good idea for you to go to the Embassy. Too many variables. And what happens when Handley finds out? Because he will find out. There are a lot of us here. He's still got plenty of loyal people who may not know what he's planning."

"Then what, Trevor? What do we do? How do I help you do what you need to do without jeopardizing the mission any further?"

Shaw approached him. "Axell, she's got a point. This could work. I know you don't want to put her in harm's way and neither do I, but if we plan it right, this could work."

———

Two days holed up in the tiny apartment and the word finally came down. Yang was due to arrive later in the evening. The plan was put into action.

Lacy tossed what few personal items she had into her bag. "I'm ready."

"Okay. We figure our best bet is to go by bus," Shaw began. "Less likelihood we'll be stopped by any potential checkpoints on the route. This place has a big-time tourist attraction and the buses leave about every thirty minutes. So they'll do what they can to minimize inconvenience for the tourists. And if we get you in disguise, all the better. Because once we get to Beijing, we'll be on foot to the embassy. I don't want to risk a cab in the event we're sitting at a light or whatever and some cop pulls up next to us. That's when we'll be at our most vulnerable."

"Hey, someone's pulling up." Caison peered over his shoulder at Shaw.

"It's okay. It's Maddox." Shaw approached the door and pulled it open. "You get what we need?"

"Well, I don't know, does a bear shit in the woods?" He smiled and held a bag in his hand.

Shaw grabbed the bag. "Yeah, yeah. Let's just see what you got." He reached inside and retrieved a wig. "Perfect. You'll be playing the part of the blonde today, Lacy." He tossed it to her. "Go put this on. We'll need to take a picture."

"A picture? For what?" Aaron asked.

"New passport," Maddox replied. "Even on the bus, they'll want her passport. And I got one for you too, Shaw."

"Hang on, I thought I was going with her."

"Hunter, you're going to need to stay here with Axell and Caison. In the short term." Shaw moved toward the kitchen and picked up his carrier bag. "I got this for you."

"A laptop. What do you need me to do?"

"You'll need to get Merrick's new passport into the database. The US database, so when they scan it, she'll be good to go."

"That's going to take time—and resources. I'll need passwords, user ID's. I can't just hack into the State Department's database. And from here?" He shook his head. "Not a chance."

Maddox opened the door again. "Meet your new partner." A young man, college-aged, stood in the doorway. "This is Yan. He's going to help you."

Aaron looked at Axell. "Do we know this guy? What the hell is this?"

"Before you get your panties in a bunch, Yan is one of the best hackers in the country," Maddox continued. "He sits in his bedroom in front of a computer and does nothing all day except figure new ways to screw over the Americans and anyone else who might've pissed him off."

"And one day, we crossed paths with him," Shaw said. "Got a

little too close to our operations. So now he helps us out. It's a mutual understanding, isn't it, Yan?"

The kid nodded. "I can help CIA."

"So, as I said, Hunter, you and Yan will get Merrick's new passport into the system so when they do scan it, everything will come back clean, *capiche*?" Maddox closed the door again as the kid entered.

Lacy emerged from the bathroom, hair tucked beneath the short blonde wig. "This is the best I can do."

"Eh, it's all right." Caison shrugged a shoulder and cocked his head.

"Thanks." She spotted the kid. "Who's this?"

"Someone who's going to help us," Shaw said. "Okay. We'd better hit the road. We're burning daylight and I want to get back into Beijing well before the embassy closes. Can't risk spending the night there. We get in. We get you out."

"The ambassador," Axell began. "Can you convince him to keep his mouth shut about this? And make sure she gets out safely? My fear is that he'll make contact with State. And if the secretary finds out, which he undoubtedly would, he'll go to the president. And then we're screwed."

"I'll have to wait and see, Axell. She'll be allowed to go home and the important thing to remember is that she stays out of the hands of the MSS or Chinese Police. There might be consequences for her returning home, but it won't be death."

"Well, that's good to know," Lacy said. "Anyway, isn't our goal here to create a diversion? Divert resources away from discovering your operation with Yang?"

"Yes. Word will get around that you're in the embassy. CIA, whoever's loyal to Handley, will inform him. And that's ultimately what we want. I'll be leaving a few breadcrumbs. Just enough to garner attention. You all won't have much time to get Yang," Shaw said.

"And then our next problem will be in ensuring we get out," Caison said.

"We'll cross that bridge when we get to it. Hopefully, this will all be over before long and Yang will be out of the picture. Once that happens," Shaw glanced to Axell, "I believe Handley, the president, or whoever else is involved in the plan will want to distance themselves as quickly as possible. Any and all connections to Yang will be erased. And it'll be like none of this ever happened."

"I need to start now." Yan walked toward the laptop. "This won't do." He retrieved his own.

"Hey, hang on there." Aaron turned to Shaw and appeared concerned.

"It's okay, Hunter. Let him use his own computer. He's done this before. We just need your help once inside. You've run into the database before when you were at Langley. You know the ins and outs of it."

"How'd you?" Aaron stopped short. "Never mind. Fine. Let's get started." He approached Lacy and stared at her hair. "You look —different."

"That's kind of the point." She gently took hold of his arms. "I'll be fine. Like Shaw said, this will be over soon. Just do what you need to do to make sure I get out of here, okay? Once I'm home, they won't keep me quiet."

"That's what I'm afraid of. I'll get you out. You just stay safe, okay?" He kissed her cheek.

Caison turned away and peered out again onto the small alleyway. "Okay. We'd better get moving."

Lacy grabbed her bag again. "I'm ready. Let's go."

"Axell, I'll be in touch when we've reached Beijing." Shaw

checked the time. "It'll be a good two, two and half hours by bus. In the meantime, Hunter, you've got about twenty minutes to get her in the system."

"That's all?"

"Yep. She's got to get on that bus. I've got my own passport. I'll be good. So just make sure she gets on that bus or this will be over before it begins."

————

The bus station was now only minutes away. And as they approached in what was called an unofficial taxi with a driver who was yet another in a string of paid informants for the CIA, Shaw peered through the windshield.

"No increased security, from what I can see." He turned to Lacy in the back seat. "That's a good sign they don't know you're here." He turned to the cab driver. "Pull up over there. Away from the passenger entrance."

The driver did as instructed and stopped alongside the curb, several feet west of the entrance.

"Thanks. I'll be in touch." He handed the man 30cny and opened the door. "Give me a second," he said to Lacy as he stood on the curb, surveying the immediate area. A moment later, he opened her door. "Okay, come on."

"Should we go in?" Lacy asked.

"Yeah. We stand out here much longer and people will think we're lost and start coming and asking if we need help. I just want to buy Hunter and Yan as much time as I can."

"Me too." Lacy appeared on edge, her eyes darting back and forth, her steps slow and deliberate.

"Relax, Merrick. I need you to look like a tourist, understand?"

"Yeah. Sorry."

"It's all right. Let's just keep moving." He reached for her hand and laced his fingers between hers. "We're just an average couple touring around, all right?" She nodded as he pulled them nearer the entrance. "First thing we'll do is walk toward the monitor with the schedules posted. And we'll figure out when the next bus is due to leave. One step at a time, got it?"

Lacy held on to his hand, inhaling calming breaths as she stepped in line with him. She needed to pull this off and get to the embassy. It was the only thing that would take the heat off of Axell and the others so they could find Yang and take care of him. Then, this would be over. Yang wouldn't be protected by security staff here. He was working against his own government and his low profile would be his weak link.

What they would face at home remained to be seen, but right now, she just wanted to step foot back onto American soil and the US Embassy would be the closest thing to that.

"Says here the next bus leaves in fifteen minutes." Shaw turned to her with noted relief. "Perfect. We've got some time."

"What now? Do we go buy the tickets?"

"Not yet. Let's grab a coffee like anyone else would. We'll give it, say, ten minutes. And hopefully, that will be enough. I see a coffee kiosk over there."

They walked toward the kiosk and Shaw paid for the coffees.

"I'll tell you, they get a Starbucks in here and this place would be booming." Shaw smiled and raised his cup. "You know they open something like a store a day in this country? Boggles the mind how they're so successful here. They're one of only a handful of US companies that've seen that kind of success in China. They have a Disneyland in Shanghai, so there's that too."

Lacy could see he was trying to put her at ease, take her mind off of the fact that if Aaron and this Chinese hacker didn't do what they needed to do, she would likely be hauled off and sent to some prison. Shaw too. Perhaps he was also convincing himself every-thing would turn out just fine. "Must be difficult in a country known for its tea to make a successful bid in the coffee industry." She indulged his efforts and he appeared to appreciate it.

"Oh yeah, for sure." Shaw sipped on the coffee and continued to survey the area.

"Should we, um, you know, go ahead and go to the counter?" Lacy asked.

"I suppose so. We've given it enough time. Shit or get off the pot, right? Sorry, no offense."

"None taken. I'm not easily offended."

"Good to know. I think I've spent too much time around Maddox." He led the way toward the counter.

"He's an interesting guy."

"You have no idea." Shaw approached first and retrieved his wallet and passport. In Mandarin, he began, "Excuse me? I'd like to get two tickets for the next bus to Beijing?"

The man behind the counter noted their Western appearance and began speaking English. "Passport, please. Thank you. And you too?" He peered at Lacy.

"Uh, yes. Sorry. Here you go." She smiled and handed him her fake passport with her blonde hair and a name she suddenly blanked on.

He proceeded to scan in the documents. Shaw's passed with flying colors and the man handed it back to him.

"Much appreciated."

Lacy noted a slight elevation in Shaw's tone. Like he was nervous. This wasn't a good sign. But she waited, still wearing a smile.

"And here you go, madam. That will be 320 yuan."

Shaw paid the man and was handed two bus tickets. "Thank you, sir." He grabbed Lacy by the arm and pulled her gently away from the counter before turning to her as they reached the terminal. "Well done, Merrick."

"I knew he'd do it."

"Hunter? Yes, he does seem capable. Or I doubt he'd be working for Trevor Axell." He stopped short and turned to her. "Do you know much about Agent Axell?"

"I think so. I've known him for a while. We're pretty close, I'd say."

"I see."

The bus opened its doors.

"That's our ride. Ladies first."

CHAPTER
TWENTY-FOUR

THE PRIVATE CHARTERED flight was about to take off from Dulles Airport with Shen Yang aboard and anxious about the news his plans might have been compromised. He'd enlisted the aid of his US intelligence partners to ensure the flight's anonymity. His ties to the MSS were compromised in the wake of Matthew Greiner's murder and the arrival of the troublesome Lacy Merrick in Beijing. And after the subway station bombing, word had reached Yang that the Ministry suspected his involvement. This could only have happened as a result of Mehmut's loose tongue. Another reason for Yang's growing anxiety about the larger plan.

CIA Director Handley wanted Yang there as much as he needed to be there, though Handley's concern was for the team led by Agent Axell no one had yet located. And their exposure of what the CIA had conspired to accomplish with the Movement and Yang himself. It was a concern Yang did not share. He had the money. He had the people. And Yang was ready to sever ties with the clandestine agency upon execution of the plan. These people, Agent Axell and his team, they did not pose a threat to Yang. The Ministry and State Police. These were the ones Yang feared.

With his wife in hiding in the US, he would send for her afterward. Yang was not so naïve to assume the CIA would continue to provide assistance or cover. Their goal would soon be reached, but Yang's was only just beginning.

———

The sun had risen high and burned through the wintery smog that reached far from Beijing and into Chengde.

"Hunter?" Axell approached him as he remained seated at the kitchen dinette. "She's fine. If she didn't make it onto the bus, we'd know about it by now. They're well on their way back to Beijing. You did good."

"What happens when they get there? What if the embassy turns her over?"

"They won't. You're forgetting the optics here. Lacy Merrick, US citizen, FBI analyst, who uncovered a dark government conspiracy. Nothing will happen to her, not here anyway. Once we get back home, that might be another story, but we'll figure that out later."

"Keep your eye on the prize, man." Maddox joined the two and patted Aaron's shoulder before turning to Axell. "When are we heading out? Best be soon. Sources tell me Yang will be arriving on a 6 pm flight."

"How long till he makes it back to Xinjiang, then?"

"Couple hours after that. He'll take a puddle jumper from Beijing direct to Xinjiang. I have a plane on standby whenever you're ready. Mind you, it won't be the luxurious ride I lined up before. Short notice and all. But we'll make it in one piece." He looked to Caison. "I suppose you're coming with us too?"

"Yes. Hunter's going to get on the next bus and get to Beijing.

He'll make contact with Shaw and meet up with him after making sure Lacy's safely at the embassy."

"Better do it quick, then. I have no idea what they'll do with her once she's at the embassy. Keep her overnight, maybe. Send her on the next flight home in the a.m., possibly. But if it goes tits up, Shaw's going to need all the help he can get. The good news is she's out of here. Word on the street is operatives are looking for her. And they know about this place."

"Keep your head down, Hunter. I mean it. Contact Shaw as soon as you arrive and find out where he and Lacy are. Hopefully, in the embassy," Axell said.

"What should I do if all goes to plan?"

Axell laughed. "Haven't you figured it out yet? Nothing ever goes to plan. But, in that event, Shaw might send you to another safe house until he can get you on a flight. Unless he's stuck at the embassy with Lacy. We just don't know. He has to protect his cover. He's risking a lot by getting her there in the first place. If she can get inside the embassy on her own, she'll be able to handle herself. I'm not worried about that and neither should you. Right now, Yang's got to be taken care of before it's too late."

"Good luck."

"You too. Make sure you get home safely. That's your only job. Lacy can take care of herself."

———

Maddox walked onto the concourse of the private airstrip that appeared to have cost him a fair bit of money to keep heads turned and eyes elsewhere. That was the one thing about Communist China. There were a whole lot of poor people here, including those with jobs. Especially in the rural areas. And offering a few extra bucks, or Yuan as it were, meant a family might get to treat themselves to an extra helping of dinner, or just dinner. That often carried more weight for them than protecting their country from the CIA, which had its own thriving economy among its paid assets.

"Hop onboard, Caison, Axell. We'll be there in a few short hours."

"Before Yang?" Caison said as he walked up the staircase.

"Good God I hope so, or else what's the point?"

Caison stepped aboard the small, older model Cessna. "Didn't know they had Cessnas here."

Maddox soon joined him, followed by Axell. "Oh yeah. Division went bust a few years back, though. The company thought it would be cheaper to manufacture them here, ship them off to the US, and reassemble them there. They ended up selling them here too, but not a huge call for personal aircraft in this country. So we picked up a few of them for just such an occasion. It'll get us where we need to go. Don't you worry your pretty blonde head about that." Maddox sat in the pilot's seat.

"Wait. You're flying this?"

"Yeah. I got a license. I'm perfectly capable of getting us there in one piece."

Caison cast a worried glance to Axell.

"Just take a seat and don't think about it." Axell sat down and secured his belt, pulling it extra tight for show.

"Gee, I feel so much better now," Caison replied.

Within minutes, they were in the air and the plane rattled hard on takeoff. "Sorry about that. We'll level off here in a minute." Maddox gave Caison and Axell a thumbs-up.

"What's our plan on arrival?" Caison appeared to create a distraction for himself with conversation.

"We'll tail Yang. He'll probably head straight to Fatima's home. Possibly to the man we pinned the leak on, Mehmut. We'll have to see. But either way, we'll take him out down there and make it look like his own men did it."

"What about the plans for the attack? His people? How are we going to stop them?"

"We won't have to worry much about that part of it. Whatever we find relating to the planned attack, Maddox will make sure ends up in the hands of the Party. They'll take care of it from there."

"I'm sure they will." Caison knew what that meant. No one in Yang's confidence was going to make it out alive.

The next couple of hours found the agents quiet as they considered how this was going to play out and whether they, themselves, would make it out alive. Yang was a powerful man with millions of US dollars that afforded him many powerful weapons. Rocket launchers, grenade launchers, AK47s; you name it, they'd have it. Not to mention the likelihood several bombs had already been constructed. And these three agents were equipped with only side arms. Not exactly a fair fight. But the hope was that there wouldn't be a fight. They had the element of surprise on their side, thanks to Fatima, and it would have to be enough.

———

Lacy adjusted her wig and began to step off the bus after the long, nail-biting journey back to Beijing. Every moment was spent wondering if the police would charge the bus and haul her away. Every moment spent wondering what was happening with the rest of her team. Now they had arrived and the time for speculation was over.

"Hang on." Shaw extended his arm across her. "Let me go first. Stay behind me. Closely." He stood and grabbed her hand to pull her up. "Just hang tight."

The true dangers lay ahead. Getting to the embassy undetected when the authorities knew who she was and what she
looked like, and in fact hunted her at this very moment. The
blonde wig might offer some safeguard, but any cop who looked at
her for longer than ten seconds just might recognize her. And
then there was the surveillance—Skynet. And that feeling that
haunted her months ago returned. They were watching and
waiting for her. Her heart beat faster the more she considered the
odds.

"Now. Come on. Let's go." Shaw twisted out from the
cramped seat and held onto her hand. "Once we step off, keep
your head down. Do not look up under any circumstances."

"The cameras."

"Yes."

They approached the front of the bus. Shaw nodded a thank
you to the driver and walked down the steps, emerging onto the
sidewalk. He glanced both ways and continued to grip Lacy's
hand almost to the point that it became painful. She cringed but
kept her head down.

"It's a two-mile walk. You okay with that?"

"I think I can manage."

"Sorry. I didn't mean to..."

"I know. Let's just get there. How much time do we have
before it closes?"

Shaw checked his watch. "We're fine. Got another two hours.
Plenty of time. Just stick close."

Lacy was so concerned about being caught on camera, that she
stared at her feet until she nearly ran into someone. "Oh my gosh,
I'm so sorry, sir."

The man, who appeared to be Chinese, bowed his head and
said something she didn't understand but assumed was an
acknowledgment of her apology. He smiled and moved on.

"Okay, I know I said keep your head down, but try not to run into anyone else."

"Well, you're the one who's supposed to be leading the way. Maybe you can try to avoid people."

"Have you seen how crowded this city is?" He smiled. "No, well, I guess you haven't. Sorry about that, Merrick."

"You know, you can call me Lacy. I'm not one of you guys."

"What do you mean, one of us guys?"

"I'm not an agent or anything. I just do civilian work for the Bureau."

"Oh, I see. Here I thought you were the one who risked her life to make sure the world knew exactly what happened last summer. In my book, that makes you 'one of us,' Merrick." He squinted through the rays of a late afternoon sun. "That's it. Up ahead. We're almost there now. Just a quarter mile or so and we'll be home. There will be Beijing Police in front."

She snapped her head toward him. "What?"

"Head down, Merrick."

"Sorry." She shed her gaze once again toward the sidewalk and her every step.

"Unfortunately, they're a recent addition," Shaw continued. "Mostly plain clothes, so we won't see them."

"Why would they be guarding the US Embassy? Because of the sanctions?"

"They aren't guarding it so much as they're keeping their citizens from entering the compound to claim asylum. See, a few years ago, a Chinese police chief ran inside a US Consulate to do just that. Shortly after, several police closed off the road to the consulate. It was a giant clusterfuck, pardon my French."

"Why would he have done that?"

"The truth? No one knows. Rumor has it he was going to be charged with corruption or something. I can't recall exactly.

Anyway, it's known that the Chinese now place a few plainclothes cops near the entrance just in case. They don't want another embarrassment like that happening again."

"Okay. So what if they recognize me?"

"They won't. Not if we're just strolling in. They won't approach us. I don't think they will, anyway."

A strange sensation crawled up her spine and the hairs on her neck stood. She gripped Shaw's hand and caught his attention. "Someone's coming up on us."

Shaw didn't look back. "Just keep walking. I'm sure it's nothing. Stay calm. We'll make it through."

———

On a small, clay airstrip, the Cessna touched ground, rolling and bumping over the divots and minor potholes on the runway. With only an hour to get into place, and the sun falling farther behind the horizon, they needed to move quickly.

Caison turned on his cell and waited for a sign that Lacy had made it to the embassy. And as the signal provided service, there was nothing. No email, no voicemail, or text message. "Should we try her or Shaw?"

Axell glanced at Caison's phone before checking his own. "No. Not just yet. They might've had their phones confiscated if they're talking to a member of the embassy. We've got to do what we came here to do. That has to stay at the forefront of your mind. Lacy can take care of herself. And so can Shaw."

"Okay. Listen, there was something I wanted to propose." He waited for Maddox to emerge from the cockpit. "Is it worthwhile to get a confession from him?"

"From Yang?" Maddox began. "You mean, ask him to admit he's getting money and resources from the CIA to plan an attack in Beijing? You can't be serious, Caison? Even if we did get a confession from him, you really think he'd survive long enough to make it back to the US? There are plenty of case officers here, unaware of the operation, who would be more than willing to take care of him for Handley. There's no point in considering that scenario. Because if they, the director, the president, and anyone else involved, discovered we had Yang's confession, they wouldn't stop at him. They'll take all of us out. Without hesitation."

"I'm sorry, Caison, but we have to stick to the plan," Axell said. "It's the only thing we can do to stop this."

"For right now. What about a year from now? The president just began his second term. He's got three more years to accomplish his goal."

"Yes, he does. And I can't say with any certainty this will end today. It might end for Yang, but not for us. That's something we'll have to consider afterward. Not right now." Axell began to emerge from the plane in the dusky light.

Maddox patted Caison on the back. "I know where you're coming from, and believe me, I've been in your shoes before. Sometimes we have to do things we don't want to do to prevent something worse from happening. Today is one of those days." He continued down the steps and joined Axell. "Are we going to be able to rely on him to have our backs? There's no telling what we're going to come up against once we get there."

"He'll come through. I have no doubt."

An old minivan waited nearby. The driver appeared to be another CIA beneficiary. It astounded Caison all the money they had access to. Here he was, always watching the FBI's pennies and these guys made it rain for whoever would do their bidding.

They stepped inside the van with Maddox in the front seat. He nodded to the driver. "Let's roll. We're on the clock now."

Caison looked to Axell. "I hope we're doing the right thing."

"So do I."

"Don't worry, boys. This is for the good of the country," Maddox replied.

"Which one? Ours or theirs?" Caison asked. "How far is it?"

"Minutes. We'll be there soon."

He wasn't far off the mark, and inside of thirty minutes, they'd arrived on the outskirts of Kashgar, the village where the beginning of a revolution was about to take place with the US government in the shadows, conducting the orchestra.

"I just got confirmation," Maddox peered at his cell phone. "Yang's due to arrive within the hour. Let's get into place." He emerged from the van as the sun had almost disappeared behind the mountains.

Caison and Axell stepped outside in the air that had turned much colder since they left Chengde. Kashgar was the region's oldest city and housed a large mosque where the head of that mosque was killed last year by members of the Party. Since then, tensions in the region have continued to rise, and this was what Yang had counted on.

"Here, put these on." Maddox handed them the hats.

"What are these?" Caison asked.

"Doppas. The traditional hats worn by the Uyghurs."

"I hardly think we'll pass for Uyghurs," Axell replied.

"No doubt, whitey. But in the dark, wrapped in a coat, it'll offer some camouflage. It's all I've got."

"Fine." Caison put on the triangular, pointed hat and pulled up the collar of his coat. "Really wish I'd grown a beard right about now."

"Wouldn't matter. The Party outlawed men with large beards from riding public buses and since most of these people don't have their own cars, they had no choice but to shave. So you're not that out of place."

"Jesus. Really?"

"Yeah. Really. The Chinese government has brought this on themselves. They've banned nearly everything related to the Islamic religion for these people. Look, I ain't got no sympathy for terrorists, believe you me. Nor this shit commie government, especially after what they did to ours. But they've turned these people into extremists, some of them anyway. And this is the price they'll pay for it."

"Isn't that what we're here to stop? An attack?" Axell said.

"It is. But this won't be the last attempted uprising. Just hopefully the last one funded by good ol' Uncle Sam. We don't need that shit hanging over our heads. That much we can agree on. I came here to keep these Chinks from stealing our tech and keeping tabs on their nukes. This terrorist bullshit? Not my thing." Maddox closed the sliding door of the van. "Time to go. We'll need to split up. I'll head to Fatima's joint. You two go to Mehmut's. I can't be sure where he'll go first. But it will be one of these two places." He tossed them walkie-talkies. "When you have eyes on the target, let me know and I'll do the same. Get your shot and take it. Once that happens, we'll meet here." He held out a map. "Two clicks in either direction. Bust your asses back to this point and the van will pick you up. He won't wait, so once you give me the signal, you best be on your way back."

"Better start hoofing it now," Axell said.

The team split up, heading in opposite directions as Caison peered over his shoulder, ensuring they weren't being followed.

"Tell me he'll follow through and make sure we get the hell out of here."

"If you're having doubts now, Caison, you're a day late and a dollar short. Don't second-guess. Just do what we came here to do. If we don't make it, then so be it."

"Copy that."

CHAPTER
TWENTY-FIVE

THE ECHO in Lacy's ears stemmed from her labored breathing as she tried to keep focus on her steps. Everything around her, all the noise, the traffic, and the people, she tuned out and listened only to the footsteps behind her. And how they seemed to escalate.

Shaw must have picked up on it too as his pace quickened, but not so much that it drew attention from anyone except perhaps the person who now followed them. "We're almost there."

His words were faint as her pounding heart replaced the shallow breaths reverberating in her head.

The iron gates of the embassy loomed large as Lacy and Shaw made their approach. On the inside, Americans stood watch. Whether they were armed, Lacy couldn't tell, but assumed they had firearms strapped to their waists beneath the heavy overcoats. Given the recent tensions between the two countries, she wasn't surprised by the presence of the guards. Relations had deteriorated rapidly in the past few months as sanctions took hold. In fact, what had surprised her was that the embassy was still open. But there were many Americans who lived and worked here, though for how long would largely depend on the success or failure of Trevor and Will's mission.

"Okay, Merrick. Keep moving forward. I'm going to have to come in with you," Shaw said.

"You can't."

"Just go." His grave tone meant this was not a request.

At any moment, the person following them could rip her from his grip. Lacy had to keep moving, knowing that Shaw was now risking exposure. "Okay."

"Good." Shaw moved closer to the entrance, holding Lacy's hand as he had the entire way. "Get your passport out of your pocket and step in front of me."

Shaw fell back only slightly while Lacy retrieved the document. He had positioned himself between her and the person who followed. But as they drew nearer, the steps seemed to fall back a little. Both now held their identification as they approached the guard gate.

"Good evening. How can I help you?" the guard asked, seemingly oblivious to whoever followed them.

"We need to replace my companion's travel visa. Seems she dropped her passport in a puddle of water and it's become difficult to read." He nodded for her to display her passport and managed a glance behind them.

"I see. You know we're about to close up for the night."

"I understand, but we've been traveling most of the day in hopes of arriving before that happened. Do you think we could go in, please?"

The guard studied the two of them.

Lacy grew uncomfortable at the length of time he was taking to make a decision and she instinctively cast a glance over her shoulder, immediately regretting the decision. The person behind them had fallen back some, but she knew he wasn't on their side. He had to have been the police, or worse.

"Ma'am? You looking for something?" he asked her.

"No, sir. Just felt a bit of a chill. It's getting quite cool out."

Shaw looked at her with a tentative glance. "It is cold."

The guard began to nod. "That it is. You can go in. But I don't know how much you'll accomplish today. They might make you come back tomorrow." He began to step aside while another released the lock on the gate.

Lacy's hackles raised as she felt the man from behind reach for her arm. "Hey!"

"What the hell are you doing?" Shaw said as he tried to pull her from his grip.

The guard reached for his gun. "Back off. They're Americans."

"We've been ordered to take her into custody. Now." The Beijing police officer refused to release her.

They found her and were about to take her away. She wanted to run. Pull away from this man and run inside the gates. They were so close. The gates were partially opened. "Let me go! I'm an American. This is my embassy. I have a right to go in."

The guard reached for his radio and called for assistance after motioning for the guards on the inside of the gate to approach. "You'd better explain yourself, officer," he said.

In his fractured English, the officer continued. "She is to be remanded into our custody."

"For what reason?" Shaw's voice raised in the growing chaos. "She's done nothing wrong. You have the wrong person."

"Okay. You need to let this woman go. Now!" The guard brandished his weapon. "She's a US citizen on embassy grounds. You're in violation of the China-US Consular Treaty. Stand down!"

Several patrol cars arrived, screeching to a halt in front of the embassy. The officer's eyes remained fixed on the guard. And as more US guards approached, the situation escalated. If this man didn't release Lacy, things were going to go from bad to worse and Lacy and Shaw would be in the crossfire.

The officer finally released Lacy's arm. She yanked it away and tried to steady herself because, beneath her coat, she trembled.

"Go in. Now." The guard continued to hold aim on the Beijing officer until they were both inside the gates. "Close 'em!"

"We're okay. We're inside now. Everything's okay." Shaw turned to see the scene that had erupted. A scene he thought he was prepared for, but in the end, had turned much uglier than he'd anticipated.

Lacy gasped for air and tried to slow her breath. "Oh my God. What the hell was that?"

"He must've recognized you. My God, if we'd been just a few more feet away. I don't know that we would've made it." He reached for her shoulder. "Are you okay?"

"I will be."

"Good. We'd better get inside while we can. There's a shit storm brewing out here."

————

Axell held up his hand. "This is the place. Hang back." He stepped behind the corner of the building beneath a dark grey sky. The fading light made it all the more difficult to continue.

Caison followed as the two waited and checked the time. "Ten minutes," he whispered.

"Assuming he's on schedule," Axell replied in the same hushed response. "We'll just have to sit tight."

"You know how good I am at doing that."

He peered back at Caison. "About as good as me." With gun at the ready, he returned to position. "Hang on. I see headlights coming. Pull back a little."

"That's got to be him, right, Mehmut?"

"Could be Yang's guy." Axell peered at the approaching car. This was the moment he'd waited for. Justice. He would finally get justice for Keith Colburn. It was Yang who brought him down. He knew it and this was how he would handle the problem. Take him out on his own turf. Axell was doing this for no one else but Colburn. And if it meant preventing greater loss of life, good. But that wasn't his first priority. Not by a long shot.

"They're getting out. Two men, I think." Caison studied them, but the absence of light caused his vision to suffer. "Yeah. One of them is Yang."

"Are you sure?"

"I'm sure. I'd recognize the son of a bitch anywhere."

Another car approached.

"Who the hell is that?" Caison asked.

"I don't know. We weren't counting on the whole damn group to show. Shit."

"We'll be outnumbered. Do we pull back? Get Maddox over here?"

"Give me a minute." Axell waited until those inside the second car exited. "It's her. Fatima. I'm sure of it."

"Oh no. What about Maddox? Should I try him on the radio?"

"No. You might draw attention. Damn it. I don't know who the other one is. Now we got four." He watched as they walked into the building several feet from their current location. But just as he was about to pull back again, the trunk of the second car popped open. "What the hell?"

Caison leaned over Axell's shoulder for a better look. And as they watched, it didn't take long to realize who had emerged. The man crouched down low and began walking away from the vehicle.

"Holy shit." Axell turned back. "That son of a bitch hid in the trunk." He smiled and shook his head. "Crazy son of a bitch."

"Maddox," Caison said. "He must've seen what was going down. That Yang showed up at Fatima's first, but he couldn't get a shot."

"Good thing for us. I'm starting to feel better about our odds." Axell watched as their colleague approached, hunched over, and kicking up dirt from the road. "What the hell?"

"Figured you guys might need some help." Maddox returned upright once he'd joined them. "Hope you don't mind."

"What happened?" Axell asked.

"Yang showed up. She started talking about Mehmut, and shortly after, he took off with another guy. And since I didn't want to expose Fatima, Yang told the other guy and her to follow them here. That he was going to get to the bottom of whatever was happening. So here we are. You got any bright ideas, Axell?"

"They're heading into Mehmut's place. We'll have to get a look inside. I have no idea how many are there. And there's a chance we could get off a shot while he's inside," Axell said.

"Sure. If you don't mind dying tonight. I, for one, would rather get back to Beijing in one piece." Maddox took the lead. "We'll get a look-see inside and maybe pick up more intel on when this crazy ass attack is supposed to go down."

———

The embassy doors opened.

"Go on. We're safe here."

"You've risked your cover. It's not too late for you to turn back. I can handle it from here."

"I don't doubt that for one second, but I'll be okay. I can handle myself too." Shaw ushered her inside, taking note of the several embassy officers that had gathered around for extra security. "We need to see the ambassador."

A man in a grey suit approached. "You caused quite a scene out there. Paperwork alone will be a nightmare." He looked at Lacy. "I know who you are. Figured that out as soon as it began. They must've wanted to get their hands on you pretty badly, Lacy Merrick. You got lucky you made it this far." He turned to Shaw. "What I don't know is who you are."

"A friend." Shaw held out his passport with a different name. "I accompanied Mrs. Merrick here to ensure she made it safely."

"That appears to have been a wise call." Once again, he turned to Lacy. "They seem to think you broke the law, Mrs. Merrick. You went into one of their banks and behaved in a disorderly manner. That'll get you in trouble here, you know."

"That's not why they want me and I think you know that."

"I think we should talk someplace a little more private." He turned on his heel.

"Can we see the ambassador or not?" Shaw asked.

"He's not here, unfortunately. So you're stuck with me." He finally offered a greeting. "Chris Macafee, Vice-Consul. Nice to meet you, Lacy Merrick, and you too—friend." He looked at Shaw, appearing to understand the nature of Shaw's background, and acknowledging he would not question it further. "So if you'll both follow me back, we need to talk."

Lacy was relieved to be safely inside the embassy but didn't like this guy and didn't know what his agenda was. She'd begun to feel as though she would become a pawn in this strategic positioning between the two countries. Not exactly as she'd planned when insisting on traveling here with Axell and the others. Which, by the way, she still had no idea if they were actually safe. The plan was for Aaron to get on a later bus. But had he arrived? Had he already known what happened out front? His safety was all but assured in her mind, but that could change depending on what was about to happen with Mr. Macafee.

A guard who'd accompanied them to the second-floor conference room closed the door on his way out.

"Can I get either one of you a drink? I feel as though I could use one right about now." Macafee walked to a cabinet that appeared to house several varieties of liquor.

"I'm fine, thank you," Lacy said.

"Same here. Look, Mr. Macafee, we just need to get Merrick on a plane back to Virginia. Back to her family."

"Before we go down that road, I'd like to understand why it is that you're here in the first place, Mrs. Merrick. It seems unlikely you, of all people, would want to visit here on vacation. And with your friend as an escort." A glance to Shaw. "You will not be officially recognized by the embassy, in case you were concerned. As far as I'm concerned, you're just a friend. Isn't that right?"

He nodded. "Yes, sir."

"I'll get to the point. The ministry wants to know why you're here. They know who you are. We all do. So what could possibly bring you here after everything that's happened back home?"

"You sound as though you're not very fond of me, Mr. Macafee," Lacy said. "I suppose you'd have been happy not to know what really happened. Probably would've maintained the status quo here, am I right?"

"I think we're getting off on the wrong foot here. Why don't we start over?" He sat down at the table. "Please, join me."

Shaw appeared reluctant to oblige but followed Lacy's lead.

"Good. Now. I need you to be honest with me, Mrs. Merrick. Have you traveled alone?"

"Yes."

"Are you sure about that? And before you answer again, just know that the ministry has provided me with the surveillance footage of you walking around the streets of Beijing. And it certainly did not appear as though you were alone."

She wondered why he hadn't mentioned Shaw and how he came to be at the hotel in what turned out to be a rescue effort. Someone here, in Shaw's inner circle, must have been responsible for keeping that out of the equation. Good thing. Meaning Shaw just might make it out of this with his cover intact. "Why does it matter? Am I not free to travel where I want? Did that change the day I decided to expose the truth?"

"Look, you and I both know, Mr. Macafee," Shaw interrupted, "that Merrick isn't safe here. Whatever you think of her, she did what any American would have done, regardless of the fact that it has made your life a little more difficult. I'm sure the families of the hundreds of US citizens who died in the mall attack wish their lives hadn't been made more difficult either. But there you go. I hope you're not considering delaying Merrick's return to the US. She should be allowed to leave on the next flight. She's done nothing wrong."

"She, in fact, did behave in a disruptive manner in a public place. That may not mean much in the US, but here, it's a different story altogether. You, of all people, should realize that. Not to mention she's travelling under a false passport. That's no small offense. I'm afraid the secretary of state has been informed of the situation, given the high profile of Mrs. Merrick."

Lacy closed her eyes for a brief moment. What were the odds the president was going to be informed too, and was he going to let her off? He had to know or at least suspect something was going on. Yang was in-country, Shaw was involved. They were exposed now. And if the president knew, he might make sure she stayed put until the plan was executed. She could say nothing and do nothing if forced to remain in Beijing under a trumped-up charge of inappropriate public conduct. A pile of horseshit in any event. If Axell and Caison didn't succeed, then in all likelihood, Lacy would be forced to stay until Yang did what he came here to do.

Shaw seemed to pick up on the same vibe as he regarded Lacy with growing concern. The writing was on the wall. They were not going to get the help they thought they would. Not now. Not after what happened outside. It was over. And all their eggs were in Maddox's basket.

————

The sky was pitch black. No street lights and only a few homes where bulbs burned on dilapidated front porches. One of which was where Yang resided at this very moment, discussing a plot to kill innocent Chinese and whoever else got in their way on the US government's dime.

The agents approached the edge of Mehmut's home. It was a detached building with obvious wear from years of neglect and erosion.

"How many inside?" Caison asked.

"Looks like five. Including Fatima."

"Any chance we got ears on her?" Caison added.

Maddox turned to him and revealed a half-cocked grin. "This isn't my first rodeo, Caison. Fatima was more than willing to help us out. So long as she's rewarded, which won't be a problem."

"No live feed, though?" Axell pressed on.

"No. I didn't have the time to set it up. And I sure as shit didn't bring the equipment. I thought this was gonna be a smash and grab, you know?"

"Yeah. Best laid plans and all that bullshit."

"Precisely. We'll just have to wait. Although these guys might take care of themselves if Yang believes he's being betrayed by his own people. No one inside looks particularly happy at the moment."

"Wish he'd do us the favor," Caison said. "It'd be better to have smaller numbers."

"Now where's the fun in that?" Maddox returned his attention to the front door. "If one of them comes out, we gotta take 'em down. No ifs or butts or coconuts."

"I don't think that's the right context." Axell tossed a glance at the shadows crossing in front of a side window. "You might get the chance anyway. Get ready, boys."

A flash of light and the crack of rapid gunfire filled the quiet street.

"Shit, shit! What's happening?" Axell said. "We need to move now!"

"Wait!" Maddox stopped him. "Wait till they come out. We go in there and we'll lose our leverage. They don't know we're here and won't see shit if they come out."

More gunfire erupted and the door flew open. Fatima fell to the ground and lay still on her back.

"Son of a bitch!" Maddox's eyes widened with anger. "They fucking got her."

"Goddam it, Maddox. They'll hear you!" Caison's tone was a cross between a whisper and a reprimand.

Four others, including Yang and Mehmut, emerged from the building, weapons aimed at the night and skulking like predators on the hunt.

"Damn it. They know we're here. And they know she was wired," Caison said. "We have to take them out."

"We fire now and we give away our position," Axell said. "Caison, go around the backside. Maddox and I will take cover at the car. That's when all hell's going to break loose. Be ready and be careful. Go! Now!"

Caison ran around to the back of the building and watched as Yang and three other men continued to peer into the darkness. His steps drew their attention, briefly, but they turned back at a disturbance ahead. It was Axell and Maddox making their way to the car. He knew what Axell wanted to do. They were in position. He'd been here before. Axell would draw their fire so he could get a clean shot. It would be hard as hell in the dark, but they had no other choice. Yang couldn't be allowed to leave. They had to take him down and now was the time.

Caison made his way to the opposite end of the building and began to move toward the front. No sign of gunfire from his side or theirs. Maybe he could take the shot before they spotted the rest of his team.

At that moment, a voice broke through. "Are you happy now? She's dead. You forced her to betray me and she paid with her life."

It was Yang. Caison had heard the man enough times to know the voice.

"We know why you're here, Yang."

"Shit," Caison whispered. He knew it was Axell and that he wanted Yang to fire. Catch him off guard so Will could do what he needed to do.

"Do you know that it was your government that sent me? They wanted to help me free the people of Uyghur." Yang continued to aim his weapon at no particular target. "And in return, I give them information on the MSS. It was a perfect solution."

Axell and Maddox remained behind the car several yards away, but it wouldn't take them long to realize that was just about the only hiding place there was in the area. Residents began to emerge but quickly retreated at the sight of what was happening.

"You're being used, Yang. The only thing our government wants is retribution and you're the catalyst. We won't let you do it. You have to know that, Yang. Doesn't matter what my government does. I won't let you do it. I know it was your people who killed Agent Colburn. Probably the Meekses too."

Caison's mouth was slightly ajar. At that moment, he realized Axell's agenda. He wanted to be the one to take out Yang. Maybe that wasn't how this started, but as sure as he was standing here now, gun ready to fire, that was how it was going to end.

"Was it you, then, Agent Axell? You who killed Wendell Turner for revenge?"

A prolonged silence was soon broken by the sound of a bullet striking the hood of the car that rang out into the streets with a ping. Trails of light sparked and faded on impact.

Yang had pegged Axell's location and fired the first shot. "You know my friends will not let you leave, even if you do manage to kill me. This will not end tonight. It will not end until the Party pays for their treatment of my people."

How long would it be before this old-fashioned stand-off drew the attention of the police? The village was rural, but the Party kept a tight rein on the region. If they showed up, Caison and his team stood little chance of leaving alive. And if that happened, CIA operatives would be exposed, relations wouldn't just be strained anymore. They'd be nonexistent.

This had to end now. And Caison was going to have to be the one to do it.

He aimed his weapon at the shadow of a target. It appeared as though the man on the right was Yang, but he just couldn't be sure. He'd have to be prepared to kill them both. But the other men were no longer in his sights. "Damn it, Axell. I hope you have them."

As Yang again fired on the vehicle, Caison took tighter aim, his eye closed and his hands placed firmly on the weapon. He released the safety. The crack of his gun echoed in the street and Yang fell. The other man turned and began firing at Caison.

Both agents emerged from behind the car at the erupting gunfire from Yang's associates. Axell marched forward and began firing. The sky lit up with flashes of light from every direction. The other men were hunkered down near a home several feet away. They fired back.

Axell ducked again for cover near the car. "Maddox! Behind you!" He turned back. Two shots, in the dark, a man fell next to Yang. It was Mehmut.

The other men had revealed their position and the agents fired on them. Caison emerged and offered cover as Axell and Maddox made their way toward them, firing along the way.

Rounds pinged nearby cars, hurled into the dirt streets and screams sounded in nearby houses. It would only be minutes before the police arrived. They were out of time.

Then the shots ended. Maddox had taken out one and Axell the other. But the problem wasn't nearly over yet. They needed a way out and Axell was pissed.

"What the hell?" Axell rushed to Caison. "He was mine!"

"I had to take the shot. It was the best chance we had. Axell, if we don't get the hell out of here before the police show, we won't get out at all."

"He's right. We need to jam. Van's waiting a mile away. Run now!"

CHAPTER
TWENTY-SIX

PROTECTED beneath a heavy hooded coat and veiled in darkness, Aaron approached the embassy. The familiar red and blue lights of patrol cars flashed as he drew near, except these spun atop cars plastered with Chinese characters on the hoods and doors. He stopped in his tracks, unclear as to his next move. Something appeared to have gone terribly wrong. Was Lacy inside or had she been taken away, detained in a police station somewhere in the city? What about Agent Shaw?

He continued to assess the situation, knowing a decision must be made now before his presence captured the attention of nearby authorities. Aaron turned around and headed in the direction from which he came. The only solution was to try to make contact with Shaw. And if that didn't work, wait until Axell was within range and try him again. Though he hadn't spoken with him since leaving for the bus station, he had to assume they made it to Kashgar, praying the job was done.

Equipped with a CIA-issue cell phone, a welcome gift from Shaw, Aaron walked to a nearby bench and sat down to make the call. The line rang as he peered onto the streets and watched the cars and people pass by. "Come on. Answer, damn it."

"Hello?"

"Shaw, it's Hunter. Where are you? Where's Lacy?"

"Aaron Hunter?"

His stomach dropped as he pulled the phone away from his ear, double-checking the number he dialed. The voice on the other end sounded nothing like Shaw. "Who is this?"

"Mr. Hunter, it would be wise for you to come to the embassy. Your safety has become a concern."

"Where's Shaw?"

"I'm not sure who Shaw is. I do believe you're familiar with Lacy Merrick. She was accompanied by a friend. He's here, speaking with the vice-consul now. And so is she. We're here to protect you, Mr. Hunter. Please, you need to come in. They will be looking for you too."

"Who's looking for me? I've done nothing wrong and neither have my friends."

"You're traveling under false documents, Mr. Hunter. You won't be allowed to leave the country until that is resolved. The Chinese government is aware. So again, I advise you to enter the embassy where we can ensure your safety—and that of your traveling companions."

"Why do I get the feeling I'm being threatened?"

"No one is threatening you. But you have broken the law and this is not a country in which law enforcement is lax. I'm sure you understand my meaning."

He ended the call without another word. "Shit." They had Lacy. They had Shaw and now they wanted him too. But was this man telling the truth? That the embassy was protecting them and wanted to do the same for him. His gut railed against what his head was shouting. Do as they asked and go to the embassy, trust his government, and confirm Lacy was safe. Or flee to a place off the beaten path and wait to make contact with Axell.

"No." He stood up. "No." He tried Axell's phone, squeezing shut his eyes. "Come on, man. Answer. I need you, man. I need your help." Still, the line rang.

"Hunter, what's going on?"

"Oh, thank God. Axell, where are you guys?"

"Landing on the outskirts of Beijing. The problem's been handled."

Aaron knew that meant Yang was dead and that they'd all made it out alive. But the relief he felt was short-lived. "Lacy and Shaw are at the embassy."

"Good."

"No, man. It's not good. There are a shit ton of cops out front. I tried calling Shaw and got someone else inside the embassy. Says we're all in trouble because of false travel docs or some shit. I don't know, man. He said I should go there so they could protect me."

"What? They aren't sending her home?"

"Not yet. I don't know if they're going to. Axell, we got a real problem here and I'm standing on some street corner in the middle of the city and I don't know what the fuck to do. Man, you gotta help me. We gotta make sure Lacy and Shaw are okay."

"Calm down, Hunter. Take a breath. As long as they're inside the embassy, no one can harm them."

"Then what do I do?"

"Stay out of sight. Go to some small coffee shop or something, off the main roads. Stay there until we can get to you. Do not go to the embassy alone. Wait for us and we'll figure out what to do."

"How long?"

"An hour. I'm sure we can be there inside an hour. I'll call you when we're near and you can give me your location."

"Yeah, okay."

"Hunter, it'll be okay. We'll find a solution."

Aaron ended the call and raised his head to gaze at the stars for an answer, only there were no stars. The sky was tainted with a milky haze that made him feel all the more isolated. He started in search of a place to take cover in hopes Axell and Caison would arrive soon.

———

FBI Director Mobley pulled on his coat and grabbed his car keys. "I'm heading out. I'll see you tonight, hon." He kissed his wife on the cheek and stepped outside to the clear morning skies.

His late model BMW started easily in the cold weather and he backed out of the driveway, the wiper blades whisking away the thin blanket of ice on his windshield. He reached for his coffee when his cell phone rang through the Bluetooth in his car. "Mobley here."

"Are you in the office yet?"

"I'm on my way. Why?"

"We need to meet. Now."

"Okay. What's the problem?"

"Our entire task force is out of the country and I just received a call from the vice-consul at the Beijing embassy. They have Lacy Merrick along with who I can only assume is one of my operatives."

Mobley turned deadpan. "Why is she there? Where are Agents Axell and Caison? What the hell is going on, Handley?"

"Your guess is as good as mine. That's why we need to meet and straighten this out before we find ourselves in the middle of some damn international incident. How soon can you be at Langley?"

"Sooner than my office. I'm on my way." He ended the call and turned the wheel, heading north to Langley. "Son of a bitch."

Heat climbed from beneath the collar of his button-down shirt. Why were his people there, more importantly, why hadn't they kept him apprised? They still didn't trust him. Perhaps it was deserved, but now he was going in blind, a disadvantage that could put them in greater jeopardy. "Damn it!" He slammed his palm against the steering wheel.

CIA Headquarters was in his sights now and he approached the guarded entrance. Presenting his credentials, the guard raised the gate and Mobley drove onto the grounds. As he made his way inside the building, the director waited for him.

"Thank you for coming down so quickly." Handley tendered a greeting.

"Sounds like we have a problem brewing. And I'd like to know exactly what that is."

———

Aaron hadn't taken his eyes off the street ahead as he waited in the coffee shop for help to arrive. Time was almost up and still no sign of Axell or Caison. He'd given Axell his location more than twenty minutes ago and expected them to have arrived by now, keeping in mind that the city was busy and it wasn't easy to move around undetected, out of sight of the cameras. In fact, it was virtually impossible, which made him more anxious.

He pushed up from his chair, nearly knocking it over. "Oh my God! Finally." He spotted their arrival.

Axell raised his hands and motioned for Aaron to take it down a notch, to not draw attention. "We're okay. We got delayed, that's all. Just tell us what happened."

Aaron walked back to the table where Caison and Maddox

joined them. "You don't know how glad I am to see you guys." He exposed a smile infused with relief. "I didn't know what to do."

"They're at the embassy? Is that right?" Caison began.

"Yeah. Yeah, like I said, I called Shaw. Some guy answered his phone. Said Lacy was there with a friend and wanted me to come in. But he didn't give Shaw's name."

"He didn't want to blow his cover in the event the Chinese were listening. And you mentioned it was because Lacy was traveling under false documents?" Axell continued.

"Yeah and me too." He shook his head. "We aren't getting out of here, are we?"

"We are," Axell said. "I just need you to take a breath and tell me. Did you do what I asked when you arrived?"

"You mean about mailing the..."

"Yes."

"I did. I went to a DHL."

"Good. That's very good. We might need to use that as leverage when the time comes."

"How are we going to get home? I mean, it sounded like they wanted to turn us over to the Chinese police or something."

"They want us to be scared of exactly that. But there's no chance, not with what we know, that we'll be turned over to anyone except our own government," Axell said.

"Right now, I don't know which is worse."

"Neither do I, Hunter."

"What are we going to do about Lacy and Shaw?" Caison asked.

Maddox rubbed his rounded chin and smacked his lips a few times. "My suggestion is we do what they want. Go down there. It's the only way we'll get her and Shaw out of this mess. What you have to remember is Shaw and I are valuable." He held up preemptive hands. "Not saying you guys aren't. What I mean to say is that we're still rebuilding here and can't risk being exposed to the MSS again. I know damn well Handley won't have that. He may be a lot of things, but going turncoat on his case officers isn't one of them."

"That's what I thought until Janz was shot right in front of me," Axell said. "I would've been too if I hadn't gotten out of there as quickly as I did. So I'm not sure where you're getting your information, but my level of trust for Handley is about at zero."

Maddox nodded. "Point being, we get inside the embassy, talk to whoever's got our people, and figure this shit out. Axell and I agree on one thing, our government's risking a lot as it is simply by us being here. It won't be long before they discover Yang's fate. And they know what'll happen if MSS gets hold of us. At least, they think they know, but I suspect none of us would give them a goddam thing." He pushed up from the chair. "So let's get the show on the road. See what we can work out to get you and your people back home."

It was hard to overlook the four men who emerged from the coffee shop, with the exception of Maddox. The rest were easy targets to spot if the right people knew what to look for.

"It's best we split up and each head in our own direction," Axell said. "No offense, but you people scream CIA."

"You people?" Maddox unleashed a boisterous laugh. "I thought you were one of us, Axell?"

Caison noted the exchange. "I'm not finding a lot of humor in this situation, so you'll forgive me for not joining in on the banter."

Axell turned serious. "If you don't think I understand the severity of the situation, Caison, then you don't know me as well as you thought you did. Look, I want her on a plane home to see her family just as much as you. But these are the cards we were dealt. Now we have to play them." He surveyed the streets. "Go over there. I'll stay on this path. Hunter, you head in the same direction, but hang back a good hundred feet from Caison."

"I know where I'm going." Maddox made a sharp turn and disappeared.

"If the cops are still there, just make contact with the guard out front. There'll be plenty of them at this point, I'm sure. But do not go in until we are all together. Understand?" He looked at Caison and Hunter, who nodded simultaneously. "Good. Now go."

Axell waited in place until they were well enough ahead before taking his own path. He knew they were afraid for Lacy. So was he. He was afraid for all of them. How long would it be before the authorities realized Yang was dead and got word back to Beijing? A few hours? A day? With the heavy presence the Party had in that village, it would likely be the former.

He thought about the woman, Fatima, and how they must've known she was wearing a wire. Maddox had been running her for some time and he must've felt responsible too, no doubt. And if he was being honest, they didn't need her to record anything. Not really. They already had evidence Yang received money from the US and his ties to the Separatist Movement were easily established. Her information was more like the icing on the cake. Concrete proof Yang was planning an attack. It would have been useful, but not worth her life.

Axell checked the time. It would be about 9 am in D.C. Would they already know about Lacy and Shaw too? That would present additional problems. And the hits just kept coming. Stories needed to be consolidated, firmed up. "Damn." As he made his way along the streets in the bitter night air, he cursed himself for not being the one to bring her back. Shaw was a good man and a good agent, but she was one of his, and Axell should've been there.

The embassy was in sight. It didn't appear the local police were out front. Finally, something that was in their favor. Because so long as any of them were on this side of the fence, they could be snatched.

He spotted the others near the guard gate and continued his approach, more hurried than before. Perhaps he was more concerned about being captured than he thought. Still, breaking into a sprint toward the guard gate wasn't advisable either. Not unless he wanted to get shot.

"I see you've met my friends," Axell said to the guard.

"You must be Trevor Axell?" The guard turned to walk back into the booth. "Good. These guys said they wouldn't go in until you arrived. I'll make the call and have them open the gate. Been pretty interesting around here for the past few hours. Don't suppose you know anything about that?"

"Nope. Afraid not. We just heard a couple friends of ours were inside. And we'd like to see what we can do to help them out."

"Sure." He made the call.

Axell nodded to the others in recognition and relief of their safe arrival.

"Okay. Let's open her up." The guard walked out of his booth again and approached the iron gates. "You all have a good evening and I hope everything turns out all right for your friends."

The gates opened and the officers on the other side allowed them through. Caison was the first to notice their fixed gaze. "Is it me, or does it look to you guys like they were expecting us?"

"Oh, I imagine word spread pretty quickly about who's inside. Yeah, I doubt these guys see that sort of excitement much around here," Maddox replied.

"How are you so calm?" Aaron asked.

Maddox stopped short. "Cause I've seen a whole hell of a lot worse things than this, my friend. This?" He shook his head. "Water off a duck's back."

Axell was curious if Maddox knew the whole story, and if he did, then God bless him because, in all his years in the CIA, nothing had prepared him for this kind of deception by his own director. Oh, he wasn't naïve and knew that over the course of the past fifty-odd years, the CIA had done its share of funding coups, arming rebels, and even covering up its own involvement in the drug wars. But something of this magnitude that could bring about a large-scale war, possibly nuclear, was nothing to sneeze at. And the weight of stopping this political machine had just about ground him down to nothing.

The doors of the building parted and inside awaited several men in suits. One stepped forward. "I'd say introductions were in order, but I feel as though I already know you all." He moved toward them. "Come in. I'll take you to your friends."

"And you are?" Axell asked.

"I work for the vice-consul. He's been working with your people for the past few hours." The man continued to lead the way through the corridor. His shoes struck the marble floor with a decisive echo. "In here, please." He opened the door, and inside, Lacy stood near a window. Shaw was in a chair at a conference table.

"You're here." Her face was masked in relief.

"Are you okay?" Caison asked.

"I am."

Axell turned to the man who let them in. "Where's the vice-consul?"

"He'll be here in a moment. Have a seat. I'll have beverages and snacks brought in."

When he closed the door and they were alone, Lacy remained still, appearing on the verge of tears. "I'm glad you're all okay. We've just been sitting here—waiting."

Agent Shaw stood. "The director and the president know we're here. Don't suppose you have a plan?"

CHAPTER
TWENTY-SEVEN

DIRECTOR MOBLEY HAD ONLY BEEN in the Oval Office a handful of times. The last was on the unfortunate occasion when he had attempted to circumvent then Deputy Secretary Turner on the discovery of the arrangement his under-secretary had with Lei Jian. In the end, he agreed to the secretary's terms, something he'd begun to regret even more so now than he did then. Perhaps this could all have been avoided. Now he sat here with the CIA director, waiting for the president to arrive so that they could discuss how to get their people back home. The same people who had put their trust in Mobley the first time and he'd let them down. That wouldn't happen again.

They both stood on the president's arrival.

"Have a seat, gentlemen." The president joined them and sat on the opposite sofa. "I'd hoped to put the events of the past behind me, behind the administration, yet here we all are, once again, as I enter into my second term. How the hell did this happen?"

"If I may, sir," Handley began, "we believe Trevor Axell traveled first to Beijing to arrange a plan with other CIA operatives in the area, then traveled to Xinjiang on this occasion to find Shen Yang. To kill him."

"And the rest of his team thought they'd join him? And we let it happen? Why weren't their passports flagged?"

"The members of our task force joined Axell and all arranged travel under false passports. Which, given the level of knowledge and access certain members of the team employ, would've been all too easy to obtain. From what the director here has told me, Axell seems to have gone off the rails."

"Excuse me?" Mobley appeared stunned.

"I, too, find it hard to believe, but shortly before we arrived here this morning, I confirmed with the ASAC at the WFO. The gun used to kill Deputy Secretary Turner was a match to a gun found in Axell's home."

"Our own CIA officer who was instrumental in helping Lacy Merrick kill Wendell Turner?" the president asked.

"It appears so, sir."

"I believe he was avenging the death of another agent who was lost at what Axell believed to be at the hands of Shen Yang. Or at least his people," Director Handley continued. "And not only that, sir, but our current predicament suggests his revenge didn't stop at Turner. And the reason he went to Xinjiang, along with his team, was to take out the man who he believed was ultimately responsible."

"Yang," the president replied.

"Yes, sir."

Mobley had to pick up his jaw off the floor. Was he hearing this right?

"So we have a team of highly trained CIA and FBI agents along with an expert data analyst and cyber-hacker sitting at the US embassy in Beijing?"

"That's right, Mr. President."

"I'm dumbfounded by this news, Mr. President," Mobley added. "I can't believe these people would be capable of such an act. And frankly, I think the only thing we can do is bring them home. We need to hear their side of the story."

"Don't you think the Chinese will object to that?"

"We returned Lei Jian to allow them to take care of him themselves. I would suggest we remind them of that and ensure they extend the courtesy to us. After all, what they're doing doesn't come close to comparing with what Lei Jian arranged with members of our own government. Regardless of how ill-advised this mission was, we can't leave our people there. And especially not these particular people. You must understand what they would do to Merrick. The government blames her for the sanctions. She wouldn't survive a week there. And I don't know what they'd do to the others, but I imagine they would eventually end up with the same fate."

The president stood. "Director Mobley, I understand your position. However, I think this is a problem the CIA must handle. After what happened to his operatives over there, Handley is best equipped to ensure the team's safety. For the sake of plausible deniability on your behalf, as Merrick is one of yours, I think it best if you excuse yourself from the remainder of this meeting."

"Sorry?" Mobley was taken aback by the request. These were his people—his task force. And the idea of leaving it up to the CIA to handle was outrageous.

"I'm sure you understand. The director will keep you informed as best he can. However, we need someone in the intelligence community to be divorced from this mission. For all our sakes. I think it'll be up to his team to take care of this in an effort to avoid starting a war."

Mobley eyed the two men and neither appeared to waver on the decision. "This is bullshit and you know it."

"Remember who you're addressing, director," the president said.

Mobley finally stood and was escorted out of the room.

After he took his leave, the president turned his attention to Handley. "He doesn't know?"

"No, sir. I kept him out of the loop. I thought it best for everyone."

"It is. Do we know if Yang is still alive?"

"I'm working on getting that information as we speak."

"Get back with me when you know for certain. That'll determine our next course of action." The president returned to his desk.

"Thank you, sir."

———

The ambassador pushed through the door where the team waited. "What the hell is going on? Do you have any idea what you've done? I've got the US and Chinese presidents demanding answers. Both are eager to know why it is that a handful of US citizens, members of the intelligence community, have traveled here on false passports and come to find out, an incident in the Xinjiang region was reported by the police there. Five dead. One of whom was a prominent Chinese businessman in the US. So, who wants to start first?"

Axell stood ready to shoulder the blame. "We have reason to believe this businessman was planning an attack in Beijing over the Chinese New Year celebrations. My team and I came here to stop it."

The ambassador pulled out a chair at the table and dropped into it. Shoulders slumped and head down, he continued. "Christ. How do you know this?"

"Mr. Ambassador, the history my team and I have with this businessman is extensive. We've been tracking his movements since the sanctions were put into place. Even before that time. It was believed his company acted in a manner as to avoid the sanctions and we were tasked with following the money and determining if any illegal actions took place. In the course of our investigation, we discovered Shen Yang, CEO of the Dalian Company, which is headquartered here in Beijing, was working with and was part of, the Uyghur Separatist Movement. I'm sure you're familiar with that organization."

"I am."

"He and others inside the organization were planning a large-scale attack in the city. Our actions were an effort to prevent that attack that would undoubtedly result in greater strains between the two countries. Perhaps worse. And with his death, we believe we succeeded."

Lacy looked to Axell and wondered if he would reveal that the president and other high-ranking US officials were footing the bill for the attack.

"You'd better show me some proof of your claim," the ambassador replied.

"I don't have it here, sir. As a matter of precaution, it is somewhere safe."

"Then what am I supposed to tell the president? The Chinese president too? Do you think he's going to sign off on letting you leave this country without punishment for your actions?"

"We stopped a terror attack. We saved his people."

"Not without proof. Right now, you and your team are murderers and illegals in this country."

"They had nothing to do with the incident in Xinjiang," Maddox stepped in. "I knew the targets. I took them out. All of them. Unfortunately, his terrorist buddies got in the way and I took them down too. So sue me."

Axell swung his head around to Maddox. "What the hell are you talking about?" You didn't..."

"Mr. Ambassador, you can tell that commie prick of a Chinese president I took care of a problem for him. I'll take payment in the form of US dollars."

"Are you confessing to murdering Chinese citizens?"

"Did I stutter? I mean, yes, sir. It was my job and I did it."

The rest of the team, including Shaw, appeared shocked, mouths agape and in disbelief at what Maddox had done. He just signed his own death warrant.

"You should let these fine people go home. They're going to have to answer for a good many things, I imagine, on return. But this, they are not guilty of. They did their jobs and it's up to the people well above my pay grade to give them the credit they deserve. This man was planning a terrorist attack from the US. Preying on the people of the region who'd been persecuted for years for their beliefs. They did China a big, fat, juicy favor whether you want to believe it or not."

"We all did," Axell replied.

The ambassador stood again and eyed each of them. "I'll do what I can to get them to allow the rest of you to leave. Agent Maddox, I'm afraid no amount of CIA pull will get you out of this one. You will have to stay and pay for your crimes. There's no way around that. And frankly, I can't assure any of you that they will in fact let you go. You broke their laws. They'll want something in exchange. Something big. And I imagine it will start with the easing or eliminating of sanctions." He began to leave. "The price the rest of you pay will be determined by the president on your return."

After the ambassador left, Shaw marched to Maddox. "Do you

have any idea what you've done? They're going to kill you. Why would you do that? Axell said he's got proof. We all did these assholes a favor."

"You really think the president is going to let any of this get out into the open? His administration, the CIA; they all conspired to help Yang plan the attack. They wanted it. Hell, they paid for it." He shook his head. "This was the only way I could make sure you get home. And to be honest, you'll all probably be in far more danger there than here, I'm sorry to say."

"I can't let you take the fall for this, Maddox."

"I already did, Axell. Besides, I got lucky once before. The time's come for me to pay the piper."

"What are you talking about?"

"I'm talking about when the Chinks took out our operatives. I should've been there when they found our people. Instead, I went home and visited my father before he passed. When I came back, I was too late. They'd found almost all of us. I found some of them. Shot in the heads. Left to rot in some stinking abandoned safe house. It should've been me. This is what I have to do to make it right. Your job." He looked at the others. "Their job is to make sure the administration doesn't get away with it. I understand why they did what they did. The mall attack was, well, it was horrific. But this would've destroyed so many more lives. At home and here. Look at what's happening at home right now. Job losses, riots, Chinese Americans getting their asses kicked by idiots who don't care that it wasn't their fault."

Shaw turned to Axell. "Still doesn't mean they'll let us go. Where is this proof?"

"Not in this country. That's all I can say right now." He cast a brief glance at Aaron. "They'll let us go. They want the sanctions lifted more than they want a few of us to rot in their jails."

"Do you think the president will make the deal?" Lacy asked. "Why would he risk exposure?"

"He'll make the deal. Because if we tell the Chinese what the US did, that will start a war."

———

The door to the Oval Office opened as the president stood behind his desk. He turned away from the window and peered at the man entering, hoping he had the answers he sought.

Director Handley's face was masked in defeat. "It was Yang, Mr. President. He's dead. And his colleagues. All were shot in an apparent gun battle."

The president slammed his fist on the desk as objects resting atop it quaked. The noise prompted a secret service agent to open the door. "I'm fine. Go." His chest rose and fell with increasing momentum. A rising tide of anger swelled beneath his collar and the veins in his neck jutted.

"I'm sorry, sir. This wasn't supposed to happen."

"No. It wasn't." He eyed the director. "What are our options?"

"With Yang gone," Handley shook his head. "I don't see how... the money, the connections. I—it's over, Mr. President." The lump in his throat, the taste of defeat, he swallowed down. "One of my operatives took responsibility for the deaths. I can only imagine it was an effort to save the others. He's being handed over to Chinese authorities as we speak."

"Did he do it?"

"I don't know. He was there, but I don't know if he pulled the trigger. It's possible he was protecting the others."

"Agent Axell."

"That's my guess. I wouldn't have chosen this outcome by any means, sir. And certainly not at the expense of a good agent. But what's done is done and I'll need to clean this up."

"Where are the others? Still at the embassy?"

The director nodded.

"Bring them home. The sooner the better."

"There's one other thing, sir. In my conversations with the ambassador, it was relayed to me that the minister, speaking on behalf of the premier, wants to make a trade for the release of our people."

"Well, it wouldn't be too hard to figure out what they want."

"No, sir."

"I'll have to speak with the secretary so we can figure out what we can do and more importantly, consider damage control. Rolling back sanctions is going to require congressional approval. This will end my administration."

"It doesn't have to, sir. We get them back here, they'll deal. I'm sure of it. Too much has happened in this country over the past year, and if this gets out, they know as well as we do the reaction of the American people. I don't think anyone wants that. Not even them. I think they thought they were doing the right thing."

"What? Letting the Chinese off the hook for killing hundreds of our citizens? I thought Merrick, of all people, would've wanted retribution. Same as us." He turned again toward the window overlooking the rose garden. "You've swept the agents' homes? Task force headquarters?"

"Yes, sir. Nothing we could find that would implicate you or anyone. Like I said, I don't think they want this out."

"Time will tell, won't it? And the Merrick residence? She will be the one we need to worry about the most. We betrayed them all, and I think she's all out of forgiveness."

"We took care of it. Her children were at school. We made sure the nanny was out. Nothing turned up there either."

"Good. Just be sure they don't bring anything back."

CHAPTER
TWENTY-EIGHT

THE DRONE of the airplane preoccupied Lacy enough to squelch the voice in her head and mask the images that replayed in her mind. They'd done what they'd set out to do, but at what cost? Agent Maddox would be dead if he wasn't already. Left to pay the price for their actions. Agent Shaw's cover was blown. The directive came down to place him elsewhere. Siberia was her best guess. Some miserable place where he would spend the rest of his days pushing papers or who knew what else. His career was over, but at least he'd get to live.

Soon it would be their turn. And as Lacy turned to Trevor, noting he slept, she worried. Aaron, who stared at the small television screen affixed to the headrest in front of him. And Will, whose career might also be over. In fact, this was likely a career-ending move for all of them, if they were lucky enough to only suffer such recourse.

Once again, they'd been deceived, and once again, they'd discovered the truth. And it remained uncertain how they would leverage that against a president she believed was trying to do the right thing, but in an unforgivable manner.

She felt Will's hand touch her shoulder and turned to him.

"You okay?" he asked.

"No. You?"

"Not really. No."

"What happens when we get home?"

"I don't know. I don't know the details of the agreement. What the president had to give up to get us home."

"Whatever it was, we'll be paying for it." She turned away. "What are we going to do, Will?"

"You did the right thing. We all did. If Yang had gone through with it..."

"I know. More lives lost. More devastation." She turned back to him. "But what if we were wrong? What if Yang had done it and the president got what he wanted? A Chinese civil war. Economic collapse. What if that's what they deserved and we stopped it? They were behind the attack."

"Lei Jian was behind the mall attack. Not the entire Chinese government."

"Yeah, well, what if we were wrong about that too?"

———

The employee returned to the counter with a small package in hand where Director Mobley waited. "Here you go, sir."

"Thank you." Mobley took the package and left the facility.

He drove back to the office, stealing glances at it, wondering what it contained. Axell had sent it to him for a reason. Postmarked Beijing. And after what he'd witnessed inside the Oval Office several days ago, he could only imagine what it must be.

On his return, Mobley closed his office door and set the package on his desk. With a pair of scissors, he sliced open the seal. Inside was a flash drive covered in layers of bubble wrap. And a note. Upon retrieving it, he inserted the drive into a secure computer and loaded the contents. He didn't know exactly what was on there, except that the note indicated it was proof of the conspiracy planned out, in part by CIA Director Handley. But no proof of the president's involvement. While he'd been left in the dark, he became suspicious after being dismissed from the president's office that fateful day. So, Axell's assumption of the president's involvement was well within reason as far as he was concerned. And when Axell asked that he retrieve the package ahead of their return from Beijing, Mobley figured it was evidence of something terrible.

Now he was looking at it. Yang's personal bank accounts with large deposits, shell companies that traced back to Dalian. Money former CIA officer Casper Janz moved from secret accounts to Yang. It was all here. Right in front of him. Proof that the CIA director conspired to fund a terrorist attack spearheaded by a prominent Chinese businessman, whose company had managed a work-around on the sanctions. Thanks once again to Casper Janz and another money man, Malcolm Ford.

"For God's sake." Mobley stared at the evidence before him. Something in him, however, seemed to know this day would come. He didn't want to believe the president was involved, but it would be impossible to ignore the clues. And by all accounts, this was more an act of revenge than betraying his country. But it made this no less difficult to swallow. In a time when the American people needed a president above reproach, an administration incapable of further deceit, they would learn of yet more. And Axell had sent him this without knowing that he was about to be charged in the murder of Wendell Turner.

He checked the time and knew what needed to be done. Their flight was due to arrive and they would be sent to Langley and held until the president could get there. However, Mobley would be there too, unbeknownst to the president or the CIA director. He would be there because Axell, Caison, Hunter, and Merrick needed him now. And he would not turn his back on them, not again.

————

It was déjà vu all over again. In a secure room, the team waited for the president. Only this time, the circumstances were much different. They were on the receiving end of an administration that wanted nothing more than to keep them quiet. Lacy would not be hailed a hero. She would not be thanked by a grateful president. But what she didn't know was what he would do to ensure their silence.

The door opened, revealing CIA Director Handley and the president. This was it. Maddox would give his life for this. Lacy hoped it wasn't in vain.

"I can't tell you what a disappointment it is for me to have to see you all here today." The president approached the table where the team sat. "I don't know if you four realize the position you put this country in by doing what you did."

Lacy held her tongue.

"The sanctions placed on China have been all but surrendered as a direct result. Because we certainly couldn't let it be known that you, Mrs. Merrick, the one bright spot in an otherwise troubling time, were imprisoned in the country responsible for killing your husband, among many other Americans. So my administration and Congress gave in. The price for such a betrayal to the public is as of yet unquantified. And there's no way to tell how public opinion will regard you as a result. My guess is—unkindly."

"And after it's revealed that you, Agent Axell, were the one responsible for the murder of Deputy Secretary Turner, well, I can only assume the public will turn against you as well. Regardless of what the man did to cover up his involvement, you prevented justice from doing its job," the director said.

Lacy shot a look at him. This wasn't in the plan. "What are they talking about?"

"We found the weapon in your apartment, Agent Axell. Forensics matched it to the ammunition and shell casings," Handley continued.

Axell stared at the men in front of him. Unmoved. Unshaken. He'd been here before.

"Axell didn't kill Turner," Will began. "There's no way. There were no casings found on the scene. I know because I was there. Where's Agent Fraser? He'll corroborate my findings."

Had she been right? Lacy turned away. She'd suspected him, but to hear it. It didn't seem possible. Especially now, in light of all they'd just been through. He wasn't there that morning and it had haunted her ever since. But she just couldn't believe it was really possible.

"He's right, Caison," Axell replied. "Turner was ultimately responsible for the death of Keith Colburn and Camden Meeks. No one's been convicted of treason in this country in years. He was going to get off. We didn't get the proof we needed to pin the murders on him. But we all know he ordered it. Even if Yang's people carried it out."

Aaron shook his head. "No. There's no way. You're only telling them what they want to hear. They want you gone and this is how they're going to do it."

"You're wrong, Hunter." Axell stared at his boss, a man he'd once admired. "At least I gave a shit about my brothers."

The door opened and the FBI director entered, flanked by several agents. "Director Handley, you're under arrest."

"Excuse me? What the hell are you doing?"

The agents approached him and grabbed his arms.

"Mr. President, Director Handley was responsible for funding, through various illegal sources, a planned terror attack against Beijing. Shen Yang was spearheading the operation and using millions of US dollars transferred to him by Casper Janz under Handley's direction. These people before you now are directly responsible for preventing that attack."

"And you have evidence of this?" the president asked, appearing thrown.

"Yes, sir. I also have evidence that the secretary of state was involved. A judge signed a warrant only hours ago that granted access to the secretary's phone records and emails. There is evidence he conspired with the director and Yang himself." He waited for a response, but the president was quiet. "I have a team at the secretary's office now and he's being placed under arrest."

The corner of Axell's lip turned up just slightly.

"Then I assume you're also here to arrest Agent Axell for the murder of Deputy Secretary Turner?"

"I'm afraid not, sir. My team, including the agent in charge of that investigation, discovered evidence the actual suspect was involved with an anti-government faction that planned and carried out Turner's assassination. Apparently, they believed he was behind the mall attack as well." He quickly eyed Axell.

Lacy noted the exchange between the men.

"The murder weapon was found in Agent Axell's apartment," Handley said. "How the fuck do you account for that?"

"I don't have to. The weapon used to kill Turner was found in the home of the shooter early this morning. I don't know what gun you found in Agent Axell's apartment, but it wasn't the one used on Turner."

"Mr. President, my team, and primarily, Aaron Hunter and Lacy Merrick, were instrumental in getting the proof against

Handley and the now deceased Casper Janz. They risked their lives to prove the US was funding a planned attack. And Director Mobley has the evidence in his possession. But what he doesn't have is evidence, concrete evidence, that you were also behind the plan." Axell held up his hand at the first sign the president was about to speak. "Don't. He knows it. We all do. But knowing isn't enough, is it? And it's possible Handley will admit it, but I've known him for a long time. Protecting you is the only thing that matters to him."

"I don't think the people of this country can handle another scandal and certainly not of this magnitude, Mr. President," Mobley added. "Trust is fragile and if they suspect you had a hand in it, you will not survive your second term."

"Are you threatening me?"

"No. I'm telling you, your only option is to resign."

The president grumbled. "You can't be serious? Even if they think I was involved, you know how many people here wanted to see revenge for what they did to us? What they did to your husband, Mrs. Merrick? You think they'll turn against me? You're wrong. They'll stand behind me. Take a look outside, Mobley. You see what's happening. They'll cheer my name in the streets for defending this country."

"The ramifications if Yang had been successful would have been war," Mobley replied.

"You're wrong. China would've gone to war with itself and that would only help us. You are so naïve."

"I guess we'll never have to find out, will we, Mr. President?" Mobley grabbed the CIA director. "We'll see how this plays out and how the public will view what you did."

———

Two weeks of discourse, riots, outrage. While the sanctions against China were lifted in exchange for the return of Lacy Merrick, Aaron Hunter, Will Caison, and Trevor Axell, the world turned against the administration, and so did the American people.

"The global impact of a China at war with itself, stoked by the US government would have brought about economic collapse worldwide," the president began. "And those responsible have been held accountable. But I have heard the cries. The calls for resignation. The rampant corruption in my administration falls squarely on my shoulders. This happened under my watch. And it is out of my deep love for this country that I stand before you today, resigning my post as President of the United States."

Lacy stood in the Rose Garden as the president made his remarks, the vice president standing beside him.

"You did it, Lacy," Will began. "You ended the corruption of an entire administration."

"We all did it. Maybe I started it, but we all finished it."

"I guess that means we're out of a job." Aaron stood on the other side of Lacy and leaned over with a smile.

"I guess we are." She surveyed the area. "Where's Trevor?"

"Up front."

"Good."

They watched the vice president take the oath of office.

"I am honored and humbled and appreciate the difficult decision the president had to make. In light of this fresh start our country so desperately needs, we have a new trade agreement with China that will bring back our jobs and help to heal the wounds between our two countries." He acknowledged China's President Zhang, who stood beside him. "It is our hope to move past this troubling time and look forward to a bright and prosperous future. And as president, it is with utmost confidence that I announce my appointment of a new acting CIA director. He has served this country with great distinction for more than twenty years and was instrumental in uncovering the deception so deeply entrenched in Washington. It is my honor to introduce Acting CIA Director Trevor Axell."

Trevor stood in the front row and waved for a moment before returning to his seat.

Lacy smiled and reached for Will's hand. "He's a good man, isn't he?"

"He is."

But there was one thing in the back of her mind. And while she would leave it there indefinitely, she would always be left to wonder. Who was really responsible for Turner's death?

———

Michelle Vogel leaned into Lacy's doorway. "Hey, you have a minute?"

"Of course. Come in. I haven't finished the reports yet."

"That's okay. It's not why I'm here." Michelle sat down.

"Oh. Everything all right?"

"Just thought we should take a moment to discuss your future. Have you decided what you want to do from here? You realize any door you want opened will open for you now."

"You must've heard the rumors."

"I might've heard a thing or two. The task force came as a mild surprise, but in this climate, I suppose I half-expected something of that nature to come to fruition, given what happened. And, of course, your involvement," Michelle continued.

"I haven't made a decision yet."

"So you're considering the position?"

"I am. It would be an honor, but like I said, I haven't made up my mind. I have to think of the kids and how often I'd be away. They could use some stability right now and so could I."

"Sure. I understand." Michelle pushed off the chair. "You just be sure and let me know what you decide, okay?"

"Of course I will." She watched Michelle leave and considered again what Trevor said. He was certain his post as acting director wouldn't last long and wanted her to make a decision before they brought in someone permanent.

The new president wanted to maintain the task force while giving Trevor and Director Mobley leeway to bring on additional help. Aaron had already accepted the offer to become a full-time member. Will's training in counterterrorism meant he too was offered a full-time position, which he had also accepted. So now it was Lacy's turn. Did she want to leave the Bureau? What would the task force become now were she to choose to dedicate herself to it full-time? Still, it had to be her choice. And she could not let the others sway her.

———

The doorbell rang and Celeste answered it to find a friendly face. "Mr. Axell, come in. It's very good to see you again."

"You too, Celeste." He leaned in to kiss her cheek. "How've you been?"

"Doing very well, thank you. And congratulations on your new position."

"Thank you, though I know it won't last."

"Nevertheless, you should be very proud. Lacy's in the living room." She closed the door. "Let me take that for you."

Axell removed his coat and handed it to her.

"Trevor." Lacy appeared in the foyer. "Thanks for coming over. You want a drink? A beer or wine?"

"No thanks. I'm okay. Got to drive back to the office."

"Oh. No rest for the weary, huh?"

"No, ma'am." He followed her into the living room. "I'm hoping your call means you've come to a decision?"

"As a matter of fact, I have." She sat down and waited for him to take his seat. "I've thought a lot about your offer. And you know, the Bureau has been good to me, but I'm not an agent, so I can only go so far."

"Right. Right."

"And the prospect of focusing solely on the task force would settle a good many concerns in my mind. But where does it go from here?"

A smile began to spread across Trevor's lips. "I'm glad you asked." He retrieved a manila folder and handed it to her. "This is the file on Malcolm Ford."

"Have we found him yet?"

"No. But I think once you see what's inside, you'll understand why."

Lacy opened the folder and began studying the documents.

"Dalian has been forced into bankruptcy, and given the nature of the deal with President Zhang, they've agreed to pull its operations out of the US. We know after Janz left SynDyn, the man you see there was put in charge of operations."

"Malcolm Ford," she replied.

"Yes." He paused while Lacy continued to view the file. "Malcolm Ford was a name he was operating under, but we know him as someone else."

"We do?"

"The CIA does. This man is Sergei Kozlov. He's Russian-born but became a US citizen several years ago. He never cut off ties to the people in his homeland."

"Wait. Are you telling me the Chinese made a deal with the Russians too?"

"No. I don't think so anyway. Casper Janz had cultivated relationships worldwide with very important people. I think Kozlov was just another man he needed a favor from, or vice-versa. And I'm sure he was paid well for it."

"What does this mean for us? Are we supposed to go after this guy?"

"I don't want to pretend China is going to sit back and be the good guys now. There will still be trade wars and each of our countries is not above getting their hands dirty to get what they want. But there will be people dedicated to continuing that effort. The task force's new target will be to discover any ties Kozlov might have to the Kremlin, CIA, or FBI. Our job will be to root out those ties. If Janz used him for this deal, he probably used him for something else. We'll be responsible for uncovering any more deals and exposing Janz's connections."

"And when we do?"

"Lacy, you and I both know the corruption won't end. It's been entrenched here for a very long time. The best we can do is whittle away at it and hope we continue to make a difference. I don't think this will involve the sort of political scandal we've already encountered. I believe the new president is a good man. He's already wiped clean the entire State Department. And he's empowered the task force to do more." Trevor leaned back. "So, will you continue your work with me—with us? Full-time of course."

"Yes. I'll accept your offer. Sounds like we'll be busy for a long time."

"Hey, there's something to be said about job security."

"You mentioned that others will be handling China. Who? What will they be doing?"

"After additional discussions with Zhang, the president was able to secure Maddox's release."

"What?" Her eyes brightened in an instant.

"As a good-faith gesture, he's going to let Maddox return home given that the man did put an end to Yang. That said, he'll be an incredible asset here. He knows the ins and outs of the region and will run things from here. So will Shaw."

"I'm so glad to hear it. You know, I think the president would be crazy not to keep you on as director."

"We'll see about that. But I know I'd be crazy to let you go back to the Bureau. I've never known anyone as dedicated to finding the truth as you, Lacy. And I know what that truth has cost you. Your talents will not be wasted. Neither will the others."

"Thank you, Trevor. I'm honored you place such faith in me. Oh, there's one other thing. I can still call you boss, right?"

"No. Absolutely not. You know I hate that."

"El jefe?"

"No."

"The big cheese?"

"Okay, I'm leaving now." He headed toward the door.

"The head honcho?" Lacy followed him out. "Okay, okay. I'm sorry. I'll stick with Trevor."

As he made his way outside and into his car, she couldn't help but give it one last try. "I got it! Chief!" She laughed as he shook his head with determination and pulled away. On closing the door, she continued to chuckle.

"What's so funny?" Celeste approached.

"Nothing. I'm just happy."

"I haven't heard you say that in a long time."

"I haven't felt it in a long time."

THE END

ABOUT THE AUTHOR

Bestselling author Robin Mahle, lives in Virginia with her husband and two children. Her Kate Reid mysteries have drawn praise for grabbing hold of the reader and refusing to let go. And the intense, fast-paced style of storytelling led her to create another series, the Lacy Merrick thrillers, which readers have called "believable, and ripped from today's headlines." With powerful leading ladies and action-packed thrill rides, Robin hopes to continue taking readers on roller-coaster adventures that will leave them breathless.

If you enjoyed Ms. Mahle's work, please share your experience by leaving a review at your ebook retailer.

For more information, visit Robin at
www.robinmahle.com

ALSO BY ROBIN MAHLE

Get **Exclusive Previews of new releases, information about giveaways and so much more just by signing up to receive Robin's Newsletter

www.ingramcontent.com/pod-product-compliance
Lightning Source LLC
Chambersburg PA
CBHW061938170626
46813CB00006B/2453